Bared TO THE Viscount

THE RITES OF MAY
BOOK ONE

CHAPTER 1

*A*pril, 1818, Village of Birchford, Yorkshire, England

MARY WILKINS WAS the very definition of plain.

Not ugly, by any means—she had no scars, no grotesque features or humps or oddities. She was just *plain*.

Her lips and eyelashes were pale, her eyes a mild gray, her nose nondescript. Her figure was slim, but lacked the mysterious curves all fashionable women seemed to have. Her cheeks were so freckled they suggested not blooming roses but something more akin to nankeen boots lightly flecked with mud. Even her one fine feature—her thick, chestnut hair—did her no good, since a respectable clergyman's daughter must coil it tight at her nape, where her curls had no chance to entangle a gentleman's heart.

Thus, here she was, at the ripe age of six and twenty, and still unmarried.

Overlooked.

A dowry might have attracted a local squire nonetheless,

but, alas, her clergyman father had been poor. And the excellent education he provided her at home made working men regard her as beyond their touch, so farmers and bargemen tugged their forelocks when they passed her in the lane and called her "Miss," but never asked her to go walking after church.

A vicar might have thought her an excellent wife, as plainness was almost a prerequisite for that position, but the only unmarried clergymen she knew besides her own brother Thomas were the bachelor parsons at Soffett and Aldham. Sadly, one seemed unaware that cleanliness was next to godliness and smelled like an unswept goat yard, while the other spoke with such glaring-eyed zeal of "evading the devil's treacherous lures," she'd much rather live a spinster than live with him.

So, now that her brother had replaced their father as head of St. Michael's, she kept house for him in the vicarage where they'd both grown up, and would likely continue doing so whenever Thomas finally took his nose out of his theology books long enough to find himself a bride. Papa's sister Eleanor had done much the same, tending house so Mama could tend the children. In the evenings, Aunt Eleanor sat in her rocking chair, knitting or mending, accepting hugs from those children whenever the children could be troubled to offer them. Which could not possibly have been often enough. No one asked if Eleanor was happy or unhappy.

Then one day she was found quite cold and still in her bed.

A shiver went down Mary's back.

She forced her attention back to folding the Lenten altar cloths she'd laundered, ready to stow them away until next year. She was not self-pitying, truly she was not. Everyone in Birchford knew her to be cheerful, energetic, always busy assisting her brother with the needs of the church and the parish, visiting the sick, raising funds to build a new hospital, teaching school for the youngest of the village children. She loved those aspects of her life, genuinely.

And yet—love of another kind was absent, and she felt the absence keenly. It kept some part of her locked away, like these altar cloths in this back closet of the storage building behind the ancient church, with the unused candles and out-of-season vestments and tins of beeswax she used to polish the timeworn oaken pews. Set aside. Unseen.

Untouched.

Oh, what would it be like to be *yearned* for by someone, to have someone to wrap his arms about her, to share her bed on a cold winter's night?

A warm flush went through her limbs.

Because the *someone* whose image came into her head was the most impossible man of all. The most utterly out of her reach.

Viscount Parkhurst.

To be sure, when they were children—he wasn't a viscount then, just *John*—they spent as much of their time as possible together, roaming the countryside, happily climbing apple trees and dropping toads down one another's backs.

But Viscount Parkhurst inherited his title at age sixteen when his father died of a pleurisy. Soon after, he left for Cambridge, and then—against the advice of all older, wiser heads—for the continent to fight Napoleon.

He was worldly now, accustomed to command. And familiar with the glittering ladies of London Society. Although he'd returned last fall to take up residence on his familial estate, he was certainly not likely to look on a drab little vicar's daughter with anything but a bemused remembrance that he'd once devoted so much time and attention to her.

Unfortunately, these days, she had no choice but to pay attention to him.

Since his return, the good people of Birchford kept asking her to bring him their petitions: to dig a new well at the far edge of the village, to tear down a stone wall around an orchard that had been commons in his grandfather's day, to provide a parcel of land to build that hospital she'd already spent years raising money for so local people might have more than one doctor within twenty miles.

Whenever they met, Lord Parkhurst treated her with the utmost formality, calling her "Miss Wilkins" now, never "Mary," and talking soberly with her in his study or riding with her across his lands without the slightest hint he was aware she was a single young woman of at least theoretically marriageable age. Or that they had once been so close.

Which would have been...*fine*. Most appropriate for their stations. Anything more familiar would have been awkward and distressing now that they were grown.

Except that it just so happened that Viscount Parkhurst had matured into a very, very handsome man indeed. He'd always been a sweet-faced boy, with his family's aristocratic good looks, but now he was something more approaching an Adonis.

The white-blond curls of his childhood had deepened into waves of manly bronze, and the boyish rosiness of his cheeks had been replaced by a soldier's tan that made his sky-blue eyes stand out with dazzling clarity. His jaw had grown hard and firm, his nose appealingly Roman, and his cheekbones stark now that all trace of childish softness had been chiseled away.

He'd grown remarkably tall, too, since he was sixteen, and his broad shoulders and chest now strained the limits of his well-tailored jackets. His long legs and tapered hips drew Mary's eye every time he was on horseback, or climbed a hill a few paces ahead of her. Or, for that matter, just sat in his armchair while they discussed parish matters in his study at Parkhurst Hall.

She gave her head a shake. Such thoughts must be shut away, just like the altar cloths in the cedar chest, to remain untouched and unsullied for yet another year.

For every year to come.

She let the lid of the chest fall closed with a soft thud.

She was just turning to leave the storage closet when she heard a key click in the front door to the storage building, and then the door bang open.

She froze.

No one else had cause to enter the building this afternoon.

The door slammed shut again, and the lock clicked purposefully shut.

With the closet wall between her and the main room, she could not see who had come inside, but whispers rose—one voice male, one female. Not the hushed, somber sort of whisper that was common enough on church grounds. No, this was mixed with muffled laughter.

And that laughter had an edge of raucousness, a hint of something conspiratorial and wicked.

Mary's heart gave a thump. *Who on earth would be up to trouble on the grounds of St. Michael's, in the middle of the afternoon?*

She crouched down to where a small chink in the plaster of the closet wall allowed her to peer out through dust and lath at the two newcomers.

Oh, dear.

It was a puzzling sight, to be sure.

One was the handsome, dark-haired young sexton, Mr. Bassett, who should be tending to his daily chores around the church grounds. The other was Mrs. Trumbull, the widowed proprietress of the village's most popular pub, The Fox & Crow. And thank goodness Mary had looked before simply walking out from the closet, because the laughter, apparently, was the result of what Mr. Bassett was doing to Mrs. Trumbull: embracing her from the rear and clamping his bare hands over the swells of her ample breasts.

Mary drew back from the wall with a little gasp.

Mrs. Trumbull did not have the most sterling of reputations, it was true—her gaudy red curls and buxom form made men's heads swivel whenever she sauntered by, and the lack of the encumbrance of a husband had made her quite bold in taking advantage of that attention.

Even so, Mary would have expected her to slap Mr. Bassett's hands away. Mr. Bassett was a year or so younger than Mary, and Mrs. Trumbull must be approaching forty.

But Mrs. Trumbull did not slap his hands away.

Quite the contrary—as Mary saw when curiosity drove her to peek again through the hole in the wall—the woman pushed her own hands on top of the man's, encouraging him, and let out a moan.

Embarrassment washed hot through Mary's chest. She was not exactly naïve; she understood, in a general sense, that people did such things, regardless of the rules of church and civilized society. And her father had been a most free-thinking clergyman. He often said the physical world was a divine gift, its pleasures meant to be enjoyed, provided no cruelty or selfishness was involved. He had not raised his children to be ashamed of fleshly existence.

But she had certainly never *watched* anyone indulge in this particular pleasure.

She really ought to shout out something to stop them, but what exactly was she to say? *Beg pardon—the vicar's sister is here. Pray find a new locale for your amorous goings-on?*

In any case, it was already too late to speak, at least

without irreparable embarrassment to all concerned. While his mouth pressed to the curve of Mrs. Trumbull's neck, Mr. Bassett's hands grasped the neckline of her bodice and wrenched it downwards, fully exposing her bosom above her stays. Mrs. Trumbull gasped and laughed again, a throatier laugh this time, and wriggled her buttocks against the front of Mr. Bassett's breeches, making him moan in turn.

Mary's heart thudded, and a strange, self-conscious tingling spread across the surface of her own skin. The shock of it all rooted her to the spot.

And things progressed so quickly, she scarcely had time to blink. Mrs. Trumbull arched her back, thrusting her bared breasts into Mr. Bassett's eager palms, and he reached down with one hand and hauled the woman's skirts up above her knees. And then upwards farther still, exposing her plump, pink thighs. One of his broad hands spanned both Mrs. Trumbull's breasts, while the other plunged straight between her legs and to caress her there as well.

Goodness.

Mary squeezed shut her eyes. How mortified the couple would be if they realized she was only a few feet away. She fought to quiet her own breathing—surely they would hear it rasping if she could not get her chest to stop heaving.

What on earth was she to do now?

How long exactly did these things take?

The only exit from the closet was the door leading into the main room where the couple was; the wall behind her was solid stone, without so much as a window.

The couple's moaning increased in volume, and Mary stood up straight and stuck her fingers in her ears—which did precious little to block the noise. She rather wished she could hum a loud tune to drown them out, but, even as absorbed as they were, they would surely notice that.

And no matter how tightly she closed her eyes, she could

7

not erase the image of Mr. Bassett's hand sliding between Mrs. Trumbull's legs.

Somehow it had never occurred to her that a man might touch a woman in quite that manner, in quite that place.

What must it feel like?

Mary's pulse pounded at the juncture of her own thighs, drumming in her belly and through her breasts.

Her imagination seemed to have heated along with the rest of her. A vision came into her mind, unbidden, of a man's hand stroking her just that way, the pressure of it, the shocking intimacy.

Viscount Parkhurst's hand.

Her head felt dizzy at the thought, and her bodice seemed to have grown several inches tighter than before.

Then, *thump*—something heavy struck the opposite side of the wall just in front of Mary's nose, and Mary nearly jumped out of her skin. It was unmistakably the weight of two bodies colliding with the wall.

The lovers had apparently decided their frolic required some additional vertical support.

Indeed, a quick glance at the chink in the plaster showed bright strands of Mrs. Trumbull's hair peeking through the gap. The curls quivered noticeably as Mr. Bassett did whatever Mr. Bassett happened to be doing to the innkeeper at the moment.

Whatever it was, it had Mrs. Trumbull making mewing noises like a cat.

Mary pressed herself backwards against the cedar chest, but the closet was too small to gain her any appreciable distance. *Good Lord*, if the plaster wall suddenly vanished, the pair would topple straight into her lap.

Why had no one ever thought to put a back door on this storage closet, so no embarrassed young maidens would ever find themselves trapped inside?

Even a secret tunnel through the floor would do.

Or a rope ladder through the roof.

If only she could turn into a vapor and disappear. She certainly felt warm enough to go up in a puff of steam.

But, as it was, she could do nothing but wait.

The couple's frantic breathing, and the rustling sound of their clothing—clothing that was no doubt being hastily unbuttoned or pushed aside—seemed to fill the air around her.

Mr. Bassett voice came suddenly, hoarsely, through the wall: "Are you ready for me, Dinah?"

"Now, Joe," came the reply. "Yes! Yes, now!"

The wall rustled with more shifting of bodies and clothing and gaudy red curls, and then another hard *thump* against the plaster, and Mr. Bassett groaned and Mrs. Trumbull cried out in apparent pleasure.

At first Mary thought that might be near the end of it, but a moment later, it became clear things were far from over. The *thump* against the wall came again, and again, shorter and sharper than before, then set into a steady, shuddering rhythm.

The candlesticks on the shelf above Mary's head began to clatter and dance, and a cloud of dust sifted down. Mary covered her nose so she wouldn't sneeze. *For pity's sake*—the couple's vigor was perhaps more than the centuries-old lath and plaster could withstand.

Perhaps more than Mary could withstand.

How excruciating to just *stand* there, burning with embarrassment, and, well, quite frankly, with something else as well. Her blood beat hard against the surface of her skin, heating her face, making all her flesh throb. Her breath was rasping whether she wanted it to or not, and she feared her pounding heart must be audible beyond just the roaring in her own ears.

Luckily, the lovers were making far too much noise now to notice any small sounds she might make. In addition to the incessant thumping against the wall, they grunted and whimpered and Mr. Bassett let loose with a string of desperate exclamations that seemed to involve a great many repetitions of the words *hard* and *wet* and *hot*.

Oh, heavens.

Maybe she did need to start humming to drown them out. But, under these conditions, she could hardly imagine attempting "O For a Closer Walk with God." She settled for squeezing her eyes tighter shut, and trying to focus her attention on something else, *anything* else—the liturgical calendar for the next two weeks, the multiplication tables she needed to recite with her cleverer pupils, a design for a new kneeling cushion she planned to embroider for one of the pews...

But it was useless. Her brain was fuming, and entirely different sorts of images arose, quite beyond her ability to suppress: images of Viscount Parkhurst—his broad shoulders, his strong thighs beneath his buckskin trousers, with their fascinating ridges and grooves, so like the powerful muscles of a hunting horse.

Oh, the idea of him embracing her, pushing her up against a wall...doing *that* to her...

Her nerve endings sparked, and warmth rippled through her belly, through her limbs, making the muscles of her thighs clench and her knees buckle.

Without her brain giving a command, her right hand strayed low on her belly, then lower still, moving towards that place where the sensations were rioting. Imagine *his* hand touching her there, *his* hand stroking her...

Oh, dear—she *was* going to go up in steam. Or perhaps in flames.

Her blood thrummed and pulsed intolerably hard, and a

wild and desperate impulse took hold of her. She simply...*needed*. Her fingers curved inward, pressing through her skirts to the joining of her legs. The instant jolt of pleasure made it impossible to hold back a gasp. *Oh, sweet heavens!*

She jerked her hand away before she made more noise, and bit at her lower lip.

Her breathing was ragged, her pulse almost painful in her throat, and it was all she could do not to groan.

At least the lovers still seemed blissfully unaware of her nearness. The thumping against the wall increased in tempo, apparently approaching some sort of crescendo.

"Yes, Joe, *yes!*" Mrs. Trumbull shouted. And Mr. Bassett let loose an astonishingly impassioned new string of profanities, including several fervent exhortations to the heavens, and the wallboards creaked and shuddered until Mary feared they'd truly crack this time and collapse in a heap of dust.

At long last, at the height of the frenzy, Mrs. Trumbull shrieked, and Mr. Bassett gave out a long, hoarse, mindless shout that under any other circumstance would have made Mary think he'd just suffered a death blow.

A moment later, the pounding against the wall came to a halt. The sound of harsh panting gave the only assurance that the couple had not in fact expired.

Then, to cap off all the madness of the last few minutes, Mrs. Trumbull laughed again, deep and low. "You're a right 'un, Joe Bassett," she declared ardently, still breathing hard. "A right good 'un."

"And you, Dinah," replied the sexton in the strained voice of a man who'd just run a mile uphill. "Always. The best I've had."

And that, apparently, was the limit of courtly romance between the two.

Clothing rustled again, no doubt being set to rights, and

eventually the couple's footsteps retreated from the wall back towards the front door.

Mary dared glance through the chink in the wall again.

Mr. Bassett and Mrs. Trumbull were not touching now, not even looking at one another. The sexton opened the door to the church yard and stuck his head outside, still tugging at his trousers, and looked both ways to be sure he was unobserved before he went out through the door. The innkeeper waited a minute more, tidying her loosened hair, before she too slipped out, just as stealthily.

The building was empty now, except for Mary, and silent again.

And Mary stood trembling in the closet, caught in a strange, inconsolable state of half-pleasure, half-pain.

What sort of insanity had she just been witness to?

Worse still, what strange feelings had it woken in her? What new visions of the viscount, a man she could never have? A high, hot tension still gripped her, deep in her chest and belly, twisting tightly with a need sharper than any she'd ever known.

She had no idea how to loosen it, and, if she couldn't, she thought it might slowly drive her mad.

The life of a spinster had never seemed so cruel.

CHAPTER 2

*J*ohn Hollings, eighth Viscount Parkhurst, followed Miss Mary Wilkins up a steep slope through a heavily wooded area, finding he almost had to struggle to keep up with her vigorous strides.

She was a funny thing, this grown-up Miss Wilkins, with all her projects and causes and her apparently unshakeable belief that noblemen had been put on earth to serve the needs of the poor.

It wasn't a bad belief, frankly. As little as he cared for the gruesome aspects of war, he'd loved one part of life as an army captain: the way the work of beating back Napoleon had given him a sense of real purpose.

Now that the wars were over and he'd returned to his country estate, life as a viscount threatened to be little more than sitting on his arse in other gentlemen's studies smoking cigars, or being hunted shamelessly by local mamas hoping against all odds to convert him into a son-in-law, or at least to give their winsome daughters some practice at charming a wealthy bachelor.

So if Mary Wilkins wished to press him into service

finding sites for good wells or new vegetable gardens for his tenants, he was more than willing to follow her.

Once upon a time, when he'd been free to address her as *Mary*, they'd spent much of their daylight hours in these very same woods, exploring the streams for good trout-fishing spots or searching for newts under interesting rocks. She'd been just as unstoppable then—fearless, and always game for an adventure.

Did it ever occur to her now to remember those days?

Thinking back, that part of his childhood had been among the happiest times of his life.

Of course, he and Mary were children no longer.

Mary was nearly as slender as she'd been back then, though taller, and with a subtle curve to her waist and back-side that hadn't been there before. It was harder to discern if her bosom was still flat—her unflattering dress was too shapeless in the bodice to reveal much, but he supposed there must be some change since girlhood. And he, of course, was a man now, not a boy—a man with quite a lot of experience doing interesting things with women's bodies, plump-chested or otherwise, that he'd never have dreamed of in those trout-fishing, newt-hunting days.

He knew Mary still spent time in the woods. She'd become the local schoolmistress, but didn't confine her young charges to the schoolroom. He'd happened upon the little group outdoors several times since he'd returned home, sitting in a circle under a spreading oak while she read to them, or rambling in the woods looking for prints left by fox or deer.

So there was still something of the wild creature in Mary, despite her fiercely bound hair and her straight spine and her extremely sensible boots.

Somewhere in the back of his mind, he wondered if perhaps it wasn't entirely appropriate for the two of them to be spending so much time alone together, especially out here in the woods, where the strict rules of civilized life felt rather less binding.

Even if their association now was all in the name of Serious Good Works.

Even if this grown-up Mary apparently had not a single flirtatious bone in her body.

Just now, she was using the walking stick she'd borrowed from him to clear a path through the underbrush, smacking aside the new spring greenery with wonderful vigor.

"Will you not let me take the lead, Miss Wilkins?" he offered, the use of her formal name still awkward on his tongue, even after all these months. "I could clear those branches for you."

"No, thank you, my lord," she answered without turning. "I must keep my eyes out for the head of the stream I found last spring. Your steward refuses to believe me when I say it runs underground here and down the hill towards the Clarkston Road, but I've seen where it disappears into the rocks, and heard it gurgling all along the hillside here when I've pressed my ear to the ground."

John had to suppress a chuckle. "Have you, indeed?" He could imagine Mary laying flat in the leaves and mosses doing just that.

She was almost a different species from the four well-coifed daughters of his nearest neighbor Lord Lawton, girls who seemed to flutter about him at every possible opportunity now that he'd returned to Birchford. He couldn't imagine any of *them* risking their fine frocks in a search for an underground spring. And if any of them had the strength to swing a stick like Mary Wilkins did, they'd rather die than let him know it.

How many hours of each day did the Misses Lawton spend arranging their costly skirts and ribbons and artfully spun blonde curls? Did they have causes they cherished beyond the quest to finish yet another bonnet with bows and silk flowers and those horrid little stuffed finches of which at least the eldest seemed so gruesomely fond?

As for conversation, they had little that didn't involve dissolving in fits of trilling giggles at the slightest joke he made. In truth, they giggled even when he said something serious. He wasn't entirely certain they could tell the difference.

And that wasn't even the worst part.

The worst part was that he had to *marry* one of them.

His mother, the dowager viscountess, reminded him almost daily of the promise he'd made to his late father—a promise everyone in the county seemed aware of—that he'd settle on one of the four pretty daughters of his father's dearest old friend.

Everyone also was aware of the fine, fat, unentailed swath of Lawton land marching alongside the Parkhurst estate that was meant to sweeten the deal, as an addition to the dowry of whichever daughter became the next viscountess. The land was on the Parkhurst side of the river that ran between the two estates, and its acquisition had long been yearned for by his ancestors, to extend their land to what they felt should be its fitting natural borders. His mother, his late father, his uncles, and his steward had drummed into his head for years that it was his responsibility to finally make it so.

Besides which, they all told him, the Lawton girls were famously lovely, and any man would be glad to take one as his bride.

John felt a distinct need to have his walking stick back so he could smack a few bits of greenery himself.

The Lawton girls were lovely, yes, but he found them about as interesting as plates of bone china.

He'd much rather spend his time tromping about with

Mary Wilkins, who at the moment was handily whacking down a thick gnarl of blackberry bramble that dared to block her path. It was no easy feat—after the unnaturally miserable cold weather of the past two springs and summers, this Lenten season was notably warm at last, and the vines were resurging with extraordinary vigor, as fierce, heavy green shoots thrust their way heedlessly through shrubs and trees and between the clefts of rocks, determined to conquer each available inch with soon-to-blossom life.

Even the thorns seemed longer and thicker and glossier than he'd ever remembered them to be. It was as if the stored-up *life* within must all burst forth at once.

"Up here just a little way more," insisted Mary. "Old Mr. Dockett the diviner tells me he thinks I'm quite right about the stream, and wishes his legs would still carry him up here to look for it. Imagine the well we could dig if we follow its path back down the hill."

John found himself smiling. "I'm sure it shall be the most excellent well in the county."

"It shall be!"

"And who needs Mr. Dockett when we have a sylvan nymph like you to lead the way?"

Mary whirled around then, a tense expression on her face. "Are you making fun of me, my lord?"

He stopped short. He wasn't quite sure what had possessed him to say something so whimsical. Once upon a time, of course, they'd spoken playfully to each other all the day long, but that was years ago, when they could scarcely imagine she'd ever actually address him as *my lord*.

"No, Miss Wilkins," he said hastily. "Not at all. Never. I quite admire your spirit."

To his surprise, she blushed then. The pink was quite startlingly vivid on her normally pale cheeks, and made her grey eyes brighten.

He was very grateful, just at that moment, for the drab sack of a dress she wore, and for the meagerness of her bosom, because something about that unexpected wash of color caused an equally unexpected pang of interest in the region of his loins.

Dear Lord.

Now *that* was an impulse he could not consider giving way to.

Mary Wilkins was the daughter of a *clergyman*, for pity's sake. The current vicar's sister. A virtuous woman. A woman given to Acts of Charity, not Acts of Carnal Sin.

And he was a man doomed to marry a lady of fashion.

"Forgive me," he said, hoping that would put an end to the tension—in all its forms. "I'm sure we shall find your stream very soon if we just press on."

Her mouth pursed. For a moment he saw a glint in her eye that once upon a time would have been the harbinger of a tart and unladylike retort, but instead she simply said "Yes" in a very cool tone, and turned back on her way.

Everything might have gone just fine between them after that had Miss Wilkins not, for just one fateful moment, overestimated her ability to bully the blackberry vines.

At one curve in the path, a particularly ancient, dense, towering thicket formed two huge mounds on either side, the muscular boughs intertwining overhead in an arch John would have to crouch to pass beneath. The thicket would no doubt have formed a solid wall across the path had not generations of local deer continually crashed their way through, leaving just enough of a tunnel for human walkers to pass. And lately, the busy growth had clearly been doing its best to close that wall back up.

Mary had been moving forward at a fast clip, and all at once she jerked to a stumbling stop.

"Oh, dear!" she said. "I'm caught!"

She began tugging at the region of her skirts that was snagged in the twisting bramble, but managed in the process to get her sleeve snared by yet another set of the rampant thorns.

"Hold still, Miss Wilkins," he urged her. "I'll get you loose."

"No!" she cried. "No need! Stand back, Lord Parkhurst!" And she pulled harder at her restraints, which only seemed to shake loose other branches from the vast green tangle, so more long, barbed tentacles whipped around her, catching her clothing in several places, and even the side of her hair.

"Blast it!" she cried, and her cheeks colored once more. The strong vines that caught her upper body now dragged her forward into a slightly contorted posture, bringing that subtle curve of her backside into more prominent sight.

Damn.

John's loins were definitely reacting, and the fact that Mary, as she struggled to free herself, let slip a few choice exclamations a clergyman's daughter probably should not have uttered in a gentleman's presence was not particularly helping.

She sounded like the free-spirited girl he'd once known. And along with the vague stirring of sexual awareness he was already feeling, her momentarily-unbridled commentary somehow sent a bright, buoyant sensation rising through his chest, loosening a tight knot of pressure he hadn't even realized was there.

He wanted to laugh.

But *no*.

He was a gentleman. He was a *gentleman*, and he couldn't afford to forget it, or to react to her current dilemma with any more emotion—or carnal interest—than if he were helping her down from an over-high wagon seat or retrieving a parcel she'd dropped.

He was not going to acknowledge the momentary lapse in her prim self-discipline, and he was most certainly *not* going to think about her backside, or the fact that her breathing had become more rapid or that the pinkish color in her cheeks now spread to her long, bare throat.

And if any fanciful thoughts came into his head that the hulking green tangle that bound her bore some resemblance to an ill-tempered dragon, and she was rather like an imperiled princess in a fairy tale, and he was the noble prince come to her rescue, he was going to crush those ridiculous musings immediately.

"Please, Miss Wilkins," he said, bending low to keep his own hair and coat from being snagged. "Hold very still, and I'll have you free in just a moment."

Unfortunately, the rioting maze of vines had her pinned all along one side, tugging her clothes in a variety of directions, and in the tight space he had to contort himself lest he set more branches swinging and accidentally cause her face to be scratched or her clothing to be torn. Which at one point required his forearms to press against the backs of her legs as he plucked her skirts away from the nasty thorns, and even brought his face into proximity with that intriguing backside he was working so hard not to think about.

And damned if she didn't smell rather delicious—clean, natural, without a trace of perfume, only the slight tang of exertion from their long climb, and a scent of womanly flesh that made him want to breathe her in more fully.

Damn and blast.

To his peril, freeing her wasn't a quick job: half the time, when he plucked a bit of her loose, the mass shifted and caught her somewhere else, as if with malicious intent to defy him. If women wore breeches, his job would have been easier, but there were folds of fabric everywhere around her, especially in that loose sack of a dress.

At one point, a particularly springy shoot he freed bounced upwards and speared a new bit of fabric on the way, lifting the hem of her skirt, baring her ankle and several inches of long, white, shapely leg.

Surprisingly shapely.

Oh, dear.

Mary gasped as the breeze hit her leg, no doubt embarrassed at being exposed to his gaze, so in desperation he gripped the vine to tear it free, stabbing his fingers and tearing a small rent in her hem.

At least he got that one bit of fabric loose, and her leg was properly covered again.

But Mary had jumped rather violently in her own panicked effort to free her skirts, and now she cried, "Ouch! My hair!"

He looked up to find a thick vine arching above her, pulling long strands out of the tight coil on her scalp as it strained upwards, doubtless causing her quite a bit of pain.

To stop the pressure, he straightened as best he could in the close space and grasped her hair near to her scalp, then used the fingers of the other hand to tease the captured strands loose.

They were lovely strands, he discovered.

The color looked dull wrapped in a tight coil at the base of her skull, but the loose strands in the vine-filtered sunlight were warm, reddish-brown, rather like the color of good brandy. And surprisingly silky to the touch.

What would her hair look like if it were all loose, curling down around her hips?

No. He *definitely* wasn't going to think about that.

He eased the loose curls down against her cheek, careful to keep them away from the outthrust branches which seemed all too eager to snatch hold again. Her face looked far softer with waves of brandy-colored hair resting against it.

Softer, and…warmer.

With her grey eyes suddenly looking very bright indeed.

His gaze fell quite unbidden to her mouth, which was also a good deal rosier than he remembered.

"John," she said again, more softly. She was looking at him too, her gaze vague and unfocused. Her breathing was quick and shallow, and her lips were parting. "John."

He was breathing faster, too.

John. She was calling him *John*. For the first time in years.

No one had called him by that name since his father died, not even his own mother, to whom he was always Parkhurst now. The sound of his name on Mary's lips moved something deep inside him. He felt as if he were…more than loosening now. *Melting*, maybe.

Not to mention that he was still staring at her lips, and his blood was heating quite precipitously, and his loins were now stirring to full attention against the fall of his trousers.

"Mary," he said, though he had no conscious intention at all of saying her name.

Oh, this was bad—this was very, very bad.

This was *Mary Wilkins* he was having lustful inclinations towards.

Mary Wilkins, the old vicar's daughter, the current vicar's sister. Not a woman to toy with, but also not a woman a viscount had any business paying serious court to—especially not a viscount all-but-affianced to one of the daughters of his late father's lordly best friend.

Mary seemed to realize just as he did that they were on the verge of something they would both regret, because she jerked her head away from where his hand—he realized just now—was cupping her cheek, and the gauzy look cleared from her eyes.

With a sharp wrench of her arm, she tried to pull her

sleeve loose from the vine that held it fast, but that only resulted in setting the whole green maze swinging again.

A fat set of vines whisked past his face, snaring his collar and coat-sleeve at multiple points, along with several thick hanks of his hair. It tugged his already lowered head down so that his cheek pressed straight into Mary's right breast.

Damn again.

His mouth was positioned just above where her nipple must be.

He twisted in an effort to free himself, but in the process, his lips swept over the fabric of her bodice, just enough that he fancied he felt the nub of that nipple harden to a peak.

He thought Mary might scream then, as well she should have.

But she didn't scream.

Instead, she exhaled audibly, a long, low sigh.

And then she did something entirely remarkable: she took her left hand and cradled the side of his head, pushing it firmly back into that little, soft, sweet-scented mound of flesh.

"John," she breathed, and this time her tone was very definitely sensuous—throaty and deep and needy—something he'd never in a million years have expected from his childhood friend. "Kiss me there, John. Please."

He could not possibly have heard her right. "Mary?"

"Please, John," she begged, and the nervous quaver in her voice told him more surely than anything that she was quite serious.

Her breathing was fast and shallow, and though he couldn't lift his head to see her face, he fancied he felt the pleading force of her gaze upon him.

"Kiss me there," she insisted, her fingers spearing into his hair, urging him closer. "If you don't, no one ever will. And I want to know what it feels like, just once."

"But—but, *Mary*—"

"Please!" Her voice broke on the word. "I won't ask anything more of you, I swear it. Just this one thing."

He was painfully conscious of how hard her pulse was beating—he could see it jumping in the hollow of her throat. And his heart was pounding just as hard.

Not to mention that his cock was throbbing.

Trying to clear his muddled thoughts, he drew a deep breath—and that sweet, womanly scent of Mary's flesh filled his nostrils and fogged his already baffled brain.

Everything rational left in him urged him to find some way to get his mouth away from her breast.

He intended to do that, truly. Immediately, in fact.

Without question.

Because he was a gentleman.

An *all-but-affianced* gentleman.

And yet what he found himself doing instead was hooking the fingers of his free hand into the neckline of Mary's frock and chemise and tugging the drab layers of fabric down. Her flesh against his knuckles was warm and surprisingly fine and silken, and the moment the tight nub of her nipple was free, he fitted his mouth over it hungrily. He gave it a flick with his tongue, then suckled her.

She moaned, and it was the most erotic sound he'd ever heard.

All she'd asked for was a kiss, but he had to give her more. He found himself wondering about the color of that nipple in his mouth. He couldn't lift his head enough to see it properly, so he pulled the neck of her gown down beneath her other breast, and looked his fill sideways even as he continued sucking the first breast he'd bared.

Lord. Her skin where the sun never touched it was pearl-white, and her nipple was as pink as a rosebud.

And surely just as sweet.

If he could lift his head enough to see her face, and have incontrovertible evidence he was doing this with *Mary Wilkins* of all people, he would never be able to do it.

But all he could see was a graceful small swell of womanly flesh and a pretty pink teat, so he strained against the thorns that bound his hair, palmed that other soft mound towards his mouth, and kissed it, just as she'd asked, before drawing the rosy peak between his lips.

She liked what he was doing, clearly. Her fingers were in his hair, at least where it was free of thorns, and urged him closer, nearly clawing him in her enthusiasm.

He licked and sucked and swirled his tongue, moving from one pink nipple to the other and back again as best he could with his head pinioned, feasting on her, making her gasp, making her push her hips towards him.

Heat rose from between her breasts, with the subtle, intoxicating scent of arousal.

If he hadn't had most of the left side of his body hooked by those damnable vines, he'd have done exactly as she seemed to be wanting and pulled her hips tight against his and pressed his throbbing erection into her belly.

She was trembling now, still pulling his mouth against her and crying, "John, oh, John, please, John!"

Without another thought, his hand was at the buttons of his fall, fumbling to free his aching cock. No thinking was involved, just desperate, red-tinged visions of hiking up her skirts and finding her hot, wet slit, and somehow angling their bodies so he could push hard inside her.

"John," she gasped again. "Sweet John."

And that was the phrase that stopped him. *Sweet John.*

Dear Lord, he was supposed to be her friend.

She was an innocent, a virgin, a decent girl.

Whatever momentary madness had gripped them just

now, it could only be momentary. And he wasn't such a cad that he would consider ruining her.

No.

He let her nipple drop from his lips, and did his best to draw the bodice of her dress back up to cover her. The buttons of his fall were difficult to manage with his cock swollen so hugely, but he got one side closed again.

She went painfully still. "Why are you stopping?"

His voice wouldn't quite seem to work. His brain was still fuming with the thought of getting his hands under her skirts. With a tremendous effort, he cleared his throat and said, "We have to stop, Mary…*Miss Wilkins.*" He was glad just at the moment that so much of his hair was caught in the vines and he couldn't possibly be expected to look her in the eye. Though he was, of course, still staring at the upper swell of her sweet little breasts. "You know how utterly inappropriate this is."

She let out a long sigh. "Yes, I know."

"On the count of three, we are both going to jump with all our strength and rip our way clear of these vines, do you understand? Even if it hurts. Even if we tear half our clothing off." He squelched that thought hastily—the image it brought into his mind wasn't going to help him tame his urges. He tried again. "We cannot afford to stay together like this even one minute longer, not if your chastity means anything to you. *Do you understand?*"

"What if it doesn't mean anything to me?"

"What?"

"My chastity. What if I…*want* to be wicked?"

The solid ground of his universe gave a disconcerting lurch. His cock pushed more insistently against his half-buttoned trousers. He had to master both sensations by sheer force of will. "No. Don't say that. You're not—you're *not* wicked, for heaven's sake. You're just—distracted by what we've just done. It works like that. You would regret it the moment we…the moment we went too far."

"I don't think so, John."

He blinked rapidly. Why did she sound so blasted *rational*?

How was he supposed to save her from herself if she was so very eager to be ruined? With his head mashed against her bosom, it was difficult enough to be the voice of reason, and her attitude wasn't helping. Certainly, the parts of him below his waist were attending to her words with the greatest eagerness, sending clamoring messages to his brain to stuff the whole notion of gentlemanly honor and get on with the business of rogering the girl.

To make matters worse, her fingers were stroking his hair in a remarkably sensual manner, and he felt the caressing pressure straight down to his toes.

"I've been thinking very hard about this, for weeks now," she said. Her voice sounded calm, very much as it did when she told him of her plans for vegetable gardens and wells. "A woman in my position has little hope of ever marrying, but that doesn't mean I don't have the same needs as any other female."

"Mary, stop talking." He tugged against the vines. "Stop talking *right now*."

"Just once, just once, I want to lay in a man's arms. I want him to touch me, *there*, and put his—"

With a strangled yell, John heaved his body to the right, using all his muscle and weight to tear the two of them free. There was noise of branches cracking and fabric rending and both his and Mary's yelps as thorns scraped them and far too many strands of hair were violently plucked from their scalps.

But to his relief, their bodies came loose from the tunnel of vines.

And tumbled right down to the ground. With Mary sprawling half on top of him, with his hand firmly planted on one cheek of her really-rather-delightfully-soft buttocks.

He pushed her away, a bit more forcefully than he meant to, and scrambled backwards like a crab, before he could give in to the temptation to gather her in his arms.

Mary fell back on her bottom, her skirts wild around her knees, most of the length of her legs bared, her thorn-mussed hair half still in its coil, half in a wild, brandy-colored halo around her head.

She was flushed and vivid and brilliant-eyed and outraged and aroused, and both of them were panting hard, and all of a sudden she was the most gorgeous, desirable vision he'd ever seen.

But he couldn't have her. He *couldn't*.

And yet, she was looking at him with such longing, such desperation.

She wanted a little taste of pleasure. The sort of pleasure a gentleman was always free to indulge in, and which would likely be denied her forever.

His heart sank.

How could he abandon his friend to *that*?

And so he did the only thing he could think of that would give her release and still leave her virginity intact: he crawled over to her on his knees, ran his palms up her bare legs, urged her onto her back, and pushed her skirts up to her hips.

With a groan, he set his mouth to the sweetly musky, glistening place between her thighs.

CHAPTER 3

*M*ary couldn't believe what was happening. She was stretched out flat on the forest floor, her hems up nearly to her waist, her bare legs spread wide.

And in between her legs, his sun-bronzed head shifting with the astonishing movements his mouth was making, was Viscount Parkhurst. *John.*

His tongue moved against her intimate flesh in the most astonishing ways, his thumbs caressing and spreading her most private folds as he licked along them, between them, and up, up to a place at the very top of that juncture that seemed to be pure sensation. Her hips bucked as his tongue swirled there, around and around. She thought she might burst from the pleasure of it.

When she'd watched the couple in the storage shed and had pressed her hand to that spot between her legs, she'd felt a sensation like this, but this was heightened, a thousand times more wondrous. Having John actually touch her—not just with his hands, but with his *mouth*—was so much more overwhelming than she ever could have imagined.

The pleasure only built and built. He seemed to know

exactly where she most needed his caress, how to lift her from one sensation to the next, how to make her body thrum with delight.

Surely she should be feeling pain from all the places the blackberry thorns had scratched and stabbed her, but she felt not the slightest sting anymore. Only swirling sensations of bliss.

At first, she feared John could not possibly be enjoying what he was doing to her, but the enthusiasm of his movements, and the wonderful groaning noises he made, told her he was quite happy to be doing it. For a time, he held both her hips in his hands, as if to lift her more tightly against his tongue. Then his hands went between her legs again, pleasuring her further. One palm pressed to her nest of curls, and pushed gently up towards her belly so that shockingly sensitive bit of flesh at the front of her stood up more exposed. He licked and bit and sucked and rubbed.

She writhed beneath him, her fingers instinctively reaching into his hair, gripping him. Surely he must want to do more—surely he must want to do what the sexton had done to Mrs. Trumbull up against that wall. And she wanted him to do it. She wanted him to, though she suspected he'd chosen to do what he was doing in an effort to preserve her virginity. And what he was doing felt so remarkably, miraculously good, she couldn't really ask for more…

At one point, he stopped and looked up at her, his eyes as dazed and unfocused as a sleepwalker's. He gasped the word "Mary" before settling between her thighs again.

He got up on his knees then, and one of his hands left her to go between his own legs. He seemed to be fumbling with the buttons of his breeches. She wished she could see more of him, but the sight of his elbow off to the side, beginning to pump forward and back, was enough to drive her arousal to a new peak.

His hand came back between her legs for a moment, skimming some of her moisture onto his fingertips then going back between his own legs to move with renewed vigor. His groans became more fervent. The idea that he was using her wetness to pleasure himself sent a jolt of new sensation through her—almost as if he had put himself inside her.

His tongue did push hard inside her, matching the rhythm of the hand he had on himself, and the fingers of his free hand continued their dizzying swirl on her sensitive nub.

The spring breeze licked over her exposed skin. Above her, the green tree branches swayed, the clouds glided through the jewel-blue sky, birds swung in quick arcs of flight between the leaves, chattering bright melodies—and all of it seemed to rush and swell along with the pleasure of her flesh, until it shifted and swirled into a mad pinwheel of color and sound.

She had to squeeze shut her eyes, or she would have fallen straight into the sky.

The memory of the couple taking their pleasure in the shed came back to her—the way they'd seemed to move towards a crescendo of pleasure—and she understood now what they had been feeling.

Her hips bucked. She was rising, rising higher and higher, her body tensing as it arched upwards. Her thighs were trembling. Some deep primal rhythm deep within her seemed to take control of her blood.

The pressure within her coiled tighter, tighter, narrowing to one sharp, blazing point of sensation, right where John's tongue laved her.

Then all at once everything exploded. Heat roared outwards, a fierce, hot wave, racing past every boundary, shattering all barriers between him and her.

They cried out together and their bodies jerked. His hands and her hands seemed to be everywhere at once, pressing into one another's flesh—though she knew she touched nothing but his hair—and she felt one more slow, deep, pulsing wash of pleasure, and a sort of glow through every inch of her.

The tension all drained from her limbs, and she fell back against the earth, utterly languid, utterly spent. Her legs were still open, her eyes closed, and the sunlight on her face had never felt so golden and pure.

"Mary." It was John's voice. Almost a sigh.

And then again: "Mary." Not so soft this time.

She opened her eyes to look at him. He'd risen up off his knees into a tense crouch. The trancelike look on his face began to clear, giving way to a look of something more like shock.

Horror, even.

"Good God, Mary," he said, and this time his voice had an unmistakable edge of anguish. "What have we done?"

Her brain was still whirling, and all she could say was the truth: "It was wonderful."

"Yes." John shook his head while hastily stuffing his shirt-tails back inside his trousers and rebuttoning his fall. "No. *No*, it was...I lost my head entirely."

"It *was* wonderful."

"I'm so sorry. I just—oh, Lord, we—we must get away from here."

Mary managed to raise herself back to a sitting position, though her sense of stupor remained. Why exactly must they get away? This spot was Paradise.

John pulled her skirts peremptorily down to her ankles then hauled her to her feet. The blood rushed from her head. She swayed a little; her legs felt numb and rubbery and not entirely up to the task of keeping her upright.

"We'll go home," he said, sounding rather thick-tongued, like a man who'd had too much ale, or who'd been abruptly roused from deep slumber. "To our own homes." His hands ran fretfully through his golden hair, trying to smooth it, but only mussing it further. "We'll just—we'll—oh, damn me, I'm so sorry. I don't know what we'll do."

He turned and set off walking in front of her, faster than was wise down the steep rocky slope, stumbling a little as he went. It occurred to her fuzzily that they'd abandoned his walking stick by the blackberry bramble, but urgently as he was moving homeward, she doubted he'd appreciate her calling him back for it.

It was a silent walk down the hill, and the springtime air seemed suddenly to have turned very chilly indeed.

As the breeze brushed her hands and face, she felt the sting of her cuts and scratches return, as though the thorns were raking her anew.

CHAPTER 4

*L*ate that evening, Mary stood in her kitchen, drying the last of the supper dishes, trying to go about her domestic routine as always, though still in a daze. One moment, visions of what she'd done with the viscount in the woods that morning sent her stomach swooping with elation. The next, their cold parting twisted it into a hard knot.

He wouldn't even *look* at her when he said goodbye at the vicarage door.

He'd mumbled vague apologies, eyes darting in distress, unable to complete a sentence. Just "We can..." or "We'll just..." or "Of course we shouldn't have..." Spots of blood welled from a deep thorn-scrape along his cheekbone, as though he'd just returned from a duel.

She couldn't help feeling that she'd wronged him in some terrible way.

And she had no idea how she'd ever put it right.

At least she had the house to herself for a few hours—the town drunkard, Donald Evans, had got deep in his cups again and was fighting with Mrs. Evans, and one of the

Evans boys had come running for the vicar to calm the man down before he turned vicious as he too often had in the past.

She was just reaching up to slide the last of the plates onto its shelf when a series of hard, urgent knocks sounded at the vicarage's front door.

She wiped her hands hastily on her apron, her fingers still stinging with blackberry scratches. People came to the vicarage at all hours in need of her brother's services, and one of her duties was to usher them inside. She felt rather grateful for the interruption tonight—if nothing else, a small emergency would take her mind off the viscount for a few minutes.

She hurried to the foyer, lit the small lantern they kept there for such occasions, and opened the door.

Out in the gloom stood Viscount Parkhurst.

A slew of emotions swept over her—half cold, half hot. Embarrassment, thrill, fear.

There was no helping it: his nearness sent a hot spark of energy rippling over the whole surface of her body, and set off a throbbing pulse low in her belly. For a moment, she could scarcely resist pulling him into an embrace, kissing him hard, and trying to draw him down on the foyer floor with her so they could repeat what they'd done that morning, and more.

But the collar of his black wool greatcoat was turned up, shielding his face, and his tall beaver hat loomed darkly. He looked quite literally like a shadow of himself.

The little she could make out of his expression was grim.

Was he angry with her, or...

Did this have nothing to do with what had passed between them earlier? People who knocked at night often wore that look, and it usually meant a clergyman was needed in a hurry.

Oh, dear.

A quick mental reshuffling was in order—from lovelorn maiden to efficient vicar's sister. She shoved her personal desires aside as though stuffing them into a sack. "What's the matter, Lord Parkhurst? Is someone ill?"

"What?" He blinked in apparent confusion, as though she were the one who'd surprised him at the door. Oh, his eyes were so startlingly blue, even in this half-light. It made her breath catch.

"Is someone *ill*?" she repeated. "At Parkhurst Hall? Your mother? Your brothers?"

"No," he said, but his brow creased as if with worry. "They're well. They're all well. Is—is your brother at home?"

So he *had* come for the vicar. Something was certainly wrong, even if he wasn't being quick to say so.

She schooled her voice to its usual rational self-control. "I'm afraid my brother was called out already. Donald Evans has got drunk again, and Thomas has gone to get him into the care of one of his cousins before he does any harm."

"Ah," John said distractedly. "I hope someone found where Donald hid his musket and took it away before real trouble starts."

Her heart flipped at the thought. "Thomas will calm him before it comes to that. I'm sure of it."

"Yes, yes of course." John seemed to realize he'd spoken rather alarmingly. "I'm sorry, Mary. *Miss Wilkins*. Your brother will know just what to do."

"Donald will need watching till the drink wears off, and he minds Thomas better than other men, so Thomas may stay some hours. But if your need is urgent, I can go for him myself."

"Oh. No. I—no, I wouldn't trouble you like that." Just then, he seemed to remember he was still wearing his hat. He snatched it off his head, but proceeded to spin it about by the brim, round and round in agitation.

She tried not to notice how the edges of his hair shone golden in the light of her lantern, how the shadows heightened the sculpted plains of his cheekbones. And, oh the dark line there on his cheek where a thorn had torn at him, for her sake.

Well, at least that proved she hadn't imagined what happened that morning.

Lord, she wanted to touch him.

Could he not say a single word, make a single gesture, to let her know he was as aware as she was of what they'd done? Even if he were angry with her for insisting that he touch her, could he not just *say* so?

Why must he be so stiff and uncomfortable with her?

Standing face to face with him in this formal mode was nearly unbearable. But sending him away seemed cruel, if he was half as troubled as he looked. "Would you like to come in and wait a bit? Thomas may be back sooner than I think. I could at least give you tea before you go home again."

His eyes widened at the offer, as if shocked.

Why on earth? Granted, it wasn't entirely proper to invite him into the house when her brother was away, but a vicar's sister could bend the rules when a parishioner was in need. And considering what they'd already done up on that hill, taking a cup of tea together could hardly be considered shocking.

He shifted foot to foot. "Well, I suppose I should talk to you in any case—first, I mean."

"First?" That word turned her stomach instantly to water. What awful news did he bear that would concern *her* directly? "Is it one of the children from the school?" A panicked inventory flashed through her thoughts: little Jack Kelsey's lungs were never strong. Tommy Harrow was

37

forever jumping out of trees. Annie and Lucy Turner's father had been to market in Leeds just last week, where they'd had reports of scarlet fever.

But John only looked confused. "Children? No. Please, Mary, may I just come in?"

Apparently he wasn't going to tell her anything until they were indoors. Her heart fluttering, she led the way into the kitchen, which seemed a more appropriate place to be alone with him than the sitting room, with its perilously soft and inviting divan and armchairs.

Once she lit the lamp on the table, she got a good look at him. In addition to the scratch on his cheek and several on his hands, he seemed rather green around the gills.

A new panic swamped her. "Oh, Lord, it's *you* who's ill! Why didn't you tell me?" She couldn't stop herself from laying a palm to his cheek. He didn't feel warm, though his skin was perhaps a trifle clammy.

He sucked in a breath at her touch. "Mary. *Miss Wilkins.* Don't."

He jerked two chairs from under the table and pushed one towards her unceremoniously.

They both sat, and impulsively, she took hold of his hand. "Please, John. Just tell me what's going on."

His fingers gripped hers like a vise. He licked his lips. A muscle in his injured cheek jumped. He started to speak, stopped, started again, his usual easy eloquence apparently having abandoned him.

She was beginning to be very worried, indeed.

And then he slumped forward off his chair.

"John!" She went to grab his arms to keep him from falling and hitting his head. But once his right knee touched the floor, his downward motion stopped and he appeared quite steady again.

He remained kneeling before her.

This time it was John who took her hands, clasping them both quite firmly in his own.

A new alarm rose in her chest.

Oh, no. This *couldn't* be what it looked like.

It absolutely *shouldn't* be.

But apparently it was.

"Mary," John said, in a tight, choked voice. "*Miss Wilkins.* You must do me the honor of becoming my wife."

Someone might as well have dumped a bucket of icy water over her—chill mortification dragged down her every limb.

Dear Lord, he wasn't deathly ill. He was *proposing.*

"John!" Her tongue tangled. "This—this—oh, gracious, Lord Parkhurst, this isn't necessary."

"Of course it's necessary." His face looked so distressed. "I compromised your virtue."

"You did no such thing." She flung off his hands and jumped to her feet. "If anyone did any compromising, I compromised *you.* You climbed that hill to look for a site for a new well for your tenants, as a charitable act. I'm the one who begged and pleaded with you to..." Her cheeks flamed as she struggled for a decent way to put it. "To—to *kiss* me."

He was still, stubbornly, kneeling. "It doesn't matter. I'm enough of a man of the world to know how to resist temptation. It was my responsibility to stop things from going where they went. You were an innocent, you couldn't know how—how things can become...so *heated.*"

Her cheeks flushed. The scratches on her face and hands throbbed afresh.

He broke off, his own cheeks going ruddy, and shifted his weight as though the very core of his body ached. "In any case, you only asked me for a kiss. I'm the one who...took it so much further. I did things with you only a husband should do."

A ripple of heat went through her, despite her embarrassment. If *that* was his view of what husbands should do with their wives, marriage to him would be a living pleasure.

She squelched that selfish thought. "Get up, John. Don't be on the floor. I can't bear it."

Just at the moment, she needed to move away from him. If she didn't, the impulses battling inside her might split her straight down the middle.

She went to cupboard for saucers and cups, searching for the few that had no cracks or chips. Tea might restore the man—might restore them *both*—to sanity. "Your offer is beyond decent, Lord Parkhurst," she said, reminding him of who he was, and therefore how foolish he was being. "But you're a peer of the realm! You need a wife appropriate to your station."

"You are a gentlewoman, Mary."

"*Impoverished* gentlewoman. With only a few minor lords in the family tree, mostly distant branches. London Society would not find my pedigree impressive. Or even acceptable, for a viscount's wife."

He stood now, a scowl on his face, his full height becoming intimidating, even from across the kitchen. "As I recall, your mother had a baronet for an uncle."

"Yes, on her father's side," she said, and fixed him with a firm look. "But on her mother's, a bricklayer and a man with a Cheapside oyster shop."

He shook his head impatiently. "You're a virtuous woman. That's all that matters."

"But this is *unnecessary!*" A terrible ache was rising, filling the space between her ribs so she could scarcely draw breath. She had to convince him he was speaking nonsense. Had to convince herself as well. "Be rational a moment, John. You know full well there will be no consequences to what we did."

"What do you mean, no consequences?"

"I mean no one saw us. No one will ever know. And it's—it's not as if you could have gotten me with child."

He gave a choked little laugh. "Always so practical, Mary."

"Yes, practical." Though her hands felt unsteady, they held the kettle firm as she lifted it from the hob and took it to the sink to pour hot water into her coarse earthenware teapot.

She had to be firm for the both of them. Had to be sensible, and squelch whatever wild fantasies were trying to slip free in her imagination. Fantasies of having him as *hers*, and hers only, for all time.

He's not meant to be mine.

"Your proposal is meant kindly, I know," she said. "But you must see that it is…beyond preposterous. Marriage to a woman of my station would make a hash of your reputation, a hash of your life."

"Mary! For pity's sake, that's not—"

"And what of *my* reputation? Great heavens—what would all our neighbors think if Viscount Parkhurst suddenly married the vicar's spinster sister? They'd all assume something quite outrageous must have happened between us!"

He laughed again. "Well, isn't that what—"

"*No!*" she said. In truth, she didn't think the townspeople could imagine what actually happened between them on that hillside. She certainly couldn't have imagined it herself before this morning. Oh, the feel of his hands on her skin, of his lips against her flesh, and his tongue pushing inside her. The memory was like a madwoman's dream.

He stared at her in expectation, his eyebrows raised.

"Well, perhaps it was outrageous," she admitted. "But they will think of it as something base and wicked. While I cannot think of it that way. It was…" She couldn't find the words for it. She licked her lips, swallowed hard. And at last abandoned the attempt to describe what it had meant to her. "Please,

John," she said instead. "We both know you were merely being—*kind*."

"*Kind?*" He took a step towards her, a sudden expression like thunder in his eyes.

"Besides," she said, raising a palm to halt his approach. "Everyone knows you're meant to marry a Lawton girl."

And that indeed stopped him in his tracks. He jerked back slightly, said nothing in reply.

He knew as well as she did that it was true. Everyone knew a promise had been made between his father and Lord Lawton. And what dishonor it would be for him to break his father's word.

She turned away from him then, fumbling with the lock to her battered old tea-chest, and her fingers shook so much, half the precious leaves she spooned out scattered over the sink.

"Can you imagine the scandal of what you're suggesting?" she said, keeping her eyes averted. "It would be an outrage for you to spurn the Lawtons. Those young ladies put off their Seasons waiting for your return to Birchford—Miss Lawton for three whole years! I know for a fact she's turned down at least two very eligible suitors, both of whom have now taken other brides. How many other chances has she wasted on your account? If you don't marry her, people may think she's on the shelf, and all her chances gone!"

John heaved a deep sigh. Clearly, he knew she was right to chide him.

There was silence between them then, and she kept her back to him as long as she could, letting the truth of what she'd said steep along with the tea-leaves.

When at long last she turned back to face him, she was instantly startled. John, who had been standing perfectly still over by the table last she looked at him, now stood just inches away, towering over her. He'd moved without a sound, and now loomed so close, she could smell the wool of his coat. The spoon she'd been holding dropped from her fingers and clattered to the slate floor.

His eyes locked on hers, but with determination, not with passion. He was being very stiff-spined now. Dutiful. A soldier. "Do you think I care what our neighbors think? I only care about what's right."

Her breath fluttered in her throat. "Well, I care what people think!" she managed to say, with some semblance of firmness. "They'll assume I seduced you, for why would a man like you seduce a girl like me? They'll assume I used some shameless trickery. And they'll assume we did...far worse than what we did."

"What we did was enough." The memory did not seem to please him.

No, he looked utterly miserable, like a trapped animal.

"*Think*, John!" she pleaded. "If people think me a wanton, Thomas won't be able to hold his head up in the pulpit. He may be asked to leave his position as vicar. He could be ruined."

That at least made John avert his eyes for a moment, his expression abashed.

But he gathered himself deliberately. "We still must do what's right. I compromised you, Mary. In—in the sight of God."

"God has seen far worse, believe me."

"Not from me. Not from you." He blinked suddenly. "Unless you've ever...."

"No! Certainly not! Never!"

"Thank goodness." The relief on his face was palpable.

Oh, dear. He was a good man. A very decent man. And he didn't want to be in this position at all.

And why should he be? He hadn't chosen it. A stand of

malevolent blackberry vines and an over-curious spinster had trapped him into it.

Still, he wasn't backing down. His face looked dreadfully pale, but determined. "Your own brother is a man of God. If his household doesn't do what's right, whose will?"

"I'll tell you what I know from being a clergyman's daughter, and a clergyman's sister. All my life, when people in this village have been in trouble, when they've transgressed, when they've done wrong by their marriage vows, they've come here. To this kitchen. Often in the middle of the night. You think I haven't heard the confessions over the years? My bed chamber is just above this kitchen. What you and I have done is nothing compared to half of what I've heard. *Nothing*, John."

He looked almost insulted. "That was nothing to you?"

A pang went through her heart. She didn't want to think about what it had meant to her. She *couldn't* think of that. All that mattered now was setting him free from the trap she'd inadvertently sprung on him.

She moved out from between him and the sink and went to the cupboard for her tea strainer, setting it over the best teacup just as if they had nothing more to discuss than which workmen to hire to repair the school roof.

"Do you know Lady Ellerby, who's leased Rosemere Cottage?" she said. "Did you know she had to leave London because she'd been having simultaneous affairs with the Prince Regent and the Duke of York, and the brothers nearly fought a duel over her? I'm not violating the sanctity of the confessional, either. She told me so herself, over tea. As she's told many others. She seems rather proud of it all."

"Please, Mary, I don't care what other people—"

"Lord Parkhurst," she insisted. "This morning was an aberration, for both of us. But I don't regret it any more than Lady Ellerby regretted her affairs, and I'm not ashamed. It was something I needed, just once in my life, and you were generous enough to give it to me. But now it's done. I won't have it lead to any suffering."

"*Suffering*? Good Lord, is that how you see it? Being married to me?"

Before she could say another word, he'd advanced on her again, wrapping an arm around her waist, spinning her to face him, and pushing her back against the cupboard.

His hips pressed to hers.

"Is this suffering?" he asked, and slipped his other hand inside her bodice, fitting his fingers around her breast.

Oh. Bright arcs of sensation shot out from where he touched her, radiating throughout her body, sending little starbursts everywhere. Her eyes squeezed shut. She only realized she'd been holding a teacup when it fell from her grip and shattered on the slate.

He ignored the crash.

"Do you want me to stop, Mary?" he said, his voice low, almost a growl.

She couldn't seem to think. All reason fled in the face of the pleasure he sent racing through her body.

She shook her head. "No, don't stop."

And he didn't stop. His hand lifted her breast so the nipple peeked above the cloth, and he fitted his mouth where his palm had been. He suckled her as he'd done that morning, and the hot pull sent a throb between her legs.

His hands both went behind her and began tugging at the laces of her dress, even as his mouth continued drawing at her breast. Soon he had the top of her dress loosened enough to tug it down from her shoulders, baring her halfway down her rib cage. With hands and lips and tongue he pleasured her, moving from one nipple to the other, hungrily.

She leaned back against the cupboard, boneless, molten. She wanted to sink to the floor with him, shards of broken china or no. The only good she could imagine in this world would be for him to lift her skirts and touch her down there as well, and undo his own clothes and sink himself inside of her.

He was groaning now, his breathing grown frantic, and his hands reached down to grasp the fabric of her skirt. It would be so easy, so easy to surrender everything to him. To let him give himself to her, right here, right now, forever.

But it wasn't what he wanted—not really. He was a man. He could take his pleasure with any woman, her as well as another, once he put his hands on her. But so much more was at stake here.

He thought he had to *marry* her. And he was a viscount, for pity's sake. He needed a fashionable wife, a lovely creature who could run an aristocratic house and waltz with dukes and host dinners for Prince George himself. Not a little country mouse with a pale mouth and flat chest and no city manners.

She couldn't let him ruin his whole life over a few minutes' animal indiscretion.

So, gathering all her strength, she pushed him away, hard. "Stop, John. Stop now."

He looked startled, half in his trance again, confusion on his face.

When he tried to move toward her, she held out one hand to block him. She yanked her bodice back to a reasonable degree of modesty and drew herself up straight. The next question would be painful, for both of them, but he had to understand the point she was trying to make. "Do you love me?"

Now he was flustered. "Mary…."

She thought about the Miss Lawtons, with all their graces and physical charms. *They* were women designed to attract men's love, *this* man's love. "Do you love me, John? Can you honestly say you are *in love* with me?"

"Mary, I—"

"Listen to me," she said. "There's only one thing that matters here. Before this morning, before we went up on that hill, did you have the slightest thought in your head about asking me to marry you?"

Every muscle in his face seemed to slacken. He nearly spoke, then stopped himself. The only possible answer was *no*, and they both knew it.

"But we did go up on that hill," he insisted.

"*Before* that happened, John. Did you have the slightest thought of choosing me for a wife? Be honest with me."

He stiffened his posture, pure gentleman and officer. "I have always liked and admired you. You—you were my best *friend*, Mary, for years and years."

"But did you ever once think of *marrying* me?"

He glanced up, considering, and then out of nowhere, he smiled. An impish grin that surprised her. "Well," he said, "I do seem to remember a scheme to run off and sail a pirate ship together."

A short, pained laugh escaped her. She'd forgotten about that.

Long ago, they'd given themselves bloodthirsty pirate names, made buccaneer hats out of paper, even drawn up maps of all the coastline they planned to terrorize. "That was when I was ten years old."

"It counts." His eyes twinkled, just for a moment—the first sign of light in them she'd seen all evening. A tender ache filled her heart.

Oh, he really wasn't making this easier for her.

But she shook her head. "As I recall, our only concern about how we'd live together was which of us got to be captain."

"Mary," he whispered. His expression had gentled and grown sad again. "Be sensible, now. We were children, then, but we're not any longer. That was all in play, but this isn't a game."

"Precisely. It's the rest of our *lives* we're talking about. So I'll ask you again: would you ever have asked me to marry you if we hadn't gone out in the woods this morning? Tell the truth." She did her best to smile at him, trying to keep her mouth from wobbling. "I know the truth already anyway."

He looked down. "Well...no," he admitted at last. "I can't say that I did."

"That's all I need to hear." She swung herself back into efficient action, moving past her erstwhile suitor to retrieve her dustpan and broom to sweep up the broken teacup. If she could just get the shattered bits cleaned up, she could put everything else back in order, too. Back the way it should be. "I would never marry for anything less than love. And I will not saddle you with an ill-matched wife for such a small indiscretion as we committed today. We would be miserable together." She looked up into the sudden shock in his eyes, and softened her words. "I would not do that to someone I call a friend."

John drew in a slow, deep breath. There was resignation in it, but also pain. He was an honorable man, and she was forcing him to compromise what he saw as his honor. "This isn't over," he said. "You will be convinced."

"That's not possible." The china shards tinkled as she swept them together and poured them into the bucket beside the door, to be tossed down the privy later. "I think things through carefully, and once I've come to a decision, I stand by it. I'm stubborn, and you know it."

Setting down her broom, she picked up her lantern again and walked briskly to the front door, shepherding him along with her. "It's time you left now. You are my friend, John, always. But it's not proper for you to be here any longer, and we will not discuss this again."

He did protest for a time, and she had to stand firm. At long last, though, he left, and as she watched him retreat out into the darkness of the woods that lay between the vicarage and Parkhurst Hall, she knew she was right, utterly right, to say no to his ridiculous proposal.

She'd stick by that *no*, even if he came and begged her again a thousand times over.

And if she still felt a sharp, hungry pulse go through her at the thought of saying *yes*, she would just have to find a way to kill that impulse.

John's life would not be ruined just because a plain country mouse had let herself come halfway to falling in love with him.

CHAPTER 5

*J*ohn took the long route home through the woods, trudging along, his head aching, and his chest feeling oddly sore and hot as well. Thankfully, enough moonlight streamed through the trees here and there to let him pick out his path, for he couldn't have borne the revealing light of a lantern. Shame weighed too heavily on his shoulders.

He'd felt enough of that emotion on his walk to the vicarage tonight—shame at his own impetuous behavior up on the hill that morning, shame at the dishonor he'd visited upon a decent girl like Mary, shame at the idea of jilting the Lawton girls he'd already kept waiting for so long. And, most of all, shame at having to break the solemn promise he'd made at his father's deathbed to keep to the plan to align the Parkhursts and Lawtons.

But when he arrived at Mary's door, and saw her in that little circle of lantern light, her skin going pink, then pale, then pink again, he discovered a whole new sort of shame awaiting him, a shame he hadn't even been expecting. He'd assumed he'd talk to Thomas Wilkins first, and that the vicar would ensure his sister's cooperation in the marriage. He hadn't expected Mary to be alone, and free to speak entirely for herself.

And he certainly hadn't expected her to say *no*.

At least not to say no quite so unequivocally. So forcefully, in fact.

He rather thought he'd been tossed out on his ear.

As he made his way home, he kicked at rocks and stamped on dry branches with considerably more aggression than those objects deserved.

True enough, he'd never considered marrying her before —which was hardly unreasonable, given the difference in their stations, and how far their lives had diverged since childhood. But he'd been quite sincere when he said he'd always liked her, liked her very much indeed.

Certainly, there was no one else with whom he'd rather embark on a life of piracy.

And he *did* admire her, genuinely so. Since he'd returned home, he saw how much she did for the good of the village and all his tenants—organizing village events, providing schooling for the children, making improvements for everyone's health and happiness. She was the heart and soul of the place. A person whose work *mattered*.

Unlike an idle viscount, he supposed.

He stopped dead in a deep patch of shadow in a dense stand of pines. A little clearing stood before him, brightened by a shaft of moonbeams, but he was all in darkness. It seemed an appropriate place for his mood, still and heavy and out of the light.

Was that what Mary meant when she said they didn't belong together? That they were *ill-matched*, and would be *miserable* together. She as well as he.

She'd spoken of *suffering* in marriage to him, for pity's sake.

Did she really think him such a useless prat?

Damn it. She'd only seen him surrounded by luxury here at Parkhurst Hall—sitting in upholstered armchairs or atop a thoroughbred horse in spotless buckskin pantaloons his valet had brushed clean for him, with piles of money to fall back on if ever he did stumble.

If she could have known him when he was a soldier—if she'd seen him on the battlefield, streaked with soot and blood, barking orders to his troops, charging at the enemy...

Well, it didn't matter what she thought of him, anyway.

He'd compromised her. A gentleman and gentlewoman just shouldn't do what the two of them had done and act as if nothing had happened. Maybe Mary could be that pragmatic, but he couldn't. Where virtue was concerned, intangibles *mattered*, rules mattered, and if everyone ignored them, where would civilization be?

His mind flashed on the image of Mary laying on her back on the forest floor, her thighs spread for him. Oh, yes, he liked her. He certainly liked her thighs. *And her scent.* And the way she writhed beneath his mouth as he'd pleasured her with his tongue.

How might she writhe if he'd done everything he'd wanted to do that morning? How might she moan?

She'd liked what he did to her, he was sure of that, at least.

Yet she was refusing to marry him.

Damn, this was a mess.

Of course, one simple way through was to talk to Mary's brother, and let him understand exactly what had happened. Thomas Wilkins was a sensible man, an honorable man. He'd see the necessity of marriage in this situation.

Though the prospect of such a conversation turned John's stomach to lead. Imagine trying to explain to an ordained clergyman that he'd had the man's sister on her back, with her skirts around her waist, and that woman would apparently rather die than let him make an honest woman of her.

Marriage was for life, and Thomas would be his brother-in-law. He'd prefer not to have to avert his eyes in embarrassment every damned time he saw the man.

And then there was the likelihood Mary would hate them both for ganging up to pressure her into a union she didn't want.

No—John had to give Mary some time to see reason on her own.

If she didn't come around in a week or two, he could go to Thomas then and force the issue. He could wait a week or two.

A sudden snapping noise startled him from his reverie.

Something was moving, something fairly large, crackling through the underbrush. With a soldier's instincts, he stepped even deeper into the shadow of the pines.

A cold weight dropped through his middle: what if it was Thomas Wilkins coming home early from tending the drunkard?

John pressed his way deeper into the cover of pine branches and squinted into the darkness. Shadowy shapes moved through the trees on the other side of the clearing. *Two* shadowy shapes.

So not just Thomas Wilkins, then.

The shapes stumbled into the clearing.

A man and a woman. Neither one of whom was the vicar.

The pair appeared to be having some sort of silent altercation—pushing at one another, struggling.

Was the woman under attack?

He was just bracing himself to spring into action when he recognized who it was: the sexton Mr. Bassett, and Mrs. Trumbull, who ran the Fox & Crow. And they weren't fighting; they were pulling at the fastenings of one another's clothes.

Mary must have been right about the frequency with which others in the village misbehaved. He certainly knew misbehavior was the wont of soldiers, but somehow he'd assumed it was different with decent country people.

He was on the verge of calling out to make his presence known when Mrs. Trumbull apparently succeeded in loosening the bit of Mr. Bassett's clothing she was most eager to get out of her way—the closure of his breeches. She sank instantly to her knees, and without any further preamble, took the length of him into her mouth.

Good Lord. John had no choice now but to stay hidden where he was.

Mr. Bassett grunted. He seized the innkeeper's head in both hands and began to work in and out between her lips, building to solid thrusts.

His own cock stirred—and immediately he thought of Mary.

And that was the wrong thing to be thinking.

He mustn't think of Mary, not right now, not this way. He'd done enough wrong by her already, and he needed to keep his head as clear as possible about her.

Instead, he tried to imagine the eldest Miss Lawton on her knees, taking him in her mouth. Just a thought experiment. To see if he might be able to muster the same enthusiasm for her that apparently came so easily to him with Mary.

He focused on a mental image of Annabel Lawton kneeling before him in some frothy Parisian frock, the top of her plump bosom bared like the swells of two ripe peaches, her lovely golden curls loose about her shoulders. Her pretty pink bow of a mouth sliding along his shaft, her moist lips opening wider to take him deep.....

He *tried* to imagine it. Got as far as her tongue stroking the seam of his cock.

And then the image dissolved.

It was impossible to sustain.

Any of the Misses Lawton would refuse to get on her knees in the first place—it would wrinkle her dress. And surely the idea of putting her lips around a man's bared appendage would horrify her ladylike sensibilities.

Even with the sight of the fornicating pair in front of him, his cock began to flag.

Marriage to a Lawton girl would probably mean a lifetime of separate chambers, of creeping in to her bed at midnight, more like a thief than a lover, touching his wife as little as possible while she gripped the bed-sheets and said her prayers, her face turned away as she wished him done with his vile manly business.

A deplorable thought.

Not that he'd expected anything different as late as when he rose from bed this morning. He'd been resigned to it then, bound by the demands of honor. But then he hadn't yet seen Mary Wilkins with her hair wild and her eyes gleaming with desire.

That image in his head, and the thought of the smell of Mary, the taste of her, her smooth legs spread open before him, her chest heaving with her desperate breaths, the sweet moans coming out of her mouth, had him rock-hard again in an instant.

Mary.

A new image took form in his mind, unbidden: Mary Wilkins on her knees before him, brandy-colored hair unbound, those clever gray eyes focused on his face as she took him into her mouth, smiling as she did it. Her tongue whipping over the length of him, laving him around and around, her excitement growing every second right along with his. That image was vivid, enduring—and arousing beyond belief.

He closed his eyes, fighting the urge to let his hands slide to his fall to undo the buttons as he had with Mary that morning.

And then he heard Mr. Bassett cry out, "Damn me, woman! Don't stop now."

John's eyes flew open. Mrs. Trumbull was still on her knees but only her hand held the man's stiff member now.

The woman laughed, quite wickedly. And then she rolled down onto her back on the carpet of leaves and mosses and drew her skirts up around her hips, spreading her legs wide to show him what awaited him there. "I don't mean to stop," she purred, and rubbed one hand lasciviously between her legs. "I just mean to offer you another chamber for your pleasures."

The sexton roared like a bull, pulled his breeches down and fell atop her.

But that sight was nothing to the thought of Mary on her back on the forest floor, of what might have been had he not just used his hand and mouth this morning, but taken her completely.

Mary, he thought, would have welcomed him, wrapped her legs around him with fervor, fisted her fingers in his hair, given as good as she got. No turning her head aside and wishing for it to be over.

He remembered how her thighs had tensed while he pleasured her. Her hips had lifted, offering her soft, slippery, fragrant core, yielding every inch of it to him. She'd grabbed hold of his head to push his tongue deeper, and writhed and clenched and spasmed beneath him.

Lord, if he could have Mary underneath him, he'd make her come again, even harder than before—and then again, and again, and again.

The blood had been drumming in his head, through his belly, a rough, hot need, and before he could swallow the sound, a groan forced itself from his lips.

The sound surely would have attracted the attention of the pair coupling on the ground, had their tryst not reached its conclusion at nearly the same moment, so they were lost in ecstatic shouts of their own.

The air seemed to echo with the noise of pleasure—and at the peak of it all, what sounded like a second female voice. A gasp.

He looked to the other side of the clearing, and caught a sudden glimpse of a pale white face peeking out from behind another tree.

Dear Lord—*Mary*.

He could barely make her out, hidden as she was, but there was no mistaking her, or the fact that she was looking straight at him.

How long had she been standing there? What all had she seen?

She saw him catch sight of her, and disappeared behind the trunk, as quick as if she were a sylvan nymph indeed.

He couldn't see or hear her retreat—now that her pale face had vanished, her dark clothes made her invisible even under the moonlight.

Instinctively, he moved to try to run after her—and in the darkness ran smack into a bush. It rustled loudly, and he hastily drew back away from it, concealing himself behind another tree.

He heard Mr. Bassett's voice, sounding suddenly alarmed. "Did you hear something, Dinah?"

"It was an animal in the bushes, Joe, nothing more."

An animal. Yes, he was an animal indeed.

What had happened to him today? He was an honorable man. *Had* been an honorable man, just that morning.

Now he was skulking in shrubberies, watching other people copulate, fantasizing quite spectacularly about the vicar's sister down on her knees—and that very girl herself had caught sight of him in the process.

It was a good thing the path in front of him hadn't been clear. If he had been able to run after Mary, if he had been able to catch her, what on earth had he been planning to do?

He liked to think it would simply be to beg her once more to marry him, but he suspected that would have come somewhere down the list after trying to get her entirely out of her clothes.

Damn it all.

His whole world had shifted straight off its axis, and he didn't know if he could ever set it right again.

MARY FLED through the woods as fast as the moonlight would permit her, stumbling over rocks and roots and still not slowing.

Why on earth had she come out here at all? It was just that the air in the vicarage had seemed unbreathable after the viscount left. The thought of the woods and the dark and the cool air had called to her, and she'd come out, thinking only to walk for a time to clear her head and soothe the aching pulses of her heart.

Even then, it had been clear to her she'd done the right thing in turning down the viscount's proposal. Duty alone had compelled him to ask for her hand. Lord knows he'd looked so ill at the prospect she'd thought one of his loved ones must be dying.

So what if some deep-buried part of her clawed at her brain with the thought that she could just say *yes*, and have him for her own, have him share her bed and her body forever.

She would never listen to that voice.

And now—well, she was more sure than ever that a marriage between them could only be a mistake.

It had been enough of a shock to discover Mr. Bassett and Mrs. Trumbull together again in the woods—she'd nearly charged right into them. But then to see John, watching them as well from deep in the shadows of a pine. She could barely make him out, would not have seen him at all except that her mind was so attuned to his shape and form that the edge of his shadow drew her eye, but it was clear enough to her how utterly absorbed he was by what he was watching.

She'd seen the naked look of lust on his face as he watched Mr. Bassett and Mrs. Trumbull engage in their carnal tryst on the forest floor. She'd heard the passionate groan escape his lips. And those things told her all she needed to know: that his desire for her was as thoughtless and base as the sexton's lust for the scarlet-haired innkeeper.

If she'd harbored even the slightest hope that his behavior up on the hill this morning had had something to do with *her* in particular rather than with circumstance—the vines that had exposed her legs, the thorns that had pulled his head against her bosom—well, that hope was utterly dashed.

He was a man. And men were mindless brutes when it came to female flesh.

And lust was most certainly *not* a basis for marriage.

He'd surely feel the same lust for any of the Lawton girls. And in the daylight hours, when the pleasure of the flesh was not a man's main motive for marriage, one of the Lawtons would most certainly be a better match for him. Fashionable. Tasteful. Able to plan soirées and play the pianoforte and move gracefully in silks. Pretty to look at, for a viscount to show off to his friends.

He would not regret marrying such a girl six months after they were wed.

So it was really just as well things had gone as they had tonight. That she'd stumbled upon the two over-eager lovers and John spying on them in the woods.

Any sentimental illusions that might have troubled her, might have tempted her to selfishness and stupidity, had been wiped away.

CHAPTER 6

*D*amn it all, but Mary Wilkins was stubborn as a rock.

John tried to talk to her after church on Sunday, but she vanished into the sacristy with a mumbled excuse about hanging up vestments—though her brother was clearly still *wearing* his vestments, right there on the church steps, while the two elderly Dalton sisters pinned him down with a long story about their tabby's new litter of kittens.

He stopped by the schoolhouse the next day, but Mary spied him coming up the walk and cued the children to sing a rousing rendition of "Jerusalem the Golden" in four-part harmony, with Mary singing loudest of all. She seemed ready to lead them through all sixteen verses, and probably a reprise as well, if he hadn't eventually taken the hint and gone away.

He even sent her a note saying he'd hired Mr. Dockett's boy to climb the hill to confirm water was indeed streaming underground, just as she'd said, and he would have men begin the well the moment she gave him her opinion of the exact spot to dig.

Surely that would bring her running to Parkhurst Hall, he'd thought, for how could she resist seeing one of her plans for the village come to fruition? But she only sent back a hand-drawn map with a large X and the words "Just here, sixty-two paces east of the willow" as though she'd become a pirate indeed.

Without him.

Maybe what they'd done together amidst the blackberries had truly been of no moment to her. She certainly didn't seem to have been affected by it. She seemed her normal self —self-possessed, confident, briskly going about the business of the church and the school and the town, quite without the need of him.

Had it really meant so little to her?

The thought hung on his chest, a dull gray weight.

He'd been short-tempered and irritable for days. His housekeeper had set out blackberry jam for his tea yesterday, in a little jam-pot hand-painted with blackberry vines, and at the sight of those green twisting branches, he'd actually *yelled* at her to take it away. She'd scorched his beef for dinner that night, and he deserved it. And his valet wasn't much happier with him. John kept shifting fretfully in his seat whenever the poor man tried to shave him, and that morning had tossed aside four different neckcloths because each one seemed tighter and more abrasive than the last.

He really couldn't let things go on like this.

Sooner or later he was going to have to go to Thomas Wilkins and confess what had happened up on the hill, but he kept hoping Mary would come around on her own before that mortifying conversation became necessary.

Unless…she was right to be refusing him.

What if he *was* being foolish in this insistence that they marry?

Certainly, she'd been very clear—painfully clear— that

she had no interest in becoming his wife, that she'd be quite miserable forced into the role of viscountess.

And he couldn't imagine it any more easily than she could: Mary Wilkins frittering away her time in ballrooms, with ostrich feathers in her hair and the Parkhurst family rubies weighting her neck. Mary Wilkins standing for hours in full court dress to make her bow to the queen. Sitting with his mother in the evenings, embroidering pillowcases and gossiping about other women's hairstyles and china settings and shoes.

It would be like...taking a wild deer and penning it up in city stables.

Unnatural.

Even cruel.

It was far easier to imagine her fighting a bout of fisticuffs in Gentleman Jackson's saloon, or arguing a bill in the House of Lords. She'd be quite impressive at those ventures, wouldn't she? Fierce and agile and utterly inexorable both in landing punches and in her line of reasoning. But, alas, neither a boxing match nor a seat in Parliament were within his power to offer her.

He heaved a sigh.

Still, they had done what they had done, and the demands of honor on that score were perfectly clear.

Of course, honor also demanded he marry one of the Lawtons.

If only honor permitted bigamy. He could marry both women, and the Lawton girl could perform the duties of viscountess during the day, and Mary could share his bed at night.

Good Lord—that was *not* an appropriate thought.

Appealing, maybe, but not appropriate.

Tuesday arrived, and the next day would make a full week since they'd got themselves snared in those inexorable vines.

John found himself skulking about the village green, restless as a schoolboy on the lookout for mischief. Mary had to show her face here sooner or later. Tomorrow was May Day, and she was, not surprisingly, head of the committee tasked with preparing the village festivities.

Men had been working all morning, pounding in the tall post for the May Pole—a huge thing hewn from the trunk of a pine tree more than a hundred years ago and stored in the Merchant's Hall most of each year. The pole was painted the same bright glossy red that adorned so many of the barges that worked the rivers here, and gleamed in the sunshine.

Ropes were strung between the living trees all around the Green from which would hang cheerful lanterns. The last few nights had been unseasonably warm, and everyone hoped the evening dancing might be held outdoors by lantern light rather than up in the stuffy assembly rooms above the Hall.

He turned on his heel for what felt like the nine-hundred-fiftieth time to walk yet again up the path between the school and the church, when at long last, he saw Mary coming, leading a little group of ladies with long, brightly-colored ribbons draped across their outstretched arms. He was a mere ten feet from the May Pole for which those ribbons were intended, so Mary couldn't possibly evade him now.

He stepped forward, trying to project a polite smile that would communicate to onlookers something like, "I've come to speak with Miss Wilkins about a matter of impersonal village business," rather than, "Please Mary, let me make amends for debauching you the other day."

Mary caught sight of him and blanched. She stopped dead, causing another lady behind her to plow straight into her back.

But a third lady, Annabel Lawton, the eldest of the Lawton sisters, did not stop. Giving a toss of her golden curls, she weaved her way neatly past the others and swooped right in upon him with a smile on her pretty pink bow of a mouth—a smile that said, "Here is the gentleman I intend to snap up in holy matrimony, and I know I will succeed, for no man can resist my personal charms."

His throat constricted.

Miss Lawton batted her long black lashes. Her armful of ribbon was held out imploringly, a clear sign that he should relieve her poor, weak, ladylike arms of the awful burden of those thin strips of cloth.

It would be a grave insult to refuse her.

"Allow me to assist you with those, please, Miss Lawton," he said dutifully, and took the ribbons into his own arms.

As he did so, Miss Lawton contrived to brush both his hands with hers, and then blushed prettily and glanced away with a little gasp, as though the contrivance had been entirely his.

Lord.

He had to give her credit for her skill.

With that distraction past, he looked around for Mary— who had already managed to climb to the top of a tall stepladder and was balancing on her tiptoes, using a long stick with a hook on its end to thread the first of her ribbons through the round ring at the top of the May Pole.

The sight of her stretched out up there struck him with erotic force.

Damn it all.

Whether any of the good townspeople openly acknowledged it or not, May Day was part of pagan tradition, from long before the coming of Christianity, a true rite of spring. The May Pole was a spear thrust up to pierce the frosts of winter, a symbol of fertility, of the surging energy of the newborn earth.

The lithe line of Mary's body made him want to see her stretched out on the grass. Completely unclothed this time.

With his naked body stretched out over top of hers.

And he could lose himself in the feel of her, the smell of her, the clench of her thighs and the wet warmth between them, her chest heaving with desperate breaths, the sweet moans from her mouth…

He willed her to look at him, to see the heat she sparked in his eyes. She'd spoken of love as a necessity for marriage, and though he might not be able to offer her precisely that, they had *this* between them, this very powerful thing, and surely that ought to count for something.

Look at me, Mary. Turn and look.

But she was paying no attention at all to him. Her gaze was solidly focused on her task.

Was it really so hard to guide a ribbon through a six-inch ring, or was she *pointedly* ignoring him?

His money was on "pointedly ignoring him."

He sighed, and the delicious heat that had filled him at the thought of their bodies coming together curdled back into a cold sensation of disappointment, mingled with a dull weight of shame.

Mary wanted nothing to do with him.

Miss Lawton, though, had no such compunctions. She tapped him boldly on the forearm to bring his attention back to her, gazed straight at him with her robin's-egg-blue eyes, and twittered, "What do you think, Lord Parkhurst? Tomorrow for the May Pole dance, shall I choose a blue ribbon to hold or a pink one? Or perhaps yellow? My dress shall be blue, but I do love the freshness of pink, and the brightness of yellow. They put one in mind of azaleas and daisies, don't you think? Most appropriate for the season. And one wishes to celebrate the coming of spring with the proper enthusiasm."

"Indeed," he said, having nothing else sensible to reply.

"And shall you join us around the May Pole, my lord?" Her lashes fluttered again. "To dance with the other young people?"

"I...I had not thought about it either way."

He glanced back up at the bright red May Pole. Oh, if Mary Wilkins were going to dance, how could he resist? As they had from time immemorial, the unmarried men would face one way, the unmarried women the other, winding their long ribbons around the towering pole, drawing tighter and tighter until the dancers had no choice but to press up close to one another, heated and laughing, their heightened blood blazing in their cheeks. Modern civilization could pride itself on whatever dignity and discipline it wished to claim, the symbolic meaning of the dance was unmistakable, almost obscene.

Desire. Pleasure. Sex.

Ah, but if he and Mary did join the dancers, she would probably slip by him each time without looking at him, avoiding the brush of his arms and shoulders. She would freeze him out.

"Oh, but you *must* dance," chirped Annabel, startling him. "The lord of the manor should join his people in their festivities. It is an absolute *duty*."

He managed to smile at her, but risked another glance at Mary. She had half a dozen ribbons strung through the ring already, and was reaching down for yet another. Most efficient.

A memory came to him suddenly, of Mary at perhaps seven or eight years old, daring him to race up the trunk of an enormous oak tree. They'd both scraped themselves mightily on the bark as they fought to gain the highest branches. And when they'd reached the top and looked out over all of Birchford and the surrounding countryside, from the mouth of the River

Burne on the southeastern side to the wide blue ribbon of the River Ouse in the northwest, they'd both gasped at the sight—all that rolling green and sparkling water stretched out beneath them, and the clouds above looming huge and white, closer than ever. And there was the square sandstone gleam of Parkhurst Hall, its usual majesty reduced to dollhouse proportions.

Mary had sighed and said, "This is how giants must see the world." They'd both been quite earnest about giants at the time.

And, eyeing his suddenly fragile ancestral home, he'd answered her: "A giant this tall could destroy all of Birchford with just a few stomps of his boots."

"Oh, no!" she'd said. "It could be a kind giant, who'd give us rides on his shoulders, and plow all our fields with his hair comb, and build new stone cottages for all the farmers using just his fingertips."

He smiled to remember it now. That had been childhood Mary in a nutshell—daring and imaginative and immensely kind, all at once. Which, now that he thought about it, was still an apt description of Mary as an adult, though she hid all but the kindness from most people who knew her.

He couldn't see her face now as she stood on the ladder, only the side of her head with its tight-coiled hair, and the length of her very serviceable brown frock. Funny how drab she could appear if you didn't know just what you were looking at.

Miss Lawton, in contrast, was all vivid color and glow. The blonde curls, the blue eyes, the radiant rosy skin, the prettily sprigged muslin of her dress with its thousands of tiny pink and green flowers, and a glossy bright green ribbon in a bow just under her very full breasts.

By rights, Miss Lawton should be the object of his sexual fantasies. She was the sort of plump, silken, scented, pliant creature most men wished to spend their lusts upon. But, no. Mary's pale stubborn mouth and those small firm breasts and that spine stiffened by a rather prickly sense of pride provoked him so much more intensely than Annabel Lawton ever could.

He'd let himself forget what Mary was over the years he was away from home. But once they'd gone up that hill and gotten tangled in the blackberries, he'd caught sight once more of the bright flame that burned just beneath the surface.

He nearly jumped as Miss Lawton tapped him on the forearm again.

"When you dance about the May Pole, my lord," said Miss Lawton, "you must hold a blue ribbon, and you must wear that waistcoat of yours with the blue stripe through the white cloth, the one you wore to the church breakfast Sunday last. You shall look quite sprightly. I daresay no man in the county shall look more like a proper celebrant of the spring!"

"I daresay," he replied dryly. "Of course, you are quite wise in such matters, Miss Lawton." He tried to smile, though his head was beginning to hurt. If he did as Mary insisted and married Annabel Lawton, conversations this inane would be his doom every remaining day of his life.

Surely he'd spent enough time mollifying the ego of Miss Lawton. He stepped up beside the ladder, his heart pounding as though he were the most callow of swains. "Are you quite all right up there, Miss Wilkins?" he asked, lifting his armful of ribbons in a helpful sort of gesture. "Perhaps I could assist you?"

Mary speared yet another ribbon through the ring. "Thank you, no, Lord Parkhurst. I am managing quite nicely."

Of course she was. Mary managed quite nicely at everything.

He was the one who was of no use to her. His heart sank.

Did she truly see him as nothing more than an annoyance, a pestering mayfly? Once upon a time, they'd been partners in all their adventures, and she'd trusted him implicitly to be as wild and brave and strong as she was.

Well, the years had passed for her, too. Perhaps she only saw *his* surface now—the civilized, privileged surface of a viscount who no longer climbed oak trees or wished to be a pirate. A *gentleman*, with all the qualities that term implied.

Miss Lawton tapped at him yet again, like a damned woodpecker.

"My lord," she said, "Do please promise me you'll join the dancing tomorrow evening as well. The proper dancing, I mean. We have so few noblemen who attend our little assemblies here, and I very much want to dance as ladies are meant to. Since I have not been to London yet, I've had few opportunities."

Ah, that was a well-aimed volley. No, Miss Lawton had not been to London yet. Lord Lawton had not let her have her formal Season, precisely because he fully expected her to become a viscountess right here at home.

Damn this whole situation.

If no marriage proposal was forthcoming to Annabel Lawton, John would be committing a grievous offense against her family. And he would bring shame to his own father's memory.

Damn and blast and damn again.

Warring impulses pulled at his insides, aching like a bruise. He wanted Mary, but Mary didn't want him—she was making that very clear. And duty demanded that he do what everyone else was waiting for, and take Miss Lawton as his bride.

Maybe it would just be easier to let Mary have her way, forget anything that happened between them, go forward with his father's plan for him, marry Annabel Lawton and be done with it.

That strategy would certainly be easier on his pride than following Mary about like a spaniel spurned at every turn. It would be the wise and sensible thing to do. The honorable thing.

The best salve for his wounded pride.

But the thought made him more heavy-hearted than he'd ever felt in his life.

CHAPTER 7

*M*ay Day morning dawned bright and clear.

Mary Wilkins was not given to superstitions, but the day was already so splendid, the nighttime mists vanishing from the field and woods almost the moment the first rays peered over the horizon, it was hard to resist the lure of the old stories.

Long ago, the pagan people here believed spirits inhabited the trees and meadows, and local folklore still held that on this loveliest day of spring a maiden would spy her true love if she went out in the morning to gather flowers.

Certainly, this morning felt a thousand times better than yesterday, when she'd felt so stiff and wooden perched up on that ladder like some scrawny old workman while John flirted right under her nose with the gloriously beautiful Annabel Lawton.

She'd seen their hands brush when he offered to carry Annabel's ribbons for her. She'd seen the startled look on his face, the hint of a blush stealing over his cheeks, the alert awareness in his eyes. Of *course* he reacted to Annabel like that. Any man would have.

After that morning with the blackberry bramble had knocked the world temporarily out of sorts, things were settling back into their right dimensions again.

A moment's madness—prompted by *her* wanton impulse—made John do what he'd done with her up on that hill, and a misguided sense of duty prompted him to offer marriage afterwards. But Mary had held firm to what she knew was right, and disaster had been averted.

It *would* have been a disaster if she'd tried to marry John. No matter what he said, they'd both have regretted it within a month of the wedding day as the ridiculousness of their pairing made itself inexorably clear.

And yet, yesterday, watching John together with blonde, lush-bosomed Annabel, flirting on the Green, she'd thought she would die inside.

But she didn't die. She was made of stronger stuff than that. She'd been raised to do the right thing, after all. She'd make what she could of her life, and not indulge in self-pity.

Right now, the morning was beautiful, as beautiful and magical as anything the pagans could have desired. The past two springs had been so cold and damp and gray, people spoke of a "year without a summer," and complained of frosts lasting into June and skies so dark even the most frugal housewives had to light kitchen candles in the afternoons. Some went so far as to say the world had fallen under a curse, and crops would never grow right again.

But this spring was proving such mournful thinkers wrong. The morning was balmy, and all around her leaves shone brilliant green and rustled in hushed, welcoming whispers. The fresh breeze caressed her skin, and tiny insects with transparent wings beamed golden in the sunbeams, flickering through the air like friendly sprites. The smell of earth rose warm and fertile—the world was full of the possibility of transformation.

While her brother still slept soundly in his room this morning, Mary had donned a frock of thin green muslin, the lightest she had. The other young ladies would follow local tradition and set out with unbound hair and bare feet to gather May Day flowers, but they would stick to the relatively civilized meadows at the other end of the village, along the riverbank, where they might stay on the well-packed earthen path and not dirty their toes too much. They'd come home with tame white daisies and pale yellow daffodils. But Mary headed deep into the woods where the loveliest wildflowers grew—the scented wood anemones and bluebells, bright marsh marigolds, sweet bramble roses and jewel-toned irises that required a good deal more exertion and exposure to thorns and mud.

She'd always gone into the woods on May Day, celebrating the coming of spring much as her long-ago ancestors had done, and that one day of the year she'd left her hair free of its usual coil, as a pagan maiden would. But this year she took an extra risk, gave herself an additional small taste of freedom: she left off not just her shoes, but her chemise and petticoat and stays as well.

It was a shocking thing to do, to have her body bare beneath her dress. A bit of sunlight behind her, and anyone could see she wore no underthings. But she'd never encountered another soul when she went Maying in woods in the past, and she couldn't imagine she'd see anyone this morning.

For just one brief hour, she wouldn't feel like the vicar's sister. She might imagine herself loose, unfettered, part of the sensuous world. It was a small compensation for forbidding herself to even *look* twice at Viscount Parkhurst yesterday, for holding herself rigid on that blasted ladder and not thinking—or at least trying not to think—about how much she longed for him to touch her again.

Now her curls blew softly across her cheeks, and the

breeze fluttered her light skirts over her legs so she felt the shape of her body beneath the linen, for once seeming not straight and scrawny, but subtly rounded, feminine. Her flower basket beat against her hip, and even that small pressure sent shocks of physical awareness through her. A strange, restless energy tinged with desire seemed to ripple through the very air as she moved. Her blood heated and sang.

Ever since she'd lain on the forest floor with the viscount's mouth between her legs, she was changed. The physical world had changed for her. She felt it all differently, felt new possibilities in it—even if it was illusion, even if it would all be denied her forever after, even if she'd never taste the pleasure of a man's touch again.

A sudden, wild impulse swept through her, to throw her body down in a field of flowers, hike up her skirts, and let the sun kiss her flesh. To touch herself wantonly where John's mouth had touched her. Where he'd pleasured her so thoroughly.

Oh, what if she *could* be here with John?

She shouldn't think of him, but the thoughts flowed in anyway. In fantasy, at least, she might have him. In this world that felt so magical, they wouldn't have to remember the restraints of civilized life. They could lie down together amongst the bluebells, loosen what little clothing they wore, and let the surge of new springtime life carry them away.

Her heart thundered at the idea, her lungs drew in deeper draughts of air.

She came up over a rise lined with sweet blooming hawthorn trees, agilely dodging their thorny branches, drinking in their perfumed scent, feeling more alive and vigorous than she had any right to feel.

And then she saw him.

John.

Standing right there in the clearing she'd been heading towards.

Not more than twenty feet away.

He wasn't dressed in his normal lordly attire. He wore no hat or jacket, and the sun made a halo of his golden hair and a bright nimbus of the loose white linen of his shirt. He did wear breeches and boots, but no waistcoat and no neckcloth, and his sleeves were rolled up to his elbows.

In nearly the same state of dishabille as she was.

His throat and a bare expanse of his chest beneath it gleamed like bronze. He was too beautiful—a young pagan god.

And he shouldn't be there—he *wouldn't* be there, like that.

She must be dreaming him up.

She stopped dead, but she made no move to cover herself. A gentleman oughtn't to see her with her hair loose and her feet bare and the sun shining through her dress with no chemise beneath. But this wasn't real. This was a dream—a fantastical bit of magic conjured by the May Day sprites.

John's gaze seemed to be raking over her form, clearly taking in the sight of her, and his fists clenched so hard, the muscles of his forearms bunched.

And then he called out to her.

"Mary!" he exclaimed. "You're *here!*"

The sound of his voice was enough to break the charm that held her. She wasn't imagining him. He was real, and flesh and blood, not a magical illusion.

And he was most certainly *not* supposed to be roaming the woods on May Day morning.

She snatched up her basket, holding it protectively in front of her torso.

"John!" she called back in a warning tone. "What are you —why are you outdoors?"

He just stared at her, giving his head a shake, his brow

furrowing, as though he could not understand the language she was speaking.

Well, whatever his reason for appearing, it was very, very dangerous to be out here alone with him, in this strange, loosened state she was in. She might not be strong enough to resist him, and she knew she *had* to resist him, for his sake, if not for hers.

No, it was for her own sake as well—she had to keep her distance so she could keep something of her inner self alive when he married elsewhere.

"Only the ladies are supposed to be out now," she admonished as firmly as she could, though her voice trembled slightly. "Gentlemen are supposed to stay at home in their beds. Until at least—at *least* nine o'clock."

And, dash it all, he *grinned* at her. "Too many years in the army," he called back, shrugging his broad shoulders. "No soldier I know could possibly sleep past seven in the morning. And this is entirely ridiculous, having to shout at each other from across the—"

"Stay back!" she yelped, and clutched her basket tighter to her chest. "And—and *go* back. Home. *Indoors.*"

Even this far away, she could see the line of his jaw tighten. "I can't bear it indoors," he admitted, his deep voice carrying easily over the distance, seeming to vibrate over her bared skin. "I feel like a caged lion inside walls. Besides, shouldn't you be over by the riverbank, where the other ladies go? Isn't that the traditional spot?"

"No, *this* is the traditional spot. The riverbank is just more—"

"Modern?" he answered. And there was that grin again. "Civilized?"

A hot flush climbed up her throat. "Easier on ladies' feet."

"No doubt." He took a step towards her. "But you are undaunted, Mary, as always."

He took another step. Two steps. Three. Casual and easy, as if they'd met quite properly dressed on the lane around the Green, but his eyes were locked on hers with an intensity that was anything but civilized. His stride was long, and the distance between them was closing faster than her nerves were comfortable with. "Never the ordinary path for you."

While he was still a few strides away, she took a step backward. "I beg your pardon! *I'm* the one following the rules this morning."

He stopped then, his blue eyes scanning her face. "Are you? Following the rules?"

She held her ground, refusing to even *think* of how many rules she had already broken today. She lifted her chin and gave him the stern, authoritative stare she sometimes gave the schoolchildren when they were being particularly naughty and needed to be cowed.

He did not seem to be cowed.

Instead, a strange wistfulness came over his expression, and he cocked his head to one side, watching her thoughtfully. "Do you remember, when we were children, you told me these woods are full of faerie folk, who love nothing more than to play tricks on foolish mortals?"

She blinked. "Those were children's stories."

"Were they? I wonder, just now. Miss Mary Wilkins, the vicar's sister, appearing from the woods on May Day morning, barefoot, with curls dancing free, just when I happen to walk by? Perhaps you're one of those faerie folk, come to bewitch me."

"Don't be ridiculous."

"I would normally think myself ridiculous for saying such a thing, but at the moment..." He grinned once more. "They say the faeries can spin visions from our dreams. And just look at you."

"What?" Despite herself, she glanced down at her soft

frock and bare feet, the wind tugging at her hem. Oh, dear. Nothing between him and her but a basket of flowers.

Duty and reason made her wish she were wearing her heavy serge skirts and sturdy boots instead of this diaphanous green. And then again, there was a part of her that didn't wish for anything about this moment to change.

"What...what *dreams*?" she asked.

He took another step in her direction. "Why do you think I couldn't sleep?"

Her heart hammered so hard in her throat she could scarcely draw breath. "Now you are definitely being ridiculous," she rasped.

He shook his head slowly, very slowly, his eyes never leaving her face. "Not ridiculous. I couldn't sleep because I was thinking about you."

"You shouldn't. " She retreated another step. "You shouldn't think about me."

"I tried not to. I tried very hard." Another stride closer.

Her legs trembled.

"I'm finding it devilishly hard to avoid thinking about you these days," he said. "*Especially* when I'm in bed."

A flutter went through her abdomen at his words. "Stay back."

But he didn't stay back. He advanced again, coming close enough now that if they both reached out their arms, their fingers could touch.

"This morning I thought of you walking in the woods," he said, his tone low and urgent. "I imagined you with your hair down, walking through the flowers. I tried to convince myself that was only a fantasy, that you'd never dare do it in truth." His breath held a moment, then released on a ragged sigh. "But, damn it all, look at you. Better even than I imagined."

The flutter she'd felt became a pulse. A hot pulse, throbbing through her breasts, through the core of her.

She dropped her basket then, folded her arms across her body to cover herself.

"No, Mary, don't," he demanded, his voice going rough. "Don't hide from me. I want to see you. I *need* to see you. Please."

She shook her head, almost dizzy with the combination of need and fear. "We can't, John. What you need is to stay away from me. You need to go back home."

He took one more step closer, close enough that she could see the dark golden hair that curled on his chest, and the pulse that beat at the base of his throat. Much closer than a gentleman should allow himself to come to a lady in her current state of undress. "Do you know what guided me here when I thought of you," he said, "when I knew all the other ladies would stay close the village?"

She meant to turn and run, but his gaze seemed to pin her to the spot. "How?"

"The other ladies are doing this in the English way. Staying in places where Nature has been tamed. But you— you understand something they don't."

"What is that?

"That the rites of spring aren't English at all. That's they're much older than that, much more powerful."

Her breath shuddered. "My father told me about the ancient Britons," she said, trying to keep her voice light. She needed all the defenses of her education now. "The little hillock our church stands on was built by them, long before the Saxons came. They called this time of year Beltane, the time of fire. The burning away of winter, the coming of new life."

Oh, why did the sun make his hair and shirt and skin glow so beautifully—he was like flame itself, like a heat that purified, that melted, while bringing both pleasure and pain.

"And long before the time of the Britons," he said, "the Greeks called this time of year the Dionysia, in honor of their great god who made the vineyards grow. When I was at Cambridge, my history tutor was obsessed with the practice. Wrote monograph after monograph, and I read them all. I was fascinated, too." His words were scholarly, but his voice became rougher still, deepening with desire. The pulse in his golden throat leaped harder. "In Greece, spring is harvest time, not planting time. But the idea was the same—the people left their orderly homes and went into the open fields to sing and dance and give themselves over to their deeper physical natures, because they believed that unleashed the energies that made the crops grow, that encouraged new livestock to be born, so all the cycles of life would be reinvigorated. In every way."

Her whole body was trembling now. He'd moved so close to her, she fancied the air was warmer from the heat of his body. His eyes locked on hers. Her breasts ached, and her womb clenched. Slick moisture gathered between her legs.

She stepped backwards, overwhelmed by the impulses that shook her.

He moved with her. "Greek maidens would gather baskets of flowers, just as you were doing. And they'd carry out jugs of wine. Intoxication was not just pleasure, it was their sacred duty."

Intoxication—*yes*. He was intoxicating her with his voice, with the intensity of his blue eyes, with his height and his breadth and the scent of his skin. She backed up more hurriedly, trying to escape the magnetic pull of his body. She felt roots beneath her feet, and knew the moment before she reached it that she'd backed herself against the hard barrier of a hawthorn trunk.

John kept coming, stopping barely a hands-breadth short of her. Every fiber of her being hummed with his nearness. "Young men would carry symbols of their desire—huge wooden carvings called *phalloi*."

A hot blush bloomed through her. Her father had taught her enough Greek to know the meaning of that word. The hard, smooth trunk behind her back seemed suddenly to have more meaning than it had just a moment ago—a rising shaft, a hard, surging energy. No wonder the ancient peoples had worshipped trees.

John smiled at her, his eyes full of heat. "And the young people would give themselves over to the pleasures of the flesh, for days. It was their duty—to shake off the cold and barren time of winter, to make the world live again."

She nodded shakily. "Fertility rites. The rites of spring."

"Yes. That was the whole point. For the Greeks. For the Britons. For the civilized world now, though we try to hide the truth from ourselves, try to call it quaint tradition. But some of us know what lies beneath. I know. *You* know."

Her own pulse beat so hard in her ears it nearly deafened her.

"Let me touch you, Mary."

Her fingers flew behind her back to brace her—the bark was sleek beneath her fingers and the scent of the blossoms was delicious, but she knew the branches just above her head were also full of ruthless thorns, sharper even than the blackberry bramble. Much like the temptation he was offering her. Sweet, but with the power to wound. Wound them both, forever, no matter what path they chose.

She had to make him stop. "You can't," she said. "You shouldn't."

"Let me see you, then. I want to see you. Pull down your dress, let me see your breasts."

"Why? Why do you even want to see them? You've seen

them—they're so small. They're not—*I'm* not—enough for you."

"Then why am I dying of need for you?" His chest came almost flush with hers, though the smallest space of air still separated them. "Your breasts are lovely, Mary. Perfect." His eyes swept over her face. "And Lord in heaven, look at this hair of yours. You should never bind it up again. The color of it this morning—where the sun touches, it's like living fire."

His warm breath buffeted her skin. The shape of his mouth as he spoke was tantalizing. She wanted to touch her fingers to his throat, to his chest.

"Your thighs," he murmured. "Let me see your lovely thighs again. I've been dreaming of them constantly."

She meant to say no, but instead she sighed and let her head fall back against the tree. Something too powerful was washing over her, through her. She couldn't think, couldn't summon the words she knew she needed to say.

And he seemed to take her sigh as sufficient permission to dig his fingers into the skirt of her frock and lift the thin barrier of muslin upwards. He bared her calves, he bared her knees, and finally he bared her thighs and the hot, slick place between them. Sunshine and spring air brushed her skin, and seemed to make her glow from the inside as well.

"Let me touch you," John said again, the words rasping. "Please." He leaned in further, laying his palms flat on the tree trunk on either side of her, still gripping the fabric of her dress so that it pulled tight across her hips. Hot need stabbed through her.

"Please say yes, Mary. Please. Say yes to me."

Her voice came out of her in a breath she didn't plan on releasing. "Touch me, then."

He groaned, and his mouth found its way into the hollow of her throat. His body surged into hers, his hands going to her waist, his hips thrusting against hers. His shaft felt hard and huge through the fabric of his trousers, and he ground himself into her, against the mound of curls between her legs. The delicious pressure sent shock waves of pleasure through her breasts and belly and through every limb, through the very core of her.

And then he kissed her mouth.

He had not done that the other day, though he'd kissed her in far more intimate places.

And it was more wondrous than she could have imagined, to feel his mouth against hers. His lips were gentle and fierce at the same time, tasting her, fitting themselves to hers, finding all her subtle shapes, giving and seeking and answering all at once.

One of his hands came up to cup her jaw, to angle her face so he could explore deeper.

There was such tenderness in his touch.

And it was...*personal*. Undeniably personal. This was *John* kissing *Mary*—seeking deep inside her, for something more than just animal release.

Oh, her heart was softening. Her body was throbbing. Her soul was rising up and offering itself to his. She would give herself to him, give everything to him, give more than she could possibly afford to give.

There was nothing she could do to stop herself.

Her arms went around his neck and she pulled him tighter against her body. He groaned against her mouth.

His hand at her waist slid up under her dress, pushing it even further upwards, past her ribcage, seeking her breast. His palm fit around the small swell and squeezed, his thumb rubbing tantalizingly over her nipple.

She groaned as well.

That had him thrusting against her with new enthusiasm —hard, deep pressure that had her gasping. His other hand dropped to her bared hip, stroking it, kneading her flesh, and she shivered against him.

She was busy touching him as well, through his shirt, delighting in the remarkable firmness of his shoulders. His chest against hers was hard as granite, but wonderfully warm; his weight pressed her into the tree trunk in a way that should have hurt, but didn't.

He pulled back for a moment, his eyes hot on hers, then reached down to his own waist and pulled his shirt up and over his head.

The fabric glowed with light as it whisked past his dark-gold curls and made a halo around him for a moment before he dropped it to the ground.

He was bared to the waist.

Oh, the glorious sight of him, his torso uncovered, his skin glowing with its own radiance in the sunshine. The muscles rippled across his shoulders, bunched hard at his chest. She'd seen engravings of Greek statues in books her father owned, and John Hollings, Viscount Parkhurst, put them all to shame.

For he was not cold marble, but living man.

She laid her hands to his chest and pushed him back gently so she might be able to take him in more fully with her gaze. Though he had the power to resist her with ease, he allowed it, and watched her face as she examined the beautiful length of his body.

His flesh was vivid with life, and the crisp golden hair of his chest tapered into a heavier, darker line as it dipped down the hard plane of his belly into the waistband of his trousers.

He was all mystery to her, and all temptation.

She wanted to dip her hand there, too, to touch the urgent press of flesh beneath the cloth, flesh that strained so hard, it seemed on the verge of ripping open his trousers.

He didn't give her the chance, though. His patience had been stretched thin enough. He yanked her towards him, his fingers going to the buttons at the back of her dress. He made short work of them, pushed her back against the tree, and pulled the loosened bodice down in a few quick tugs, baring her completely to the waist.

The look in his eyes as he took in the sight of her was something she'd never seen before from her friend. Nothing of the polite gentleman remained in that gaze, none of the courteous self-control she was so used to. The look was dark and animal and commanding.

His chest heaved with the force of his breathing.

And then his mouth fell on her, drawing first one nipple and then the other against the wet heat of his tongue. He suckled her until she could barely hold her legs steady, and small whimpering noises were escaping her lips.

And then he gathered her in his arms again. Skin to skin.

She had never felt anything quite so wonderful, her flesh to his flesh, her exquisitely sensitized breasts against his chest, his crisp hair biting lightly into her even as the rest of him was the most extraordinary combination of silk and solid rock. His mouth still worked its magic against hers.

So much heat, everywhere.

He pressed his hips more firmly into hers, writhing against her until he wedged her legs apart. The hard bulge of his shaft rubbed up and down at the juncture of her thighs, sending shock waves through her. The fabric of his trousers seemed rough in contrast to the silken smoothness of his skin.

She needed to touch him. See him. There.

Her hand worked its way between their bellies, over the firm ridges of his muscled abdomen, lined with still more crisp hair, and then down into the waistband. She wriggled her fingers beneath the cloth, feeling his muscles flinch at her touch. And her fingers touched his shaft at long last, feeling it strain into her hand, hard and hot like fever, and yet velvety soft.

It seemed to jump into her palm, eager for more of her caress. John let out a groan so deep she thought it might rend him in two. His hands at her waist gripped her hard enough to bruise the skin, his whole body tensing as though he were preparing for battle.

His breath rasped as he broke the kiss and buried his mouth against her throat. He was beginning to tremble, too, seemingly reining himself in, letting her take her time exploring him.

With her fingertips, she stroked just the tip of his shaft at first. It was so big and round, it filled her palm, and seemed to swell more and more against her fingers. This was meant to go inside her? It seemed impossible that something so hard and massive could enter into such a tender part of her.

As she stroked along the silky-hard head, a spot of mois-ture appeared at the tip of it, wonderfully slick...she slid her palm across it, working it around his flesh, discovering the intriguing ridges, the way the head widened outward then tapered back again to the main part of his shaft.

His body went rigid against her. He gasped and moaned, "Oh, Mary, please, Mary..."

She slipped her fingers downwards, grasped the thick, heavy column of flesh. Squeezed it.

That seemed to make *him* go weak in the knees. His weight pressed more heavily against her breasts. "Jesus," he breathed. His hips seemed to move of their own accord, thrusting into her touch. "Please...."

She was making this happen to him. *She* was.

She felt...*beautiful,* suddenly. Desirable. Powerful.

The trousers were constricting her movements; she wanted to grasp him more firmly, more fully; she wanted to pump him with her hand the way she'd seen him with his own.

John seemed to want exactly that. His hands were shaking now, but he undid his own buttons, and his shaft sprang completely free. She glanced down between their bodies again to get a look at it. It was thick and long, startlingly so. But the color was bronzed, and the curls at the base gleamed golden in the sun.

So strange. So masculine. And, somehow, despite its strangeness, enticingly beautiful.

She wanted it in her mouth. She wanted to taste it.

A thrill went through her—a pure impulse of daring.

She *would* taste it.

Wriggling from his grip, she dropped to her knees, and took the shaft in her fingers again. He was swelling even harder than before, and she found she was unable to bring her fingertips together around its throbbing breadth.

She was face to face with this most intimate part of John.

His musk filled her nostrils—a shocking, mesmerizing scent that was every bit as strange as the sight of him, and every bit as tantalizing.

Not stopping to think, she brushed her lips over the head, opening her mouth wider as she followed the sensuous broadening, then closing slightly again as she took the whole top of it inside her mouth and drew her lips tight.

Her tongue pressed against the silky hardness, tasting the strange, thrilling salt of him. She swirled her tongue, letting it slide around and around the smoothness of the head, her fingers squeezing and stroking the length as it did.

This was perhaps not as personal as when he was kissing her, but it was even more intimate in many ways—to have this most private part of him inside her mouth.

John groaned and shuddered and strained, clearly fighting the urge to thrust hard down her throat. His thighs shook. The fingers of one hand raked her curls, gripping and releasing convulsively as though he could barely restrain himself from yanking her mouth harder against him.

She glanced up at him and saw that he had braced the palm of his other hand against the hawthorn trunk. His blue eyes were locked on her face, the gaze intent, his brow furrowed. The bulging muscles of his arms and even the ridges of his abdomen seemed to be clenched rock-hard.

He was trying to let her keep control, and she savored it.

She gave him a wicked smile even as her mouth still held his shaft.

Inch by inch, she swallowed him deeper. The slick head moved against the roof of her mouth, and by instinct she began to suck him, to draw him against the slippery lining of her cheeks and to the entrance to her throat.

One of her hands slid beneath to caress the soft swell of his stones, while the other reached back behind him, yanking at his trousers so she could pull them farther down and stroke the magnificent muscles of his buttocks. Just as she'd predicted, he was as strong and sculpted as a racehorse.

She pressed against him there, urging him deeper and deeper into her mouth.

It was terrifying, thrilling, hard to breathe, and the frantic moaning sounds he was making fueled a fire inside her.

His member was a beautiful, powerful thing, and she began to yearn to feel it inside her, between her legs. Her womb blazed and clenched, turning to delicious liquid. She could do it if she wanted: she could let this powerful man with his huge shaft mount her. She could let him drive up hard inside of her, to where the desire tightened into a white-hot knot. The thought drove her wild. She wanted it. Wanted it desperately. She wanted him to thrust inside her as the sexton had done to Mrs. Trumbull. She wanted him to claim her entirely.

Every instinct cried out for it.

And John seemed to feel the same thing, because all at once his hands went under her arms and he was lifting her, pulling his member from her mouth and pressing her back against the tree.

Her skirts were up around her waist again before she could think, and when he pressed his hips against her again, his bared shaft was what pushed against her curls. A small shift in angle was all it would take for the rigid thickness of it to spear between her thighs and push up inside her wetness.

She was made for that—a sheath to his blade, a harbor for his seed.

The spring day seemed to cry out for it—the very sunlight and warm wind seemed to command that they join and mate.

His breathing was ragged, and so was hers. They both wanted it.

His mouth pressed to her ear, his voice ragged and urgent.

"I want to take you, Mary. Do you know what that means?" His tone was utterly unfamiliar. Uncivilized. His shaft ground against her frantically. "I need to take you."

But he hesitated. Why was he waiting?

She wanted him to thrust up inside her. Her blood was mad with her need for it.

She wriggled her hips against him, spread her thighs, urging him forward with her hands against his buttocks.

But he went still. Harder than stone.

And he pulled back from her. His eyes studied her face.

She heard herself whimper. "What, John? Why do you stop?"

His eyes were squeezed tight shut; his head was shaking side to side. The look of him was anguished, as though he fought a powerful internal battle.

Now it was her turn to beg. "Please. Please, John. Do it." She ached. She burned. The pagan magic of the day hummed all around them. It seemed to very survival of the world depended on him...*taking* her, like he'd said. "Please, *now*."

But he didn't.

His hands were on her hips, clutching spasmodically. Hungrily. His shaft strained between them. But he didn't thrust inside her.

His face was a portrait in agony. The muscles of his mouth moved, seeming to struggle for the coherence of speech. "You will..." He fought for every word. "You will marry me then, Mary?"

She could scarcely recall the meaning of the word. *Marry*?

Oh, God, she couldn't think. She just wanted, wanted. Needed.

He lay his forehead against hers, panting into her face. "Answer me. You have to answer me. Quickly."

Marry? Oh, Lord—the word's meaning hovered at the edges of her consciousness. They weren't supposed to do this unless they'd done that...other thing. It would...it would ruin her otherwise. *Ruin*.

That was an important word, she remembered that much.

It was supposed to be an important word.

But it was so very hard to care just now....

"Damn it, Mary." His hands against her gave her a shake. "*Answer*."

But how could she answer? And how could he think of such a thing, now, of all times?

She was supposed to say no to his offer, she knew that. For some reason. Marriage to her would not be good for him. It would hurt him.

He was John. Her friend. And she loved him.

She loved him.

She couldn't hurt him—even if everything in her body

screamed at her to do anything, say anything, to make him part her legs and push himself inside her.

He…was…her…friend.

Her *friend*. And that had to matter more than anything.

She fought to gather enough breath, enough sense, to say the words she needed to say. "No. No, John." It was painful to say it. She knew that *no* meant she was also saying no to everything else she so desperately wanted. But she had no other choice. "I can't. I can't marry you."

The groan that ripped from his lips this time had no sign of pleasure in it. It was a groan of pure pain. "Damn you. Damn all this. How am I to stay away from you, then?"

With a mighty effort, he pushed himself back from her, stumbling unsteadily. He bent over, his hands bracing his weight on his knees. The breeze that ran between them felt suddenly, shockingly cold after the heat of his flesh.

She wanted him against her again, wanted his warmth, his strength. His desire. She felt frozen against the tree.

Long moments passed, the two of them breathing in harsh rasps, and he looked to be in as much pain as she felt.

"John, please…"

"You have to marry me," he said. "We can't go on like this."

Oh, the reasons for her refusal poured back into her mind as she watched him. He was so beautiful. So perfect. And therefore not made for the likes of her.

He was made for a Lawton girl, the sort of lovely, elegant, blue-blooded girl who could make him happy, night and day, for a lifetime.

What was happening between him and her right now— this was just…*lust*. Just their animal natures. Like Mr. Bassett and Mrs. Trumbull. Not the basis for a life together. And not enough to save them from misery in the long run.

"I can't," she repeated wretchedly. "You know I can't let that happen."

Pain was wrenching something loose inside her, something she thought might make her bleed. But she couldn't let lust destroy him, this good man who was so precious to her. If she said yes to him now, he'd regret it soon afterwards, the moment their pleasure was done.

He told her exactly that himself that first day upon the hill, when those vines had caught her and he'd first put his mouth to her breast. She'd told him then that she didn't care about virtue, that she wanted him to take her, and he'd said she was just...*distracted* by what they'd done, that it worked that way with bodies, that desire fogged the mind.

Indeed, lust was a form of madness....

John had straightened again, and he looked magnificent, torso bared, his flesh vivid with the heat of his blood, his shaft still boldly erect and his trousers low around his hips. Like a satyr. Like a beautiful, golden-haired satyr.

At the sight, the rush of primitive energy roared through her again.

She was a nymph, a half-naked nymph, and nothing in the world could be more natural than to part her soft thighs for him and welcome that hard flesh inside her.

For a moment, she teetered on the precipice. It would be so easy. To open her arms to him and let them both taste the magic of pure desire, pure elation.

But the best part of her heart would not let her. She had to protect him from himself, from herself.

Hastily, she worked her bodice back up to cover her breasts, and straightened out her skirts so they fell completely over her legs. "You were right that first morning," she told him. "When we climbed that hill together. We can't do this; we simply can't. We should both go home now. To our own homes. And forget this ever happened."

"Mary!"

"I'm the wrong woman for you, John. We aren't pagan

creatures, you and I, not really. We must live in the civilized world, and in that world, a viscount and a poor vicar's daughter do not marry."

"Listen to me—"

"I have listened. I listened to you when you were in your right mind. I'm only recalling your own wisdom to you now. Please don't make this more difficult than it already is."

He shook his head slowly back and forth, a wild, desperate look in his eyes. His chest still heaved with frustrated desire. But he must have known on some level that she was right, because he remained enough of a gentleman to stay where he was and not grab for her by force, as a true satyr would.

She retrieved her basket from the ground and turned back towards the vicarage. Over her shoulder she spoke the words she knew she must: "Go and marry Annabel Lawton, Lord Parkhurst. She's the one you really need."

CHAPTER 8

*H*e was in love with Mary Wilkins.

There was simply no other word for it.

When he had her up against that tree this morning, so heated, so pliant, with her hair flaming around her shoulders and her breasts bared to the morning sunlight, he felt he would die if he didn't claim her.

And when she fell to her knees and took him in her mouth...he'd fantasized about her doing that, but the fantasy came nowhere near the reality of having her look up to meet his eyes and smile at him while her lips circled his throbbing cock—such a purely lascivious smile, so full of pagan delight, showing her pleasure at pleasuring him.

When he'd lifted her again, ready to take her fully, to finally consummate this strange and wonderful bond that had been building and building between them, she'd been willing, more than willing.

He had come so close. So damn close.

And then he'd ruined everything.

He'd said the wrong words maybe, though heaven knows every word he said was only the truth. And those were the only words that would come to him with the blood pounding through his head and through every throbbing inch of his body. But what he'd meant was so much more. He meant he needed *her*. Had to become part of her. Bring their bodies so close together they could never truly be parted again.

If only he'd been able to let the demands of honor slip a few seconds longer, and just done what they both wanted without speaking of marriage.

Good God, what did honor matter in this case? He needed her, with every ounce of his being. And if he'd taken her...no, *made love* to her as fully as he longed to do, she'd have seen that, too. She couldn't have walked away from him again after that.

They'd have been bound together, and even her stubborn pride couldn't argue against it.

Damn it all, though.

She *had* walked away.

Sane and sensible and stiff-spined as ever.

Why was she so proof against him, when everything in him was falling apart without her?

He went through the rest of the morning like an automaton, wound up and jittery and mindless. When the time came for the May Pole dance, he found himself on Birchford Green without intentionally deciding to go there. Surely Mary would come—a more civilized Mary, granted, with her stays and petticoats on and her hair tightly bound, but still Mary.

He took his place among the dancers, scanning the crowd for her, hoping she'd just kept herself out of view until then. But no matter how many times he went round the May Pole, she did not appear. Girl after girl passed, all in bright springtime clothes, with bouncing curls shining in the sun, but nowhere, nowhere amongst them was the gray-eyed, freckled, brandy-haired, sweet, passionate, stubborn, clever creature in a plain little dress he truly longed to see.

His heart gave an aching pulse. Mary really was refusing him.

Other eyes met his: Rosamund Lawton, Lucinda Lawton, Vanessa Lawton...and of course, Annabel Lawton herself, flushed and giggling and full of flirtatious looks. Wearing her blue dress to match his waistcoat just as promised. She also wore a bonnet sporting one of those hideous stuffed finches she seemed to favor, and as the dancers wound closer and closer, he became ever more horribly conscious of the blade-like little beak and disturbing tiny black glass bead eyes.

Miss Lawton, for her part, seemed to assume she was charming him. She angled her body toward his as she passed, dipping at the waist to display her full bosom, eventually daring to bump her hip against his, to brush his forearm with her breasts. After the May Pole dance was done, she hovered near him, eventually imploring him to fetch cider for her from the tables set up under a spreading oak tree.

It would be insufferably rude to refuse.

Miss Lawton fluttered her lashes at him as he handed her the glass. "It's wonderful, Lord Parkhurst," she told him silkily, "to have you back here in Yorkshire where you belong. The strength of a rural society like ours depends on the full participation of its best men. We cannot thrive without your good example and leadership."

He took a long draught from his own drink, trying to think of a polite way to respond. She'd lobbed him a puff-ball of silly flattery, and he could think of nothing duller than batting it back to her.

Not that she seemed particularly interested in his deeper thoughts. As she swirled to a seat on a bench by a stand of lilacs, with her graceful posture displaying her figure to advantage and her soft smile reassuring him of his own illustrious importance, the true point she wished to make was obvious enough: a viscount needed to take his place in the world, and for that he needed a well-bred and elegant wife.

Clearly, Miss Lawton was more than ready to fill the position—to clasp the Parkhurst rubies about her throat, to choose tasteful menus for visiting dukes, to domineer over the housekeeper and debate with his mother over whether flocked wallpaper or watered silk would do best for the morning room. No doubt she believed human society would be better for her taking on that role.

And she wasn't the only one who thought so. Townspeople and farmers alike were glancing over at the two of them knowingly, giving indulgent smiles.

Lord, this was a difficult tangle. No gentleman could be outright discourteous to Miss Lawton, but he couldn't bear the thought of marrying her either.

Unfortunately, she seemed to need no encouragement from him. "Life here in Birchford will improve greatly now," she said, her bright eyes glowing, "with our viscount permanently back in residence."

He raised an eyebrow in surprise. Perhaps, after all, he had underestimated her. Perhaps she did wish to do some good for the local people as their viscountess. Did she have an interest in expanding the school, or founding a decent hospital?

"Improve in what way?" he asked.

"Now that Parkhurst Hall is actively your country seat again, we shall have proper visitors here," she said. "Peers of the realm, I mean. My father often speaks of the house parties your father used to give, how dozens would come at a time when the Season ended, straight from London. He says Birchford seems a backwater now, compared to what it was then."

Oh. So, no, he had not underestimated her. She wasn't

concerned about the poor, she was concerned about the qualities of the local *entertainments*.

"Of course," she added coyly, "no one could expect you to host in quite your father's style while you are still a bachelor." And she smiled at him meaningfully.

Well, that was bold as brass. He had to take another swallow of his drink, or choke.

"In the meantime, my lord," she said, flicking a fallen lilac petal from her skirts with a look of slight irritation at its intrusion on the unsmirched perfection of her clothes, "you should avail yourself more fully of my father's hospitality. You know he would welcome you for supper any night of the week."

Bolder and bolder. Miss Lawton wanted her proposal of marriage, and she wanted it soon.

He felt rather sick. Was this really how people of the *haut ton* arranged their lives? With such bloodless interest in luxury? Aligning themselves with partners for whom they felt nothing so they might amplify their riches, and hold their chins up higher than other people's?

It was madness, when the world held such magic as he'd felt with Mary in the clearing that morning.

Something had changed in him, very definitely, since he and Mary had gotten tangled in those blackberries. He wanted more from life than he'd wanted before—he wanted passion, and he wanted...*connection*.

Yes. That was it. It was what he'd felt that morning, the moment he'd kissed Mary—kissed her mouth for the first time—that the *connection* between them was far more than just physical desire. From the time they were very young, something between them made it easy to wander the woods together for hours, laughing and exploring and telling foolish stories and egging one another on with dares. It had been so effortless, he'd always taken it for granted.

But he could see more clearly now: the person he was with Mary, that was the person he wanted to *be*, all the time. He wanted to talk with her and laugh with her and find a meaningful place in the world with her, not with anyone else. He didn't want to trade that for anything—not even for the rules of honor that said he must keep a promise made to his father.

Couldn't Miss Lawton find something like that for herself, with a man who could truly love her? What good would it do her, to gain the title she wanted, but no true marriage?

He set down his glass on the bench beside her, and bent his head to look her forthrightly in the eye. "Will you be quite honest with me, Miss Lawton, if I ask you a difficult question?"

His tone was that of a philosopher, not a lover, and Miss Lawton's comfortable expression faltered. "Of course," she said, but she sounded wary.

"Have you ever thought of leading a different sort of life? Of ignoring what everyone else expects, and deciding for yourself what you truly want to be?"

The question clearly caught her by surprise. Her mouth dropped slightly open. And, for just an instant, something sparked in her eyes that he'd never seen in them before—a sharpness, an intelligence, and a flash of emotion that might have been fear, or perhaps even yearning.

She expelled a short breath. Her fingers twitched in her lap.

For just that instant, he thought that she might be about to give him a serious answer, that they might be on the verge of actually understanding one another.

But the moment was over as quickly as it came.

Miss Lawton seemed to catch hold of herself. Her lips closed back into a perfect Cupid's bow, and her countenance went smooth and impenetrable as porcelain again. "Why should I want a different sort of life?" she said, her tone perfectly complacent. "I should think people like you and I are the luckiest people on the earth. My father always says so."

Her father always says so. "Of course," John said, and tried to keep the disappointment from his voice.

Miss Lawton stood, confident as a queen once more, and laid her fingers on his forearm. "So will you call on us soon?" she asked, and her eyes were so placid he could scarcely believe he'd seen that brief flash of honest turmoil in them. "You know you need no invitation to visit us at the Grange."

"Your father is very kind," he said. He bowed over her hand as politely as he could manage and watched her walk away, his heart full of dread.

There really was not question in his mind any longer: he couldn't marry Annabel Lawton. He just *couldn't.*

He felt nothing for her. She felt nothing for him.

If they were to marry, they'd do it to please their fathers, to combine their family fortunes, to do what Society told them to do. And they'd both end up miserable. Society and Nature were entirely at odds here—and Nature's urgings seemed vastly more likely to lead to happiness, for everyone concerned.

But how on earth was a man of honor supposed to put an end to their presumed engagement?

Well, he had to find a way. Mary would never so much as consider his proposal while she believed he was bound to a Society marriage. And the longer he let things go on, the worse harm he'd do to the Lawtons.

And so, an hour after the May Day dancing was done, he found himself riding through the woods on the way to Lawton Grange. The day was warm and lazy, and it seemed more than a few of the local inhabitants still held to the ancient pagan customs of May Day—sultry, drunken laughter sounded from the shrubberies here and there, and at one point a fully naked man dashed across the trail not fifteen feet ahead, buttocks flashing as he ran. One of his tenant farmers, John was fairly sure, doing his part to ensure abundant vegetative growth for the coming year. John rode on quickly to avoid making the acquaintance of whatever equally-naked farmwife might be in hot pursuit.

Coming up over a rise of red crag, he had a sudden view down into a slanting hollow left where a heavy length of sandstone had sheered off some years ago. A hoarse shout made him glance down through a veil of pine branches into the rubble that was left, where he caught sight of none other than Mr. Bassett and Mrs. Trumbull.

Mrs. Trumbull was bent forward over a sandstone boulder, her bodice down to her waist and her skirts pushed up, while Mr. Bassett, trousers around his thighs, was taking her roughly from behind. After a moment, Mr. Bassett spun his lover around and lifted her under the hips to set her arse on the rock. She lay down on her back, like a sacrifice on a pagan altar, her breasts bare, staring into the sky. Mr. Bassett pulled her knees up over his shoulders, and went back to thrusting enthusiastically while Mrs. Trumbull threw her head back with an ecstatic cry.

Good Lord. With all the time the pair spent fornicating, it was a wonder Mrs. Trumbull managed to run a pub and Mr. Bassett managed the keeping of the church grounds.

Well, if the ancient Greeks and the Britons had been right, every farm in the region would have a bumper crop come harvest.

A sudden vision of Mary filled his mind: Mary stretched out like that, the sunlight gleaming on her bared flesh, her hair spread over the sandstone, her legs spread for him.

Flames of desire speared through him, and the heat

seemed to clarify his mind. *That* was what he wanted. That was what would bring him life. Only that was real, and all the minutiae of civilization was a thin veneer laid overtop—a distraction from what truly mattered.

He spurred his horse faster along the trail.

By the time he arrived at Lawton Grange, he was almost surprised to find the footmen and the parlor maids fully clothed.

The perfection of the foyer seemed absurdly chill and artificial, with the tidy black and white squares of the marble floor, the polished mirrors in their gilt frames. Even the sculpture of a half-naked nymph at the base of the staircase seemed cold and sexless—bone white, eyes blank, breasts smooth as eggs, no tempting triangle of brandy-colored curls between her legs.

No, a life focused on this barren elegance was not a life he wanted.

The Lawtons, however, made a very different assumption about his purpose in coming. The moment his presence was announced, he felt the household ripple with anticipation as servants scurried off in every direction. Lord Lawton greeted him grandly, ushering him into the sitting room with the self-satisfied pomp of a grandee about to sit down to a feast. Three of the Lawton girls came in in a rush a few minutes later, clearly shepherded from upstairs, where they had no doubt been resting up for the evening festivities. All three were blonde and pink and very pretty. Lucinda, the sister third in age, looked like she still belonged in the schoolroom, and seemed terrified by his presence. The youngest, Vanessa, was a smaller but perfect copy of Annabel, though she lacked the smug expression her eldest sister wore as Annabel swirled to a seat on the settee nearest him. Clearly, as the eldest, Annabel was ready to stake her claim.

The missing girl, Rosamund, the second sister in age, was

herded in shortly afterwards by a grim-faced parlor maid. Judging by a streak of gold pollen on her skirts and a blotch of mud on her hem, Rosamund had been in the gardens. She had something hidden behind her back that she stashed guiltily under a cushion as she sat. Was it a book?

God forbid a gentleman should catch one of the Lawton girls reading.

Or thinking.

He tried to smile.

Another maidservant brought tea, and Annabel quite naturally did the pouring. Her graces were on full display— every gesture polished, her hands flawless and smooth as the porcelain she handled, the cups and saucers making not the slightest rattle, the tea not the least slosh. Did the girl have no nerves at all?

She cast a self-satisfied glance at him as if for assurance that he saw the superb hostess he was destined to procure. "Cream and no sugar for you, Lord Parkhurst, isn't that so?" she asked.

"Oh—yes. Please." Lord, she'd been studying him.

As she passed the cup, she leaned towards him slightly more than was necessary, displaying the creamy bounty of her bosom. An impressive bosom to be sure, one he'd admired in the past, but somehow it seemed excessive to him now, lacking in subtlety. The pale gold of her hair seemed cold and insipid. She was, objectively speaking, lovely. Just... all wrong for him.

Her inviting smile made his stomach churn. Did she genuinely have no idea what he was thinking and feeling? Had she not read his hesitation this morning, and his distress? Or had she read them perfectly, but dismissed them as quite irrelevant to her wishes?

Though he could remember none of the content of it later, he managed to engage the family in polite conversation for the requisite fifteen minutes, during which the girls did much simpering and giggling and a sharp pain grew steadily in his temple. At last, he could bear it no longer. "Lord Lawton," he said far too abruptly. "Might I have some private words with you in your study?"

A sort of jolt went through the line of pretty girls. It was obvious what they all assumed: that he'd been overcome with passion for Annabel and could not refrain from asking for her hand as soon as possible.

Well, there was no helping it. Let them assume what they wanted to assume. He needed to have a serious conversation with Lord Lawton, and he could not in good conscience postpone it even another minute.

He followed the older man out of the room with all the enthusiasm of a criminal heading for the gallows. How exactly was he to tell his late father's lifelong best friend that he was rejecting Annabel, in fact refusing all four of his daughters?

They settled into leather armchairs, and Lawton—no doubt attributing his tongue-tied discomfort to a smitten suitor's bashfulness—poured them each a snifter of brandy.

"Here," Lawton said. "Drink up, lad."

The brandy was no doubt superb, but just at the moment, it was as welcome as glass of vinegar. John choked down a sip.

Lawton smiled at him indulgently, laying a hand on his own embroidered waistcoat over his swelling patriarch's belly. "Come now, dear boy—you've always been like a son to me, you must know that. I daresay I rejoiced nearly as much as your father did on the day you were born." The smile took on an edge of sentimental melancholy. "Parkhurst was the finest of men, and his loss has never gone from my heart. It never shall. But you've grown to be his spitting image, John. He would be so proud to see you now."

A lump of lead formed in John's throat. This really couldn't be much worse.

Mary. He had to focus his mind on her, and he could get through this.

Lawton seemed to think a broader hint was in order. "You and my Annabel have seen quite a lot of each other lately."

"Yes, yes." John seemed to have forgotten how to sit in a chair without shifting his weight about. "It's been a privilege to get reacquainted with all your daughters."

"Annabel especially?"

"Well, of course. She's—she's a lovely young woman."

"No one more lovely in all the county, if a proud father may be forgiven for saying so."

"Indeed."

Lord Lawton gave him an odd, considering look. Surely he had begun to notice the lack of enthusiasm in John's tone. "And perhaps," Lawton added, a bit more forcefully, "I can also be forgiven for mentioning that many suitors have come to persuade me to allow them to court her."

"Naturally. Naturally." Oh, Lord, he was making a hash of this.

But perhaps Lawton himself had just given him the opening he needed.

John sat up straighter, and looked his father's old friend in the eye. "Miss Lawton is of course a charming and spirited young lady. With—with a...warm heart." He had no idea, really, if Annabel Lawton even *had* a heart, but it seemed wisest to speak as if she did. "She might, perhaps, have formed..." What word would be appropriate, and not imply that the young lady was loose? *Attachment? Fondness?* "A...a preference of her own. For some particular gentleman?"

Spots of color rose on Lawton's cheeks, and his fingers tensed around his brandy glass. "If you are inquiring as to her chastity," he said in a clipped, offended voice, "I can assure you that Annabel has always conducted herself according to the highest—"

"Oh, no! Sir! I have no doubts as to her conduct. Quite the opposite, in fact. I meant that, perhaps, out of a sense of duty and obligation, she might have forced herself to renounce any...*liking* she may have had for some other—"

"Parkhurst!" Lawton said firmly. "Do not be absurd. Like all my daughters, she has lived her life almost in seclusion. And far more importantly, as you and I both know, my Annabel is not a lady for the common sort. Not even for the usual run of the nobility. She deserves the *best* of men. A man of true breeding, and the highest caliber of honor. The sort of gentleman only a peer like your father could raise."

Guilt stabbed John's gut. Nothing he could say now would make his actions any more acceptable to Lord Lawton, or to Society, or to his father's memory. But he had to push forward with it. *For Mary.* "Sir," he said, "you must know I hold your family in the very highest esteem, as did my father before me. Annabel is an exceptional young lady, beyond any doubt. However—"

Lawton's eyes narrowed. The man was no fool. "If Annabel is not the match you seek," he said, glowering like a thundercloud, "I have three daughters more." The look in his eye very clearly said, *and only the most shameless cad would dare reject them all.*

"And all three are extraordinary as well. My admiration for them is unwavering. And, believe me, sir, my respect for you and for my father's memory is absolute. I...I am well aware of the understanding between the two of you, made many years ago—"

"As well you should be!"

"But that is just the point. Your daughters and I were mere children, back then. Annabel was an *infant*. We could give no meaningful assent to the match. And the world has changed greatly since those days. The modern ways of society—"

"Are an abomination to honorable men!" Lawton was red as a boiled lobster now. He slammed his brandy snifter on the side table, rattling the lamps. "*Tradition*. Tradition and tradition only forms the backbone of England. Our place is to uphold that tradition, to bind society together with the order and the dignity and the *honor* that have made our nation the greatest on this earth!

"Sir, I have no intention of destroying the backbone of—"

"Nonsense! That's exactly what you're suggesting! You think I was never young, lad? You think I was never tempted to shape the world to my own youthful, foolish desires, to flout the wisdom of my own forebears? But I have learned better, from experience. The old ways—"

"Will never make your daughter happy!" There. *That* was what truly needed to be said, the very crux of the matter. "I do not love Annabel, and she does not love me. And I cannot see how the nation benefits from loveless marriages."

Lawton's eyes had gone wide in shock. "Such marriages join *families* together. They secure lines of property, true ownership of land. It is not about the selfish whims of...of *children*. If the young are permitted to follow their hearts helter-skelter, then the land will be splintered, the great family names dragged down into dirt! You may be too callow to truly understand it, but you have a *responsibility*, boy!"

John stood. "I am no boy," he said forcefully. "I am a man. And I will not be dictated to."

Lawton stared at him in disbelief, his expression furious. "Enough!" His breathing rasped coarsely, and it seemed the very air might shatter with its force. "Call yourself what you will. You need say no more, *Lord Parkhurst*. I understand your meaning. I should not have thought I'd live to hear your father's son say such absurd and abominable things."

Fury and shame combined shook John's chest, but he held his ground.

Mary. He had to stand firm through this, or Mary could never be his.

Angry silence stretched between him and Lord Lawton for what seemed like an eternity. At long last, the older man's breathing slowed, and the high color gradually receded from his face. He looked rather ashen, and much older than he had when they entered the study. "Well, then, I see how it is with you," he said, his words bitter, but slow and measured. "As you say, the *modern* world is what we must deal with now. And to hell with England."

"England will survive well enough, sir, I am convinced."

Lawton regarded him with mournful, disappointed eyes. That look was far worse than the anger. "For the first time in my life," he said, "I am glad I have no son of my own. I could not bear to see him turn out as you have. Now get out of my house, and let me contemplate how I shall break this scurrilous news to my daughters."

The words pierced like a dart. But, truly, John knew that if those daughters were to have any hope of real happiness, there was no other way. "This will be for the best, sir," he said, "for all of us. I promise you."

"Don't dare speak to me of *best*. This scandal will be the most dreadful this county has seen in a century or more."

"Surely, sir, it cannot be so very much. No formal contract was ever drawn up, no public announcement made. People will assume they jumped to conclusions, if they expected anything."

Lawton shook his head grimly. "Easy for you to say. You'll be thought a fine catch regardless, with your title and your money, but Annabel's turned twenty now. Gentlemen will wonder what's wrong with her, that she's sat unclaimed so long."

"No one could think such a thing, not of her. You said yourself that's she an exceptional beauty. You'll see—give her just one Season in Town, and she'll be the toast of London."

Lord Lawton snatched up his glass again and drained the brandy in one gulp. "If you've ruined her life, boy, you'll pay for it, believe me."

John could not resist taking a hasty sip of his own, if only to stop himself from saying something he'd truly regret.

Then Lawton leaned back thoughtfully in his chair. The light of calculation gleamed briefly in his eyes. "I tell you what," he said with great deliberation. "I'll give you a day to think on your words, and come to your senses. I won't tell my girls what you've said, not just yet."

"I won't change my mind."

"Maybe not. But maybe so. In the meantime, don't say a word to Annabel at the dancing tonight. Promise me that, at least. I'll wait a day, as I've said, and if you really are as stubborn and dishonorable a fool as you seem, I'll tell her in my own way. Not that her heart won't be broken, regardless."

The tension in the room thickened, but there was no way around it. "As you wish. I'll say nothing to anyone, for now. But you will need to tell your daughters tomorrow. And one day, when you see Annabel truly happy, you will know as surely as I do that releasing us both from this expectation is the right thing to do. For her heart, as well as mine."

"The right thing," Lawton repeated flatly.

"It is, sir. And I hope one day you will understand."

Lawton looked at him as if he were a slab of spoiled beef. "Oh, I understand you already, boy. I understand you very well."

Nothing else John could say would make things any

better. So nothing was left to do but bow civilly, then turn and walk away.

Heaviness hung on him as he left the house—he could scarcely help feeling his dead father's disappointed gaze on his back.

But rising up from beneath that weight came a buoying feeling.

He knew what he'd done was for the best. He'd accomplished what had seemed all but impossible just a few hours before: he'd cut himself and the Lawton girls loose from the bond that held them all fast almost since birth. And all it had taken was speaking honestly…and following his heart.

Annabel Lawton had no more claim on him, nor he on her.

He was a free man.

And now maybe Mary would listen when he told her he loved her.

CHAPTER 9

*M*ary lied about a headache to avoid the May Pole dancing, but no lies would be needed for the evening—as the sun began to set, she sat at the little dining room table staring into a steaming cup of tea, and felt like the sides of her skull would split. The day-long struggle to imagine a future in which she could be happy was not going well at all.

And her brother was clearly growing suspicious about the true nature of her ailment. Empathy was one of Thomas's God-given gifts as a clergyman, and he seemed determined to exercise it on her now. "What's wrong?" he asked, hovering over her. "You've never stayed away from the May Day celebrations in your life."

She puffed a breath into the steam of her tea and watched it whirl.

What could she possibly tell him about the last few days? How could she explain why she felt so heavy and dull and empty inside? How she couldn't even sip her tea because all she could think when she touched the teacup was how she'd held its now-smashed mate in slackening fingers while John pressed her up against the cupboard and robbed her of all sanity with his mouth and hands?

She tried a joke instead. "Maybe I've just become more serious and sober in my old age."

Thomas laughed his cheerful laugh. "Don't be a goose— you're a year younger than me! And if you don't go, who'll organize the rest of us? No one will know where to put the cakes and punch. The dancers shall forget their steps and collide together, and the musicians shall all play in different keys. You know everyone in the village depends on you to keep things in order, Mary."

"Nonsense," she said. And then more ruefully, "I organized all the committees two months ago. Everything shall go like clockwork."

Thomas chuckled. "All the more reason to attend, then— the hard work's been done. You're the one always telling me to go have some fun, and not let my preaching collar strangle me."

She turned away from her teacup then and took her first really good look at her brother that evening—and was startled. Lost in his books as he usually was, Thomas tended to ignore anything to do with fashion. Most days, he looked rumpled, with his thick curls uncombed and his waistcoat buttoned askew, but this afternoon he'd groomed himself with unusual care.

He wore the new blue waistcoat and crisp linen shirt she'd sewed for him for Christmas, which he'd left in a drawer until now. His neckcloth was not only clean and starched, but neatly tied—a feat that must have taken him hours, since he hadn't asked her help with it. His chestnut hair was carefully arranged, up off his forehead in a rather stylish sweep so the vivid blue of his eyes stood out brilliantly. He looked…straight-backed and strong, very much like their father. *Handsome*, even. Thomas really had gotten all the good looks in the family.

Under her sudden scrutiny, Thomas blushed and stared at his feet. Lord, even his shoes were polished. For a dance that was to take place at night.

"Please, Mary," he said, an unfamiliar vulnerability in his voice. "I want you to enjoy yourself, but I confess I need you to help me as well. Don't make me arrive at the assembly all alone. Not tonight. I find I need an ally."

Thomas needed an ally? He was *nervous*? Amongst his own parishioners?

"What's going on, Tom?" she asked. "Why are you all gussied up?"

Now he blew out his breath in what sounded suspiciously like a sigh.

Oh. "Thomas Edgar Wilkins," she said, "Has some young lady caught your eye?

His blush deepened. "Hush. It's nothing."

"It's not nothing if you spent time starching your own neckcloth! Tell me." Mary's heart began to lift a bit. She might be miserable, but maybe Thomas at least could end up happy. He certainly deserved to be. "Which young lady is it?"

"I've already told you, it's nothing." His mouth quirked, and an odd expression flickered in his eyes. "I mean, it's no one appropriate. A lady who wouldn't have me anyway, and who'd make a terrible wife for a man of my vocation."

Great heavens—Thomas had been tempted toward an inappropriate match of his own? Whom did they know who'd make a terrible vicar's wife? Lady Ellerby? Mrs. *Trumbull*? Or…

One of the beautiful, spoiled Lawton girls. Oh, dear.

Just how much had been going on inside her brother that she knew nothing about? Well, to be fair, *he* had no idea what she'd been doing with Viscount Parkhurst—and Viscount Parkhurst was the very definition of inappropriate. In more than one meaning of the word.

"It doesn't matter," said Thomas, with an attempt at his former cheer. "I can forget her. More importantly, I've set my mind to finding someone who *is* appropriate."

Mary's heart gave a squeeze. Lord knew, she didn't want to go anywhere near Birchford Green tonight. But if anyone in this world ought to find love, it was her warm-hearted brother, and it wasn't in her nature to abandon him when he needed her moral support.

It was just a country dance, after all. And, more importantly, this was her own village. She could scarcely live her life if she avoided all events that might include the viscount.

She patted her hair. She hadn't coiled it into her usual tight bun after she came home this morning, just twisted it loosely with a fall of curls at the nape. Other young ladies would be wearing much the same flattering style tonight.

Why shouldn't she as well? Why shouldn't she go and...*dance*? With any man willing to stand up with her.

Viscount Parkhurst wasn't the only man in Birchford with legs. Even if his were unusually long and well-muscled.

Today was the first of May, after all, and she deserved to partake in all the rites of spring.

"Stay here," she told her brother. She ran to her room and opened the little oak box her mother had left to her. She pulled out her one bit of finery—a small cameo suspended on a string of tiny seed pearls—and fastened it around her throat.

Her dress would have to do as it was. She'd already put on her stays and shift and petticoats when she came home from the forest. And no one would see the wrinkles in the green linen in the lantern light.

Before she knew it, she and Thomas were walking down

the lane between the vicarage and the church, headed for Birchford Green. The lovely promise of the morning had held all day, and the evening was as warm as everyone hoped, clear and dry, with balmy air. As the sun dropped below the horizon, gold and pink clouds streaked the sky, and the first bright stars appeared in the dome of deepening cobalt blue above them.

The world held just as much enchantment as it had at dawn. Pure magic.

As they approached the Green, she studied Thomas out of the corner of her eye—he was scanning the crowd almost anxiously, his whole body tense. Mary couldn't help noticing that several young ladies, the moment they caught sight of him, stopped whatever else they were doing to simper prettily at him.

Well, goodness. Perhaps Tom's interest in romance wasn't quite as one-sided as he feared. Now that she thought about it, her brother had matured quite a bit in the past couple of years, finally shedding the gangliness of youth. He'd put on muscle walking and riding so far each day to visit his parishioners, often helping one family repair an outbuilding, another build a stone wall—he was, after all, a loving pastor to his flock, one who did charitable works as naturally as breathing.

And if the charitable work broadened his shoulders and bronzed his skin, the local maidens could hardly be blamed for noticing. From the looks of things, Mary would be moving down to the housekeeper's quarters sooner than she'd expected.

"Thomas," she said under her breath. "I believe there are several young ladies here who'll be glad to dance a reel or two with you."

A blush once more stained his cheeks.

And then she saw him flinch.

Following the direction of his gaze, she spotted Rosamund Lawton. Rosamund held herself aloof, unaware of Thomas's approach. Or perhaps *pretending* to be unaware of it—given that she stared fixedly at the wooden sign of the Fox & Crow, an unlikely focus for a wealthy young lady's rapt attention.

Rosamund's beautiful profile was etched against the sunset sky, and her golden hair gleamed. Thomas made a sound in his throat that suggested a sudden blockage in his lungs.

Oh, Lord. If a Lawton girl had ensnared her brother's heart, he'd do well to break the attachment as soon as humanly possible. Lord Lawton would never give one of his precious daughters to a poor clergyman.

"I'll make a deal with you, Mary," Thomas whispered, leaning close. His voice sounded tense, but determined. "I think it high time for both of us to be looking for some sort of happiness in this life. *Appropriate* happiness. We will both dance with as many partners tonight as we possibly can. And keep our minds open. What do you say to that?"

She felt a rush of tenderness for her brother. Look at the two of them—all duty and responsibility on the surface, but underneath, as human as anyone. She might be doomed to misery, but if Thomas could find a way to be happy….

"All right," she said. "And whoever dances least must wash all the dishes for the next month!"

Thomas laughed. "I'll take that wager! And make it two months!"

A little orchestra of sorts had formed at one end of the Green, made up of local people who regularly practiced together at the church. They were in the midst of a sprightly tune, and before long, she and Thomas were both standing up with a throng of their neighbors, dancing and whirling beneath a glowing full moon.

Thomas was good as his word, going down the lines of clapping villagers, first twirling pretty Betsy Pike, whose father owned a fine dairy, then all three of the high-spirited Marston girls, one after another, and then their giggling mother for good measure. And, goodness, at one point he was capering arm-in-arm with the beautiful and scandalous Lady Ellerby, who threw back her head and laughed at something he said.

He didn't dance with Rosamund Lawton, she noticed, though Rosamund stood conspicuously close and turned down two other men who worked up the nerve to ask her.

For her own part, Mary danced vigorously as well, standing up with the blacksmith, the baker, and several broad-shouldered young farmers. When she stopped for a mug of lemonade, silver-haired Mrs. Simpkins, the apothecary's wife, squeezed both her hands and told her warmly, "So nice to see you dancing, Miss Wilkins! It's about time!" And Mary realized that her usual habit at such events was to focus on ensuring that fresh platters of food came out regularly to the tables, and that elderly ladies had conversational partners and something cool to drink.

Well, she felt different tonight, with curls bouncing on the back of her neck, and the pretty cameo and pearls brushing the very top of her breasts. Men seemed to be looking at her in a new way, too. She rather liked the look of surprise she'd get when each caught sight of her, and more than one told her he didn't recognize her at first glance. Old Mr. Dockett, the diviner, smiled at her, his blue eyes twinkling, and said, "Good for you, Mary Wilkins. I knew you had it in you, my girl!"

Her cheeks were flushed and her heart beat strong, and

she didn't think once about Lord Parkhurst. Well, maybe just once. Or twice. But she didn't see him anywhere amongst the revelers, so the terrible lonely ache in her chest scarcely bothered her at all.

Sam Brickley, a tall, dark-haired young farmer, asked her to dance three different times. He was strongly built, and handsome in a rough sort of way. Not educated, but intelligent, and he had a good sense of fun. "You've got roses in your cheeks tonight, Miss Wilkins," he told her in his rumbling, deep, country-accented voice, and gave her a wink. "It suits you."

His hands were warm and strong in hers, and as he spun her and led her down the line, the pressure of his palm at the small of her back felt pleasantly masculine. For such a big man, he moved with surprising grace and great confidence. His eyes were dark brown and long-lashed, and really rather lovely—and they sparkled at her whenever his gaze met hers, as though he had some delicious secret he couldn't wait to share.

Well, well.

"I'd never imagined you were such a good dancer," he said while they waited for the couples at the top of the line to take their turn. "You usually keep to the sidelines. Making sure everybody else's glass of punch is full." The words were perfectly innocent, but Sam managed to say them in a teasing, playful tone that made them seem vaguely bawdy.

Mary couldn't help laughing, which Sam didn't seem to mind at all.

He gave her a beaming grin. "I'm glad you've mended your ways tonight," he said. "The rest of us poor sinners need the company." He waggled his eyebrows at her. "And such bonny company, too!"

The hanging lanterns burned brightly now, and their

flickering orange glow against the planes of his cheeks and the length of his arms made her wonder what it would be like to share a home with such a man—sitting by the firelight in the evenings, just the two of them. Eating their evening meal and talking.

And then preparing to go to bed together....

Well, well, indeed. Such a possibility would have felt out of her reach just a week or so ago, but now the look in Sam's eye suggested it might be something she could make real, if she wished it.

Well, she owed that change to John. He'd brought something out in her, something she'd kept locked down and hidden without realizing she was doing it.

The thought of John brought a pang to her chest, and a painful, ferocious longing.

No. She couldn't think of him. What had happened with John had been...an *illusion.* The perfume of a moment, nothing more. Entirely out of her reach. She had to do just as Thomas was doing—forget what was impossible, and focus on happiness that could be within her reach.

Focus, for instance, on a man like Sam.

With deliberate force of will, she brought all her attention to the good-natured, attractive man in front of her.

What might Sam look like in his shirtsleeves, or out of his shirt altogether? What would it be like to let him kiss her? Let him touch her?

Her heart began to skip in a rougher rhythm, though whether it was pleasure or disquiet she felt at the thought, she wasn't quite sure.

Other couples were wandering away from the dancing here and there, slipping quietly into the shadows. What would it be like to do such a thing with Sam? Walk through the moonlit fields, perhaps, or find a hayloft?

Rather shocking to even consider it. She *wouldn't* have considered it, just a week ago, but she saw the world rather differently now.

There really was no reason why she couldn't allow Sam to kiss her, if she wanted that. She could even let him slip his big, calloused hand under her chemise, and cup her breast. And his mouth had a nice shape, good for smiling...and perhaps for *other things*.

A hot blush stole over her.

What if she let him? *Could* she really let him?

The idea felt so utterly unfamiliar, she could scarcely tell how she felt about it.

Strange as it seemed, it might be a way to break the spell she was under. To drive Viscount Parkhurst forever from her mind.

As the music came to a close, Sam took her arm in his and guided her towards the refreshment tables. As he handed her a mug of cider, he scanned her face speculatively, as if reading her mind. He leaned in close, and the subtle scent of his body came to her—warm and dark and manly. "It's hot and noisy here," he said. "Mayhap we could take a bit of a walk."

She tensed. It would be so easy.

And it might even be the wise thing to do, so that she could move on with her life. Part of her wanted to go with him.

But another part of her felt an almost desperate panic, and thought of John.

John—whom she could never have.

She might need to move on, but she wasn't ready yet. She disentangled herself gently from Sam's arm and gave him a demurring smile.

He actually looked disappointed. "Maybe another time,

Miss Wilkins?" He gave her a rueful grin. "Perhaps a walk after Sunday services, if that's more to your liking?"

A knot formed in her throat, but she forced the words through it. "I would like that, Sam."

"Good," he said. And then he actually raised her hand to his lips in an almost courtly fashion, and kissed her fingers. "Then I'll sit in the front pew and stay wide awake through your brother's sermon. You have my solemn promise."

"I'd like that, too," she said, and now she felt a genuine smile curve her lips. "Your usual snoring tends to make the babies cry."

He laughed, and his eyes gleamed with warmth. "Ah, well, I'm a hard working man all week long. I've got to catch up on my sleep sometime."

And, *goodness*, he made that sound somehow bawdy as well.

She felt herself blushing anew, and Sam's grin implied he noticed. He still held her hand. "Will you make me a promise too, Miss Wilkins?" he whispered, putting his lips very close to her ear, so close she felt the warm vibration of his breath. "Wear your hair like that again on Sunday next. In fact, you should wear it that way always."

Another wink, and he was gone. And the inside of her chest was left fluttering, just a bit.

Goodness.

Had she really just been *flirting* with a man? She really had changed from what she used to be. And she couldn't regret it.

The full moon had risen higher while she'd danced with Sam, the bright circle of white illuminating the Green. Perhaps its influence had affected the gathering, for as she looked around now, she realized that something in the mood of the townspeople had shifted subtly from the light pleasantness with which the dancing had begun.

A different sort of energy crackled in the air. Something wilder, more fractious.

The sexton and Mrs. Trumbull broke off abruptly from the end of a line of dancers, squabbling about something. Mrs. Trumbull had her chin up and was marching off with an offended look. The sexton trailed after her, a stormy expression on his face.

Rosamund Lawton came hurrying from another direction, her hands balled into fists, her forehead creased and her mouth pursed as though she might be on the verge of bursting into tears.

And someone had evidently brought some liquor stronger than cider, because a cluster of men under one of the oak trees was laughing rather too raucously, and two of them were shoving one another in a way that seemed good-natured now, but might at any moment spark into a fight.

Donald Evans stood amidst them, looking shifty and irritable, and a bit unsteady on his feet. *Blast.* Most of the townspeople knew not to give him anything intoxicating to drink, but Donald always seem to find a way to pour something down his throat.

Oh, dear. And the evening had started out so sweetly. Where had all the May Day magic gone?

She really ought to find Thomas and alert him to the possibility of trouble. She turned in the direction she'd last seen him dancing—and ran straight into what felt like a sun-warmed wall.

But it wasn't a wall.

It was Viscount Parkhurst.

Oh, damnation.

That little flutter Sam Brickley had created in her chest shifted instantly to an avalanche. Blood rushed from the top of her head straight to her belly, and the pulsing desire of their encounter beneath the hawthorn tree returned in a hard, hot, swelling wave.

So much for forgetting the viscount by paying attention to another man.

John seized hold of the hand Sam had just kissed, and Mary felt the jolt of his touch clear to her toes.

"Dance with me," he said.

CHAPTER 10

*J*ohn wasn't surprised when Mary tugged her hand away.

"Are you quite mad?" she hissed in an accusing undertone. "We shouldn't...we're supposed to be staying away from one another."

"I don't remember agreeing to that," he said, trying to keep his expression reasonably serious. Happiness at being near her—knowing he was now a free man, able to offer for her with an undivided heart—frothed through him, making a smile almost impossible to suppress. "In fact, I think staying away from each other is a terrible idea."

She frowned. "Nothing has changed since this morning, Lord Parkhurst."

"*Everything* has changed," he said, and his breath hitched as he gazed at her. Lord, she looked pretty tonight—flushed from dancing, with curls shaken loose all about her face. Not quite the half-naked sylph he'd held in his arms in the woods that morning, but still, more of the *real* Mary than he'd ever seen in public before. "You absolutely must talk with me. I have news to tell you."

"No. No, I absolutely mustn't. And I'm—*busy*. I need to find Thomas."

"Thomas can wait. I can't."

"Oh, stop! Leave me be!" Her eyebrows raised, and her eyes looked bright with a slick of tears. "This is…this is *cruel* of you."

"*Cruel?*"

"To keep coming after me, my lord, when I've been quite clear about my wishes."

My lord. She made those words sound like some awful insult.

"Mary, please," he said. "You *must* hear me out. And you can't run off now—everyone is watching us. If you go tearing off with that look on your face, it's sure to start a scandal."

"What look on my face?"

He mimed a quick grimace.

"Oh, for pity's sake. I look nothing like that. And no one's paying attention, anyway." But she stole quick glances out of the corners of her eyes, and the tightening of her expression told him she could see they did indeed have an audience.

A very intrigued audience.

Including Annabel Lawton, who stood staring from beside the lilacs, her gaze speculative and suspicious.

Mary quickly schooled her face to blank calm, as she was so remarkably good at doing. "Of course, Lord Parkhurst," she said in a louder voice. "I should be glad to dance and discuss the digging of the new well. I'm sure we can solve the problem of the…the sliding shale."

"Clever girl," he whispered to her, trying not to laugh, and pulled her into the dance.

It was a country dance—fast-paced and rowdy. Some of the dancers formed rings and spun about in giddy groups, but other couples dared to dance in pairs, hands on each other's waists and shoulders, galloping and whirling about. John wisely chose the latter approach.

"So we can talk," he said.

And, ah, it was glorious. Mary fit so neatly into his arms. The small swell of her breasts bumped against his chest now and again, and her skirts brushed his legs. His heart was pounding, and he could see the pulse jump at the base of her throat.

The darkness was a blessing—he could scarcely disguise the intensity in his eyes when he looked at her. This close, though, the delightful little cinnamon-colored freckles on her nose were just visible in the lamplight, and he wanted to kiss each one.

She was clearly trying not to look at him, but he felt the response of her body—felt her begin to soften against him. Her spine arched where he put his hand to her back; her lungs drew air more deeply.

He whirled her around and around, one of his hands clasping hers, the other at her waist, and as they sped up, she had no choice but to clutch at his shoulder with her free hand. It felt marvelous. They belonged together. He knew it, and somewhere deep down inside, he was sure she did, too.

Though she certainly seemed determined to fight against it with all her stubborn will.

"Where have you been all evening, my lord?" she asked, keeping her voice calm and polite despite their exertion.

"Where were you this morning?" he countered, spinning her around once more. "When the rest of us danced about the May Pole?"

"I was at home, avoiding you."

Now he grimaced for real. "Well, there's an honest response. I was afraid that was your motive."

"And what was yours, for coming so late to the dancing this evening? Hopefully you were at least *trying* to avoid me."

"Quite the contrary. I was trying to figure out how I could get you to talk to me. I knew if I showed myself openly that you'd flee in the other direction. So I decided an ambush would be the best strategy."

She was showing him only the top of her head, her gaze fixed on their feet as they looped their way across the Green. "Ambushes are dishonorable. And we have nothing to talk about. I said what I had to say this morning."

"Ah, but I have something I must tell you. Something new. Something important. Come for a walk with me."

She stiffened suddenly, and jerked in his arms. "No, John. There's no point. We are both who we are, and nothing will change that." She pulled her hands away and stepped back so quickly, he stumbled. "I'm sorry," she said, loud enough for onlookers to overhear. "I've overdone the dancing. I must sit down awhile. Pardon me, Lord Parkhurst. We'll have to discuss the well some other time."

Damn it. He wanted to grab her arm and tug her back to him, or to cry out that he was now a free man and could marry her. But far too many eyes were on them now, and he had promised Lord Lawton not to make his decision public until after Annabel heard the truth tomorrow.

That, at least, was a promise he had to keep.

He had to be patient, just a little longer. So he swallowed hard, and let Mary walk away.

For now.

Just for now.

She would learn his news soon enough, and then he could tell her how fully and utterly his heart was hers.

MARY LURCHED over to one of the wooden benches and dropped like a sackload of spoiled onions.

All her powers of self-control could barely stop her from bursting out weeping. Why couldn't John just leave her alone? And why couldn't she stop feeling as if her whole body began to melt the moment he touched her?

She wished the dark night would just swallow her up.

A whiff of perfume wafted towards her, with a rustle of silks and a shimmer of golden hair. Oh, Lord—Annabel Lawton plumped down on the bench right beside her.

Perfect.

"A lady can be exhausted by these affairs, can't she?" said Annabel, fanning herself. "This is the first I've sat down all evening. Gentlemen are so very demanding."

Blast. Discussing *gentlemen* with Annabel Lawton was the last thing Mary wanted to do right now. Well, the last thing other than go back to dancing in John's arms.

Annabel leaned in with a conspiratorial giggle. "But you must forgive Lord Parkhurst, at least," she said. "He may have reason to be in especially high spirits just now."

Mary's shoulders tensed. Why was Annabel Lawton speaking for the viscount?

Annabel chattered on. "I should not really complain about being tired tonight. I do enjoy dancing. And after a lady is married, she can hardly dance so much as she is free to now."

A slow cold prickle went up Mary's spine at those words.

After a lady is *married...?*

She swallowed, and it was as if a rock were stuck in her throat. Oh, dear Lord—John had told her he had *something important* to tell her. "Do you have...news to share, Miss Lawton?"

"Oh, well. I can't really say." Annabel's fingers fluttered prettily about her throat. "Not news precisely, but I suppose I can tell *you*, Miss Wilkins, since I know you are no gossip, that I expect I shall have some very significant news to share before long."

Oh.

Oh, oh, oh.

That was what John had been about to tell her.

Annabel Lawton was about to be married.

About to be married to...*him.*

Mary's stomach dropped towards her shoes.

He took my advice. He listened to me when I said Annabel was the proper match for him. And it only took him a few hours...

So that was why he'd wanted so badly to talk to her. He wanted Mary to learn of their engagement before the general public did, in an attempt to spare her feelings. As a loyal childhood friend would surely want to do.

Her fingers clutched the edge of the bench as a wave of dizziness spun her head around.

"I tell you in confidence," said Annabel, her blue eyes darting meaningfully in the viscount's direction, "a certain gentleman of our mutual acquaintance ensconced himself with my father in the study for quite a long time this afternoon. Of course, men feel they have so many details to iron out before the ladies can be consulted. As if their thoughts on the matter were really so much more important than ours. Men are silly creatures, after all, but I suppose we must indulge them."

Nausea rose in a choking billow, and despite the dizziness, Mary found herself once more on her feet.

John was going to be *married*. Married to Annabel Lawton.

Which was, of course, precisely what was supposed to happen. What she herself had so adamantly insisted *must* happen. But she could not even begin to lie to herself that she was gratified by John's coming happiness, or take comfort in the fact that this inevitable union was in every way the right one for her friend to make. A terrible dark hole seemed to be opening inside her, turning everything cold and black.

In a sort of daze, she excused herself to Miss Lawton.

She stumbled her way across the Green, the world blurring around her, until she found Sam Brickley. He was standing with his younger brothers Geordie and Ben, downing hard cider. He grinned when he saw her.

"I think I'd like to take that walk now, after all, Sam," she said.

Sam looked surprised, but damned pleased. The mug of cider thumped down on a table, he took her arm, and before she was even sure what was happening, she found herself alone with him in the shadows behind the schoolhouse.

With no more preamble, she pressed herself back against the bricks and pulled Sam towards her by the thick lapels of his coat.

He gave a throaty chuckle. "Well, this is a surprise, Miss Wilkins." They were both breathing hard, in and out, their rhythms falling slowly into sync. His breath had a tart sweet smell from the cider.

His big, rough hand came up to where her necklace rested, and he ran his finger just beneath the line of pearls, from the upper curve of her breast to the tender skin of her throat. Her pulse kicked.

Yes. This was just what she needed. John was going to marry Annabel, and it was time to move on with her own life as well.

Sam's fingers continued to stroke, the heavy pad of his thumb playing in the space between her collarbones. "I most definitely like this change in you," he murmured.

"Do you?" she said stupidly.

"Mm. I do. And I like touching you as well—your skin's so soft."

"Is it?"

"Very." Now his whole hand swept along her neck, the palm warm, and his fingers teased their way into the curls that tumbled loose by her ear. "I always thought you had fine eyes," he said, "but who'd have thought you had such soft skin? And such lovely hair?"

Nobody, she thought. *Nobody but John.*

No—she was most certainly *not* going to be thinking about John right now.

She put her hands very deliberately on Sam's broad chest, feeling the hardness of him through the rough wool of his waistcoat, sliding her palms up towards his shoulders.

"That feels good," he said, and his other hand slipped around her waist and brought her closer. His body had a nice smell, of fresh air and clean earth. He wasn't...he wasn't *John*, but he was an attractive man. A good-hearted man. A man she could be an appropriate wife for, if they both wished it.

She felt an impulse to flee, but she fought it down.

She steeled herself. "Kiss me, Sam," she said, trying to keep her voice from shaking. "Will you, please?"

"Gladly," he said, and he did.

As he leaned in, Mary had to stop herself from squeaking or pushing him instinctively away. It took a conscious effort to relax, but as his mouth touched hers, she managed not to flinch.

It wasn't...terrible. In fact, his lips felt firm and pleasant, and his big body was a intriguing weight as he leaned against her. His tongue pressed against hers, spiced from the cider.

She had to fight down the sense, though, that his weight wasn't the right weight, that his body didn't fit to hers quite as it should, that this was wrong, just *wrong* for her...

He pulled back. "Is something the matter?"

"No." She shook her head frantically. "No, kiss me again. Touch me."

He chuckled, and pulled her against him again. "You

surprise me again and again, Mary Wilkins. I should call you Mary now, I'm thinking." And his mouth pressed into hers again, and his hands began to move, sliding first over the curve of her hips, then around to cup and squeeze her bottom, then up along her bodice, sliding over her breasts. A rougher, less subtle touch than John's, but not unpleasant.

Don't think. Don't think too much.

Just let it happen. Just go through with this, and put the memory of John behind you.

Sam's lips were at her throat now. He leaned his weight in closer until his hips pressed against her, and she felt him hardening. "How far do you mean for me to take this?" he whispered huskily against her skin. "I don't mean to push you, but I do want you, Mary."

"Far. Not far. I don't know." She felt the prickle of tears, and blinked to banish them. "Put—put your hand under my skirt, Sam."

He pulled back again, and she could see his eyebrows raise. "Well, you're in a fine mood tonight. I'd enjoy doing that, Mary, but not if you don't truly want me to."

"Do it. Truly, I want you to. I—I need you to."

He squinted at her thoughtfully for a moment, then shrugged. "Never say I refused a lady an honest request."

And his hand went where she'd asked him, lifting her hem and sweeping up over her knee and then to the sensitive place behind it, stroking it enticingly. He moved his fingers no higher after that, as if waiting for her to demand more.

Did she *want* to demand more?

She tried to focus on the sensation of his touch, to fight down the impulse to wry free like a stray dog first put to collar. She made herself breathe.

Sam's hand was strong and calloused, not a gentleman's hand. It was a working man's hand—confident, no-nonsense, accustomed to accomplishing its tasks. His lips still brushed her throat, and his other hand reached behind her and curved around her buttocks over her skirts, kneading gently as pressed his hips once more against hers. She felt his arousal…and his dark eyes studying her.

"I'll do whatever you like," he said, his breath coming shorter. "I think you're a fine woman, and I'd be proud to call you mine. But, Mary, you have to tell me what you're thinking."

"I don't want to think." She'd known for a long time that people did such things, without benefit of marriage. What she'd told John in the vicarage kitchen about the misbehavior of the local people was true: in the parish register, nearly half the time, wedding dates and dates of baptism for couples' first children were notably less than nine months apart, and she knew Thomas had more than once risked his career by hurrying the banns to keep a bride from showing shamefully at the altar.

Why should she be so different from everybody else?

She just had to let Sam do what other men did to other women. And then she'd be free. She'd have her heart back.

So she touched him. Wriggled a hand between them and cupped her palm to the thick bulge at the front of his trousers, running it up along the fullness of him.

He groaned in a most gratifying way. "You're sure?" he asked, his voice gone hoarse. "I don't generally doubt a woman's enjoying herself with me, but in this case…."

"I'm sure." She swallowed hard. She *had* to do this. She pressed her palm against him more boldly, gripping him through the wool. That seemed to stop his questions.

"Ah, Mary," he groaned. He drew in a big breath, and in his broad chest it sounded like a furnace drawing in air. A string of soft profanities fell from his lips. His hands under her skirts, which had stilled, began to move again, stroking and exploring slowly upwards, with a gentleness and finesse she wouldn't have expected from such a man. Not rushing her, still going no higher than her thigh. His eyes closed in pleasure, though, his big body swaying.

Goodness. She was having this effect on a second man within the span of a single day. Amazing she had this power.

She didn't feel lost in the moment as she had with John, didn't feel that surge of overwhelming need, that strange and magical spell drawing her under, but it—it wasn't unpleasurable. It could even *be* pleasurable, perhaps very pleasurable, if she could just will herself to relax.

Sam's hips rocked against her hand. "That's good, Mary. So good."

She could do this.

It wouldn't be difficult. Just let nature take its course, get through it, be rid of the strict cage of her virginity. Break John's spell over her.

And she might even build a life with Sam. A home. Have children of her own.

All she had to do was shut her eyes, focus on the sensations of his fingers stroking her thighs, urge him to move them up and up, touch her where John had put his mouth. If she did, his strong arms could lift her against the schoolhouse wall. It would all be settled in moments.

And if a deep pulse of sorrow was rising up through her chest—well, she could ignore that.

Sam stilled again, and one of his hands slipped from beneath her skirts to cover her fingers with his. "Have you done this before, Mary?" His breathing rasped.

"No. Yes. Some of it."

"It's a serious thing."

"I know that." Oh, Lord, why did men have to *talk*?

But he was examining her face in the shadows. "You're a lovely girl, Mary Wilkins. And clever. Bright as a new penny."

Not the most romantic of compliments, but she got so few, she couldn't complain. "Thank you, Sam."

"I wouldn't want to do wrong by you, is what I'm saying. You make good things happen for the people around here. You're a true and honest soul. And you'd make a good wife for a man."

Was he...proposing? Or warning her?

How did such things work?

It didn't matter. "Please, Sam. Just get on with it."

He laughed then, low and deep and warm, and shook his head. "You're sure? Not even a bit of poetry first?"

She responded by tugging loose one of the buttons of his trousers, and then another. "No poetry."

"Sweet Jesus." And then his mouth met hers again, and his kiss became hungrier, even as he worked the rest of his own buttons free. He seemed more than willing to cooperate with her now.

Something very near to panic swamped her, but she pushed that feeling away. She put her arms around Sam's neck instead, her forearms resting on the big, bunched corded muscles of his shoulders.

Let it happen, just breathe and let it happen....

His hands went under her buttocks, lifting her. His mouth pressed hot against her ear. "Be mine, then, Mary Wilkins..."

Oh, sweet heaven, was she really going to let this happen?

Could she?

She drew in a hasty breath to say...*something*. She wasn't really quite sure what.

And then, from out on Birchford Green, a woman screamed.

The yells of men erupted a moment after—from the sound of it, the fight she'd sensed brewing earlier had begun.

Sam eased her back to the ground again. "Damn," he said. "That's trouble."

"Yes," she said with a sigh, and tried not to recognize the sweet sense of relief that swept through her.

And they both tugged their clothing quickly to rights and ran back to the Green to see what was happening.

CHAPTER 11

*A*mazing how strong and belligerent Donald Evans could be with sufficient whiskey in his veins.

John gripped the struggling man from behind, locking his arms around the man's torso. Although he was both taller and broader than the drunkard, John could scarcely hold on as Donald kicked and punched and twisted, wriggly as a greased pig.

The young sexton Mr. Bassett had bloodied Donald's nose, and now did his own desperate wriggling just a few feet away, clamped in the burly arms of the village blacksmith.

The source of Bassett's fury was obvious: one of Donald's fists still held the skirts of the innkeeper, Mrs. Trumbull, and in his flailing, he hauled the poor woman around so violently she could scarcely keep her feet. She was shrieking loud enough to wake the dead—not to mention punching and kicking at Donald herself as best she could manage, with half her blows landing on John's knees and shins instead.

"Leggo a' her, ye damned lout!" Mr. Bassett shouted, clearly as drunk as his opponent.

"Why should I, then?" Donald Evans hollered back. "It's not like she's yours, is she?"

Mr. Bassett squirmed furiously against the blacksmith's huge forearms. "She's not *yours*!"

"Ha!" yelled Mrs. Trumbull, pausing in her screeches to give Mr. Bassett a bitter glare. "Fat lot you care, Joe!"

A ring of townspeople and his tenants formed to watch the scene—everyone from the local cobbler to the elegant Lawton girls. Mrs. Evans, the drunkard's wife, stood amongst them, sobbing helplessly at her husband's misbehavior, her face wobbly and wet as a bowl of porridge.

The Reverend Thomas Wilkins was doing his level best to calm the men, coming between the would-be combatants with one palm outstretched to each of them, saying sensible vicar-ish things like, "Come now, you should be friends. We are all peaceable people here!"

Donald Evans responded with a string of curses so vile, he'd be ashamed to show his face in church for months—assuming he remembered his words once he sobered up.

Now Mary came running into the ring of onlookers. Thank goodness. He'd wondered where she'd gone off to. She looked even more flushed than before, her hair more unruly. "For heaven's sake!" she cried. "Lord Parkhurst! Make him let Mrs. Trumbull go!"

And—*oh*. Sam Brickley came hurrying up behind her. Looking a good deal flushed and rumpled himself. Adjusting his clothing in none too subtle a fashion.

Damn it all.

Jealousy slammed through John, hot and hard, and his muscles tightened to steel. At once, Donald Evans squealed in pain...and let go of Mrs. Trumbull's skirts.

The innkeeper stumbled forwards out of the drunkard's reach, milling her arms for balance.

"Well done, then, Donald!" exclaimed Thomas Wilkins,

looking greatly relieved to see the crisis lessening. "That was the Christian thing to do."

John's fists still clenched against Donald's ribcage, making the man whimper. What in hell had Mary been doing with *Sam Brickley*? The farmer was a good fellow, to be sure—a hard worker, owned a good chunk of his own land, was steadily prosperous. But Sam was no proper match for a woman like Mary.

Mary was...Mary was *his*.

She stepped closer, but to talk to the still-wriggling drunkard, not to him. "This is why you must not drink, Donald," she said earnestly. "You've upset the whole party."

Donald wriggled a moment or two more, then, after all his violent resistance to the use of manly force, fell abashed under Mary's kind, bright gaze, and stilled. "Sorry, ma'am," he said in a more subdued voice.

Good Lord. She really was some sort of sylvan nymph: her very presence soothed savage beasts.

The blacksmith seemed to feel this was his cue to release the sexton, and Bassett—thank goodness—ignored Donald in favor of rushing to Mrs. Trumbull and trying to put his arms around her. Mrs. Trumbull, in her turn, gave a loud *harrumph* and walked haughtily away. Bassett followed quickly in her wake, spouting drunken but profuse apologies.

Mary was just inches away now, her full focus on the drunkard. With her handkerchief, she dabbed at Donald's bloody nose as though she were tending one of her school-children.

Her brother the vicar finally lowered his outstretched arms. "There, now," he said. "Peace is restored. Lord Parkhurst, you can let Donald go now. He's coming to his senses."

"I am not so certain of that," John replied.

But Mary looked up to meet his gaze, and he felt dazzled. "Please, Lord Parkhurst," she said.

What could he do but comply?

He eased his grip from around Donald's middle, and the drunkard lurched forward.

Mary stepped neatly out of his way, but the surrounding crowd of ladies was not quite so agile. Donald had apparently been depending on John's grip to help him keep his balance, and now his knees wobbled beneath him. He pivoted like a weathervane in a strong wind and pitched forward—straight onto Rosamund Lawton, who had nothing like Mary's athletic reflexes.

The pretty girl shrieked and fell back against her sisters as Donald's weight struck her full force—and shrieked louder as the man tried to regain his balance by clutching at her shoulders. His unsteady hands slipped on the silken fabric of her frock, and a moment later he was attempting to support himself by clamping his hands over her breasts.

Panicking, Rosamund batted at his head with both palms and let out a piercing scream.

"Oh, quit yapping!" slurred Donald, stumbling harder against her. "You're no better'n me!"

The Reverend Mr. Wilkins, who had been so calm a moment before, turned scarlet and swelled with outrage. "Get your hands off of her!" he shouted.

Before anyone else could move, the vicar thrust his left hand between Rosamund and Donald, seizing the drunkard's coat. Wilkins spun the man around with surprising force, wrenching him off the lady, and then, so fast and hard Donald had no chance to see it coming, slammed his right fist into Donald's jaw.

The blow struck with an audible crunch, and Donald hit the ground like a dropped hammer.

So much for the vicar being a peaceable Christian.

At least where Rosamund Lawton was concerned.

Interesting.

The drama over now, the crowd began to move. Women circled Rosamund and Mrs. Evans both, cooing words of comfort. A group of men carted the groaning drunkard off to the pump to sober him up under a stream of cold water. Two fiddlers, hoping to salvage some fun from the occasion, scraped out the opening bars of "Blowzabella, My Bouncing Doxy."

The vicar, meanwhile, was busy jumping from foot to foot, cradling his injured fist.

And John needed to talk to Mary.

He took her by the hand and pulled her away from the crowd.

"What are you doing?" she hissed at him. "I have to help Thomas."

"Your brother seems surprisingly capable of handling himself."

She tugged backwards. "I don't want to talk to you."

"No? I suppose you'd rather be back behind the schoolhouse with Sam Brickley."

Her eyes widened in outrage. "*That* is none of your concern."

"Of course it's my concern!"

"Oh—pardon me, Lord of the Manor." Her voice held a bitterness he'd never heard in it before. "I'd forgotten your rank amongst us."

"Mary! *What?* That isn't what I meant."

"To be very clear, I do not need your permission for what I do! Or your approval. Any more than *you* need mine." She sounded…*furious.* Like he'd been guilty of some unspeakable offense against her.

"What on earth are you talking about?"

She tugged again. "Let me go."

"For God's sake—it's my concern what you do with Sam Brickley because I *care* about you, damn it all." He had to make her listen. He had to make her see. "Do you truly want to end up married to that man?"

"Maybe I do." Her eyes looked almost accusing. "So what if I do?"

His chest ached terribly. "Please don't, Mary. Sam Brickley's not worthy of you."

"Now, *that* is the most snobbish thing you've ever said."

"It's not snobbish. I don't think *I'm* worthy of you either."

Some complicated emotion went over her face, but the moonlight made it hard to interpret.

He squeezed her hand tighter, drawing her with him down the lane that led behind the hillock of the church and towards the woods. Miraculously, she followed him this time without too much resistance.

When they were under cover of the pines, he turned her to face him. "Do you love Sam? Isn't that the question you told me had to be asked in these matters? The only one that matters? Can you honestly tell me you love him?"

Even here in the dimmer light, he could see tears begin to sparkle in her eyes. "What difference does it make whether I love him or not?"

"All the difference in the world."

She squeezed shut her eyes now. "Please. Please just let me go."

"Come on, now," he said, laying his hands on her shoulders and willing her to look at him again. "Where's the Mary I know? What difference does it make whether you *love* him? Have you taken leave of your senses? Love is the only reason to choose a mate. You're the one who taught me that."

She shook her head fretfully. "I was wrong about it, then."

Had the whole universe just gone mad? How could she say such a thing?

John's heart was a cannon ball, jammed heavily between his ribs and his throat. But he had to get through to her, and he had to get through to her now, before she made some irrevocable mistake. Before he lost his chance with her.

"No, Mary," he said. "*No*, you weren't wrong. You've always been wiser than me. You've made me understand things that I never fully understood before. You've made me want to be true to myself. To live life as it should be lived."

Her expression tightened warily, and the tears he'd seen earlier in her eyes squeezed out from beneath her closed lids.

"I'm glad for you, John," she said. "Truly, I am." Despite her words, her voice seemed choked with misery. Even in the moonlight, he could see that she'd gone a shade or two paler than usual. "I do think you've done the right thing. Made the right decision. Honestly, I do."

"What decision?"

She pulled her hands free of his. "I understand completely. There's no need to break any of this to me gently. I know what you have to tell me. About your...your discussion with Lord Lawton this afternoon."

"You...do?" If she knew he'd ended the arrangement with the Lawtons, then why was she pulling away from him? His heart began to sink.

"Yes. And I—I approve entirely. You will be much happier for it."

She *approved* of the end of his agreement with the Lawtons. Well, that was a good sign, at least. So why was she only talking about *his* happiness, not her own?

"I will be far happier," he affirmed. "As shall Annabel, I have no doubt."

"Good. That's excellent. It's absolutely the best possible—" Her words broke on a sob.

"What? Mary, what's going on?" He reached for her, but she ducked out of his way.

"No," she said, wiping at her eyes with a fist. Her voice came out choked. "Don't mind me. I'm—I'm delighted for you, truly. Annabel Lawton is the perfect bride for you."

He stopped dead. "What?"

"You and Annabel. She's your proper match. It's no wonder at all you've fallen in love with her." And now the tears flowed more freely. "But that doesn't mean I have no feelings at all, John. It doesn't mean you should flaunt your happiness in front of me! There are limits to the charity I'm capable of, even toward you."

Annabel? His *bride*?

Mary thought *that* was what he'd brought her here to tell her?

He couldn't help himself—he laughed.

"Oh, for pity's sake!" Mary cried, hitting him on the arm with her fist. "You don't have to laugh at me!"

He laughed harder. "Are you mad, indeed? What do you think I've been trying to tell you?" She thought he was engaged to Annabel—and she was in tears about it? Hope soared inside him. "Sweetheart, I don't love Annabel Lawton. I can't love her. I never will love her."

Mary stiffened in surprise. Her eyes flew wide and she blinked at him as though she couldn't quite absorb the meaning of what he'd just said.

Her mouth moved tentatively several times before she spoke, as though she were weighing her words. "But...you're marrying her anyway?"

"*Please* stop saying that. Just listen to me. *Hear* me, Mary, the only thing that matters, the one and only thing: I'm going to follow my heart."

Color flooded back into her cheeks. An extraordinary series of emotions flickered across her features—surprise, relief, joy, consternation. "But, John—you're meant to... Annabel thinks you...everyone expects—"

"I don't *care* what everyone expects. I don't care what the world thinks of me."

"Oh, but…" She gasped for breath. "I've told you, you owe me nothing. We haven't done anything that requires…"

This had gone on more than long enough. He took hold of her by the shoulders and backed her up against the broad trunk of an oak tree.

And kissed her.

He pressed his body to hers, his mouth to hers, and suddenly everything was right. For just a moment, she resisted, flattening her hands against his ribcage, but then she stilled, and she softened against him and opened her lips so his tongue could slip inside and tangle with hers. The shape of her mouth fit perfectly against his, the taste inside of it sweet and warm. Her arms went around his neck and he felt the swell of her little breasts against his chest, and the slight curve of her belly against his cock.

A delicious heat spread through his limbs, and he could tell it was warming her too because her back arched, and she rose up on her toes to press against him, and her fingers slid up his chest to curve and tighten over his shoulders. Her mouth became urgent against his.

He kissed her long and hard, and when he finally released her to let her catch her breath, he said, "There. *That's* what requires it."

She let out a heartfelt sigh, and the sound made his insides flip over.

He brushed back the curls that had fallen against her cheek, and looked deep into her bright eyes. "When I say I'm going to follow my heart, I meant my heart is yours, Mary," he said. "I *need* to be with you. Not because anyone or anything else is telling me, but because I feel *this* when your arms are around me."

She stared back at him, hope shining in her eyes, but still tinged with worry. "But—but the *Lawtons*? Annabel said—"

"I don't care about Annabel. It's *you* I care for. *You* I want. I'll never be happy if I'm not able to be with you."

"Oh, John," she said, and her voice quavered with emotion. "Oh, John, John, *John*."

His heart pounded at the sound of his name on her lips. Relief and joy flowed into him like sunlight. He couldn't help himself: "Not Sam, Sam, *Sam*?" he teased her.

"Not Sam," she whispered back fervently. "Never Sam. *You*. Only you."

She robbed him of breath.

So he set his lips to hers again, and pressed her back against the tree, and she tangled her fingers in his hair to draw him closer against her. Fire lit inside him—blazing in his heart as surely as in those regions lower down.

How could he ever have missed how passionate Mary was, how lovely and silken and warm? She hid so well in those plain sack-like dresses of hers, making her body so unobtrusive, concealing the flaming beauty of her hair.

He'd so very nearly missed seeing her for what she was, so very nearly stayed blind to the beauty within her. His whole life could so easily have been thrown away on his father's plans for him. Only a convenient strand of blackberry vines had saved him.

God, he loved her.

He had to have her now—finally, fully.

He seized her by the hand again. "Come deeper into the woods, Mary, where it can be just the two of us. The moon is bright, it's the first of May—magic awaits out there."

She hesitated only a moment, and then she laughed suddenly, bright and joyous. And they ran together, hand in hand, finding their way down the paths as easily as if it were broad day, as if elemental forces guided their steps.

A canopy of shimmering leaves seemed to bow over them, fretted by starlight. No sound from the village reached them here—only the breeze through the treetops and the sweet shrilling of young frogs in the shallow spring ponds.

Even the moonlight seemed brighter, purer, than before. It dazzled against the surface of Mary's neck and shoulders, turning her to pearl.

He pulled her into the shelter of a small circle of evergreens, where a bed of fallen pine needles made a sort of natural bower just the right size for the two of them, as though fairy creatures had prepared it for them specially.

As though she were his Fairy Queen.

For pagan creatures, they were both wearing far too much clothing.

He smiled down at his beloved. "I need to see more of you," he said. "All of you."

And he set his hands to her laces.

CHAPTER 12

*M*ary's head swam.

John's hands were tugging at the back closure to her dress, loosening it with expert speed. His fingers trembled slightly, though, and his breath came in hard pants; a strange energy pulsed through them both, and she fancied she could hear his heartbeat thundering. Certainly, her own beat wild.

She hardly knew what to think. He *wasn't* going to marry Miss Lawton? He didn't love beautiful, lush, radiant Annabel? He didn't *want* a woman like that?

Was it really possible a man like Viscount Parkhurst wanted *Mary Wilkins*, clergyman's daughter, clergyman's spinster sister, instead? Was it possible he would *choose* her, willingly?

Apparently he did. Even as he drew apart the back of her gown, baring her shoulders, John feathered kisses along her brow, over her ears, down the line of her jaw. And while he kissed, he murmured extraordinary things: "My Mary. Sweet Mary. My sweet, lovely Mary."

"*Lovely?*" she said, astonished. "I'm not lovely."

"Lovely," he insisted.

"I think the moonlight is addling your brains."

He stilled. He placed his palms on either side of her face, forcing her to look straight at him. "*Lovely*," he repeated firmly, his eyes gleaming with emotion. "You are beautiful, Mary. I don't know how you hid yourself so long, in those awful dresses, with your curls bound up, refusing to dance, hiding the light inside you. But I see that light shining now. And I swear to you, I will never fail to see it again."

Her pulse tripped. He couldn't mean it. And yet, he was here with her, not with Annabel, and his hands were warm against her skin, and such passion heated his gaze, it seemed impossible to deny that he meant it very much indeed.

He dropped his hands to her shoulders then, slid the gown down and off her arms, down and off her hips, dropping her petticoats after it, until she was standing in only her shift. "No more hiding, Mary," he said. "No more."

Mary inhaled deeply. All around them, the sweet scent of hawthorn blooms and early musk roses filled the night with a rich, caressing perfume that muddled all her senses. This was madness—but such a sweet, seductive madness, Mary couldn't stop herself from falling right into it.

Little by little, he undid her. His quick fingers pulled the last of the pins from her hair, and combed the long strands out until her curls flowed in a nimbus around her.

Her stays went next, and then her shift and her stockings, whispering down into the pine needles, until she stood quite naked. John kissed and caressed as he went, stroking her everywhere, tasting her, and the unseasonably warm breeze seemed to kiss and stroke her, too. The glow of the moonlight seemed palpable on her skin. Before long, she was shuddering with the pleasure of it, and with a hotter desire.

John went to his knees, still stroking her as she stood

above him, turning his attention now to her lower belly, to the small curve of her hips, to her thighs.

"Sweet wood nymph," he whispered between the nips and kisses he was giving to her flesh. "Little sylph."

When Sam had kissed her, it had been like a pattering rain, but this...this was a thunderstorm, roaring and rumbling through her veins.

She wanted him to touch her between her legs, in that one spot he'd given such wondrous, lavish attention to that first morning by the blackberries, when he'd made her whole world heat and burst. But now that he had her unclothed and trembling, he was taking his time, exploring her little by little. When they'd been together before, there'd been desperation in the way he touched her, a hurry born of uncertainty, but now something seemed decided between them, and, with no words necessary, he began to take his time.

His fingers found every rise, every hollow. He was learning her, mapping her. And as he touched her, she too became aware of the shape and outline of her body born anew, as though she had never truly felt it before.

His fingers traced the subtle outline of her hip, then back to the curve of her waist, and back further still, to follow the cleft of her buttocks, then down under the curve her bottom.

Oh, his touch on her skin was a miracle. It transformed her. She felt wanted. Cherished. Lush and womanly.

Lovely.

She arched against his touch, her belly nearly pressing into his face, and he responded by reaching upwards again, his palms cupping her breasts, rubbing over her nipples. His mouth kissed the soft curve of her abdomen, along the little grooves between her belly and the tops of her legs, nipping and sucking at every curve. Everywhere, everywhere but between her thighs...

She was floating, trembling; she could barely keep to her

feet, and had to brace her hands on his shoulders to keep from falling down.

He rose up a little then, fitted his mouth over the skin that covered her lowest rib, and sucked against her flesh, sucked harder than he ever had before. It burned a little, just on the edge of pain, and yet the suction seemed to draw pleasure from deep in the core of her, spiraling outwards with a new heat that made her moan.

He was marking her with his mouth, she understood suddenly—though how she felt so sure of his purpose she could not know. She had never heard of such a thing, but she was sure of it: he was marking her as his very own. John was claiming her.

And when that was done, at long last, he did what she had most been craving: he pressed his mouth to that sweet, swollen, throbbing place at the very juncture of her thighs. The place he had kissed her that very first morning, and opened up the universe for her.

He flicked out his tongue, just on that extraordinarily sensitive nub, and light and heat streaked through her, straight to the top of her skull. She cried out, her knees buckling. She didn't want the contact to stop, but she didn't think she could hold herself upright against the waves of pleasure shooting through her as he flicked his tongue again.

She dug her fingers frantically into the muscles of his shoulders. "I—I think I need to...be lying down."

She felt his grin against her flesh.

"You are wise, madam," he said in a deep, husky voice. "You are wise, indeed."

He stripped off his jacket and laid it out over the pine needles, creating a small but extraordinarily inviting bed. She sunk downwards, and his hands came around her waist, easing her down onto it.

The pine needles made a soft cushion beneath the jacket,

their scent resinous and delicious, mixed with the perfume of violets hidden beneath that she and John had crushed with their feet.

John rose up over her now. "Let me look my fill at you," he said, his voice rasping.

Except for his jacket, he still wore all his clothes, and she found herself suddenly self-conscious, stretched out naked beneath him. She put her hands over her breasts.

"No, Mary," he said softly. "I told you—no more hiding. And there's no need to hide from me. I'm meant to see you. And I love what I see."

"Do you?" she asked. It still seemed so hard to fully believe. "Do you truly?"

"You are beautiful," he told her. "Utterly mesmerizing."

She couldn't seem to remove her hands, so he did it for her. Taking one hand in each of his, he stretched them upwards above her head.

She squirmed with embarrassment.

"Relax," he murmured. He leaned forward, reaching for something just beyond her reach above her head, and tugged at whatever was there.

Suddenly something was touching her wrists—something like smooth twine.

"Ivy," he said. "Just to remind you not to cover yourself." He was winding the long strand of ivy around and around her wrists, the sleek vine and the soft leaves tickling her flesh. She felt a little tug and realized he had wound the ends of it around something solid—the trunk of a sapling, no doubt. Nothing so strong that she couldn't free herself if she truly wanted to. But just at the moment, she didn't want to be free.

"There," he said, chuckling. "That should hold you for a bit."

"Good Lord, John," she said. "You *are* still a pirate."

He cocked an eyebrow at her. "And you are my captive, to have my wicked way with."

The pulse of pleasure that went through her at his words turned her almost to liquid.

He began to stroke her once more, down the sides of her face, over her breasts, over her belly. She had never felt so exposed, so vulnerable...and so adored. His gaze was utterly worshipful, utterly loving.

He looked at her as though she were made of magic.

And so was he. His touch was sending sparks through her as he made his way ever further downward, caressing her hips, caressing her thighs.

"Now open your legs," he said in a hoarse whisper. "Let me see the treasure I've won."

Shuddering with desire, she complied.

It felt so strange, so daring, to expose herself to him so fully, there under the moonlight, in the fresh breeze. But he seemed delighted by her. His eyes sparkled at they gazed down between her thighs. "Luscious," he said.

And, as if drawn by magnetic force, he bent low and set his mouth once more to her cleft, sending shock waves of sensation through her, making her hips buck upwards against his touch.

His fingers and tongue together made a feast of her, licking and stroking, swirling and sucking, and she felt as if every joint and sinew in her was softening and melting away, even as a great surging pressure built between her thighs.

Oh, his touch was heavenly.

She pulled at the ivy twined about her wrists, but he'd done a better job of tying her than she'd first thought—the vines wouldn't release her any more than the blackberry vines had the first time they'd come together like this.

So she grasped him with her knees instead, squeezing his

ribcage, urging him closer to her, letting him know her pleasure and desire.

He moaned in response, and slipped a finger into her cleft.

She gasped and her back arched, her hips trying to drive him further inside her.

"Easy now," he whispered, lifting his head for a moment. "A little at a time." He slipped another finger inside, pushing gently against her walls. He wasn't trying to preserve her chastity this time, she knew. He was readying her for his ultimate possession.

And she wanted that. And she didn't want to go easy, she didn't want a little at a time. They'd been building towards this moment for so long, and she wanted him inside her. She wanted him to lay claim to her once and for all.

With maddening slowness, though, he kept up his steady, gentle pace, a third finger joining the others, sliding deeper into her slick wetness, firing her almost beyond endurance. She lifted her hips again, finding a primitive rhythm as his fingers pushed into her and withdrew again and again, slowly building in pressure, while his thumb and his tongue worked together to play with that sensitive nub at the front of her, making her writhe and whimper beneath him.

She gazed up at the dark sky, at the stars, at the dancing leaf-shadows above her head. The world seemed to be changing shape around her; her head swam, her pulse beat hot and hard inside her—everything, everything was pulsing, shifting, heating, rising.

Now four fingers were inside her, thrusting in and out, and the whole palm of his other hand covered her sensitive nub, the heel of it pressing, working, driving her upward, upward.

"Come for me, darling," John murmured. "Come, my little pagan goddess. Come, and let me watch you as you come."

And she was helpless to resist him. At his words, at his touch, a dam seemed to break loose inside her, and waves and waves of pleasure rushed through every limb, every sensitive nerve. Her hips surged upwards, her sheath clenched and clenched around his fingers. Her head tipped back and her mouth fell open and she heard herself cry out in a voice that hardly seemed like it could be her own.

"Mary," he was saying softly, almost reverently. "Yes, Mary. Come for me."

And she came and came, swirls of light and pressure and sweetness cresting through her, making her eyes squeeze shut, making her all but lose consciousness of anything but the sensation of his touch.

"Yes, sweetheart," he whispered, over and over, "yes."

She had no idea how much time passed before she came fully to herself again, and felt the clear contours of her body once more, and the ivy twined about her wrists, and the soft cushion of pine needles beneath her back.

John was still leaning over her, on his knees, smiling at her.

"That," he said, "was without doubt the most gorgeous thing I've ever seen."

She smiled. She was too languid, too warm and soft and melted, to be embarrassed. She was stretched out naked before him, legs spread, skin flushed, but she felt no shame.

No, indeed. In fact, she was far from being done with him. She wanted more, and more, and more.

And so did he apparently. His arousal strained hard against the fall of the trousers he still wore.

He saw where her gaze was focused, and he laughed. "See what you do to me, Mary? You haven't even touched me yet, and I'm stiff as an oak branch."

"And what will happen if I touch you?" she asked.

He gave her a piratical smile. "I'd be only too delighted to show you, love."

"Untie me, then."

"Not quite yet," he said with a dark chuckle. "I'm rather enjoying seeing you like this. Having you at my mercy."

"John, please," she said. "Before we go any further…"

He glanced at her face warily. "What?"

She smiled at him. "I want to see you, too. I want to see you without your clothes."

His grin spread wide now, and without hesitation, he pulled his shirt off over his head, exposing his broad shoulders, his beautiful sculpted chest. He gleamed like diamond in the moonlight. With a wicked grin, he straightened his back, and began to work the buttons on his fall. His hard shaft sprang free, jutting against his abdomen.

He lifted himself away from her for a moment, stood to pull off the boots he still wore, to peel away his trousers. His movements were so pure, so strong, so utterly male, and when he stood there, finally naked, glorious, glistening in the moonlight, his muscles rippling, he seemed something more than simply human. He was surely partly a creature from the spirit world.

She wanted him, every inch of him.

She struggled up against the restraints at her wrists, trying to lift her head towards him. "Come closer," she said. "I want to put my mark on you, too."

"Your mark?"

"Like you did on my rib. With your mouth."

John made a sound in this throat that was almost a growl. "Oh, indeed," he said. "Bound or not, you are clearly a pirate still yourself." He straddled her again, shifting his weight until he was leaning low over her, his palms braced against the trunk of the tree to which he'd tied her. She could feel the heat of his legs against her ribcage, the surprising softness of his skin and the crispness of his hair.

If she stretched her head, she could touch her mouth to his rock-hard abdomen.

"Make your mark, then, wench."

With him this close, she could smell the dark musk that rose from his sex. The velvet hardness of him pressed against her cheek, almost as if straining for her attention.

Closing her eyes, she set her mouth to the base of his ribs and nipped and sucked at the skin there, just as he had done to hers.

He groaned now, deep and full.

She sucked harder, adding the slight pressure of her teeth, until she felt his skin strain and draw into her mouth. "There now," she said, releasing his flesh, pleased to see a spot of darker color blooming where her lips and teeth had touched. "You're mine now, and no one else can have you."

He gasped. "I am yours, Mary. Truly yours."

An almost overwhelming emotion soared through her chest at his words, more than she knew what to do with all at once. To distract them both, she darted her mouth sideways, fitting her lips around the tip of his rigid shaft. He caught his breath sharply, and his palms slipped from the tree and hit the ground hard on either side of her head.

"God, Mary," he moaned. "You undo me."

And he undid her as well. Her heart thundered in her chest as she took in all the sensations of being like this with him: the heat of his body above hers, the silk of the head of his shaft, the warm, intoxicating scent of him, the grip of his fingers as they came against the back of her head to steady her, the pull of the ivy around her wrists. Something about it was more magical, more dreamlike even than when she had knelt before him in the morning sunlight.

They could not possibly be doing this. They could not

possibly be the people called Viscount Parkhurst and Miss Wilkins, the vicar's sister, who just minutes ago had been fully clothed and dancing in a civilized fashion on the Green with all their friends and neighbors.

And yet it was real—the most real and true and undeniable thing she had ever experienced in her life. The most purely natural. The most profound.

She opened her mouth wider to take him deeper, flicking her tongue around the breadth of him, round and round. In response, his fingers tightened against her scalp, tugging at her curls. She could see the muscles of his belly contract, his hips begin to flex.

She began to suckle him, drawing him in tighter with her lips and cheeks. Hard as it was to move her head, she managed to slide her mouth at least partway up and down his length, causing him to groan and shudder. Looking up, she could see his face above her, his mouth parting, his eyes pressed shut, as if in agony, or on the edge of ecstasy.

She could tell he was fighting hard not to thrust down her throat. Without her hands to guide him, she had to trust him not to lose control. He eased himself in and out as gently as he could, softly drawing her head towards him and away again.

It was an extraordinary intimacy, beyond anything she could have imagined. And yet a sharp, new need was building in her. She knew still greater intimacy was possible, more total joining of their bodies, and every instinct in her clamored for it.

As if he shared her thoughts, he pulled himself out of her suddenly. "Damn me, Mary—you'll have me bursting in a moment."

She smiled at him teasingly, surprised at her own wantonness. "Isn't that a good thing?"

"A very good thing," he said. "But not just yet, love. I want to be inside you when it happens tonight. I—I need to be inside you. I want us to lay together, fully. I want the act to bind us together, the pagan way..."

"Oh, John..."

Something seemed to pulse through her—all the power of the earth, surging and singing through the two of them, glowing from inside their bodies, drawing them together, in tune with the night sky and the warm breeze and the gurgling creek and the song of birds and the scent of the flowers.

He knelt beside her again just long enough to untwine the ivy that had held her wrists. "No more of this for now," he murmured. "Now I want you to feel your hands on me. I want you to put your arms around me. To welcome me inside you."

"Yes, my love. Yes," she said. As the last strand of ivy dropped away, she flexed her fingers. Their tips seemed more sensitive than ever; new warmth flowed through her limbs.

John stretched himself full length over her, his fingers reaching down between her thighs again, readying her once more, though in truth she needed no readying. She was hot and slick and open for him, her blood rioting inside her, the aching pressure in her belly so hard and urgent at her core that it could only be soothed by his touch deep, deep within her.

His abdomen came down to press against her belly, his hipbones fitting themselves against her own, his cock forceful and urgent and hot as a brand between them. And he kissed her deeply. Her hands fisted in his hair, drawing him hard against her mouth. Tongues tangled, breaths seemed to merge.

He was hot, electric, pulsing with a strange, rhythmic

energy, and an answering pulse pounded within her. She pressed desperate kisses to his neck, his shoulders, his mouth. Her fingers moved down to press along the bare skin of his back, finding the ridges and grooves between his glorious muscles. He was so beautiful, so perfect—and suddenly so much a part of her, she was losing track of where her body ended and his begun. "Oh, John," she cried out. "My John."

He paused to brush her hair back from her forehead, to gaze deep into her eyes. "My Mary," he said simply. "My own sweet Mary. I don't want to be without you. Not ever again. This is what I need. This is what's right. I want to worship your body properly."

And with that excruciating, reverent thoroughness he had used before, he kissed and stroked her everywhere, all over again, until she was desperate for completion.

Finally, she could bear it no longer. Her body would soon melt or fly apart if she did not have him fully. "Please, John, please," she begged him. "Come into me now. I need you now. I can't wait…"

He let out a sigh she thought might rend him in two. And pressed himself full-length on top of her again. "Now, Mary, now…now and forever."

And he took his hand and guided the tip of his shaft to the entrance of her wet slit, pressing just the head gently against her entrance. She yearned for him, yet still felt a shock to think he was going to enter her at last, with his long, thick hardness. He pressed a bit harder, and they both groaned. Her flesh seemed to press back against him, barring his progress. It seemed she might not be able to take him in after all, after everything, and a sort of panic took her for a moment.

But he slipped his fingers in ahead of his shaft, and spread her wetness on himself. His fingers worked her flesh more fully open for him, and slowly, the length of him pressed further. And further, easing inch by inch.

She bit her lip as the pressure built suddenly, stretching her.

He thrust—a moment of quick, gasping pain—and then he slid fully into her. He held still for a few throbbing moments, letting her adjust to the size and fullness of him within her, while he kissed her gently, passionately, and found her hands with his hands, twining their fingers together, a comfort, a claim, a union.

John, she thought. This was John, John she'd known all her life, John, whom she must have loved as long as she could remember. He was fully with her now, atop her, inside her.

The two of them were together, exactly as they were always meant to be.

Such fierce, strong joy soared through her, she thought she might burst. And his eyes were on hers, full of astonishment, as if he were thinking exactly the same things about her.

And then he began to move again. Pushing deeper into her, withdrawing, pushing deep again. Setting up a rhythm that somehow she already knew, as surely as she knew her own heartbeat and the rhythm of her breath, a knowledge coming from very deep inside, older even than the trees around them, old as the moon.

She couldn't get enough of him—his mouth, his shoulders, the silk of her curls, the hot glorious pressure of him moving and moving inside her. She urged her hips upward, meeting him, claiming him even as he claimed her.

Her thighs gripped his; her calves pressed themselves to his powerful buttocks.

He drove into her again and again, then stilled suddenly, gave a sort of growl, and rolled so that suddenly he was the one laying on his back, and she was above him, straddling his hips.

"What are you doing? Why did you stop?"

"I want to see you better," he said, reaching up to stroke her cheek with one hand, even as the other hand gripped the side of her hip and urged her to keep moving up and down along his shaft. "I want to see you with the stars and sky above you. Ride me, Mary."

Ride him? What exactly did he mean? Wasn't he supposed to be above her, guiding everything that happened?

Could the meaning be as obvious as it sounded? Suddenly shy again, she rose up on her knees, then came down again tentatively. The sensation was different than having him thrust into her. He filled her differently, and the pressure against the sensitive place at her front was more full, more sweet. She gasped at the pleasure of it, tested it again. She liked the ability to control what was happening, and began to increase her speed, until at last she gripped his shoulders with her hands, began to ride him more vigorously, her head thrown back.

"Jesus!" he cried out. "Gods, Mary—I wish you could see yourself. So beautiful. You are Boadicea, a warrior goddess. My goddess."

And then he could speak no more.

His breath went ragged as his hips surged up against her, as his hands gripped her by the waist, his fingers pressing into the curve of her buttocks, holding her steady as she began to fall apart.

She *felt* like a goddess, full of spectacular power, full of light even in the darkness of the night. And this glorious man beneath her: he was her pagan god.

She rode him and rode him, the pleasure inside her swelling and heating, until it seemed she was shimmering with sunlight just beneath the surface of her flesh, sunlight that pierced through all that was dark in her, that splintered all conscious thought, that shattered her solid self, and sent her flaring out in flashing, swirling stars.

She could not tell how far she flew, but he flew with her, all the light inside of him, the two of them wrapping about each other, coalescing, becoming one molten, scintillating gleam.

Then slowly, slowly, the solidity of their bodies returned to them. She felt the muscles of her thighs once more, aching as they pressed against him. She felt the hard bones of his shoulders beneath her palms.

They were both breathing so hard, their lungs rasped. Sweat gleamed on their skin.

And he was gazing up at her with undisguised wonder, his eyes shining as if with tears.

She collapsed against him then, nuzzling her face into his throat, and his arms came around her back and pressed her tight to his chest. She felt his pulse pound clear through her ribcage, beat for beat in sync with her own.

He pressed kisses against her ear, against the line of her hair. "God, Mary. That was—" he broke off, sighing. "I've… I've never felt anything…anything even remotely like that."

"Nor have I." She kissed his jawline, breathing in the scent from his throat. He was hers, hers completely. And she was his. The miracle of it all took her breath away. "I never imagined such a thing."

He brushed back her hair with his fingers, then tipped her face up so their eyes met. "Promise me something," he whispered.

"What?"

"Never forsake me, Mary."

"Never," she swore fervently. "I never could."

Why had he even asked such a thing? Didn't he know her by now? Didn't he know how completely bound she was to him—how completely bound she had been, heart and soul, even before they'd come into the woods tonight?

It was as if they'd been coming to reach this place from the first time they set out roaming together as children.

And now they were finally, finally coming home.

She smiled at him. "Forever, John."

"Forever."

Such happiness gripped her as she never could have imagined. She could never have imagined this would be her reality—could scarcely have believed John could feel this way about her, give himself to her as eagerly as she gave herself to him. And yet, here he was in her arms, his face alight as he gazed at her, warm as the sun. And it all felt so right, so perfectly, inevitably right.

They just stared at one another for a very long time, quiet now, and sated. The warmth of his skin against hers was a perfect balm, the sight of his wondrous face was the dearest thing in the world.

It wasn't until an owl hooted in a pine tree above them that they realized how much time was passing, how the breeze was cooler than before, and they were lying naked on the forest floor.

"We probably ought to go back," John said, sighing again. "People will realize we're missing. And I haven't exactly made an honest woman of you."

She laughed. "A dishonest woman. That's what you've made me." But she could not think it a sin, what they'd done. And she knew now that they would marry. She wouldn't refuse his proposal this time. Now that she knew he wasn't with her out of obligation, that he really, truly wanted her of his own free will, somehow her other objections seemed less weighty.

She would make him happy somehow, make a

viscountess out of herself, although the thought still made her stomach plunge in panic.

Though she still straddled his body, John reached out one long arm and pulled her fallen dress back towards her. "I'm afraid you'll have to make yourself respectable again, at least for a little while."

Sighing, she lifted herself off of him and began to dress. He got reluctantly to his feet and did the same.

Subtle worries began to fill her once more as the warmth of his body left her and the heady magic of their lovemaking began to ebb away. "Thomas will surely notice soon that I've gone missing," she said. "I'm not quite sure how to explain things to him. And you'll certainly be missed by Annabel Lawton. I don't think she understands your true intentions towards her. She scarcely took her eyes off you all…"

"We won't speak her name, Mary. Not here. Not now. Put her out of your mind." His voice was firm—but then his eyes twinkled. "Think only of you and me, my love. Only the two of us."

"All right." She smiled, but the tingle of anxiety rising through her wouldn't go away. She whisked her hands down the front of her rumpled dress, then patted at her hair, which was a messy billow of tangles. "Oh, dear. I'm afraid I don't stand much chance of looking respectable at this point."

John grinned and pulled her hard against him, kissing the curve of her throat. "But you do look beautiful. As for the respectable part, perhaps I can arrange to knock down a few of the lanterns on the Green, if you like. Dim all the lights."

Despite her worries, she laughed. "Unless you knock every last lantern over, people are going to notice the state of my hair. I'd best circle around to the vicarage before I go back to the Green, and find my hairbrush. You go play lord of the manor. Let people see you without me. For the time being, anyway."

"Yes, of course," he said. "You are wise, as always." And he tipped up her chin with his palm and kissed her soundly.

They walked for a time with their arms around each other, until they were close enough to the Green that it seemed wiser to take separate paths out of the woods.

Parting was almost physically painful, but at least it was only for a little while.

CHAPTER 13

*J*ohn scarcely needed his feet to carry him back to the Green—he was all but flying, buoyed by sheer joy. Mary was his. Mary was his forever. She'd promised it, at long last.

He hadn't wanted to let her walk away from him to go back to the vicarage, but he understood her concern about preserving respectability. The vicar's sister could hardly appear on the Green with her hair flying wild about her head, and her cheeks flushed, and her gown rumpled in such a way that it would be perfectly clear to everyone that she'd just been quite thoroughly tumbled in the woods.

But tomorrow, he would resolve the issue. He would go to Thomas Wilkins formally and ask for her hand, and beg him to say the banns as soon as possible.

They could be married right here in the village church, at the first possible opportunity, with all the local people, all her friends, and the children she taught in the school, present as witnesses. And they could hold their wedding breakfast outdoors on the Green. It would be full spring soon, and they could fill the tables with wildflowers he and Mary would pick themselves. Any excuse to be out in the woods with her again...

He felt joyous laughter rise up through him. No, he didn't like being separated from her, even for a moment, but he still felt the warmth of her presence as surely as if she were still beside him. The pleasure of laying with her still glowed within him, making him feel drunk on starlight.

It was if he hadn't even realized that something within him was torn and empty, and now it was whole, and radiant, and full of happiness. Soon Mary would be his wife, his viscountess, and he would find a way to make her happy in the role.

As he emerged from the cover of the woods, he heard shouts and laughter coming from the Green—happy sounds this time, sounds of celebration. He craned his neck to try to see what the occasion was.

The first person he saw was Annabel Lawton, who stood with her back to the crowd, scanning the line of the woods as though searching them. She caught sight of him, and a look of sudden alarm crossed her face, her eyes going wide, her posture stiffening.

He stopped short for a moment. No doubt he looked a bit rumpled himself, though he'd been careful when he took off his trousers, and his hair was short enough that it would be hard for anyone to tell the difference from Mary's fingers tangling in it. He felt the slightest twinge of guilt—Annabel would no doubt still be expecting his proposal. But the great expanding joyous light inside of him left no room for remorse. And he had no real reason to be sorry for her. Annabel was free to find her own true love now, and be as happy as he was.

"Lord Parkhurst," she called out to him in a tremulous voice. "There you are! I have been looking for you."

He had no choice but to address her. "Forgive me, Miss

Lawton. I…" He broke off, not quite sure what to tell her. "I went walking."

She gave him an uncertain smile. "Indeed."

Should he speak with her now? Tell her honestly what he had told her father? Surely she could understand. She was young herself, she must have a heart somewhere within her. And she most certainly was not the least bit genuinely in love with him.

"Miss Lawton," he began.

She drew in a sharp breath, and her eyes grew wary—that intelligence he'd seen in them yesterday morning glinted there again. Tinged with something like fear this time. "Yes?" she asked.

"Miss Lawton," he said again, trying to gentle his voice. "There is something I must—

something you and I must—discuss…"

And then he saw her do what she had done yesterday: *compose* herself. Just as if she'd drawn a silken veil across her face, the wariness in her eye faded, the tautness in her expression relaxed. She was complacent again, confident, with a look of dreamy expectation on her pretty features. "Yes, Lord Parkhurst?"

The change was quite unnerving. How exactly was she able to do that? But he had no choice but to forge ahead. "Long ago," he began, "when we were children—when you were indeed but an infant—our fathers…came to a certain agreement."

She managed a pretty blush, or at least the sort of demure expression that usually accompanied one. "I am aware, my lord."

"But, Miss Lawton, we…are grown now. With hearts and minds of our own."

"Yes." Surely she had some idea of where his argument was heading, but she looked not discomposed in the least.

"And surely, it is *love*, and not the agreement of fathers, that must be the essential ingredient of a happy marriage. Do you not agree?"

"Indeed. No one could wish a marriage that was not grounded in deep affection." Far from seeming discouraged at his words, she seemed to take confidence from them. Her smile became even more generous, her eyes even more bright. "I could not bear to be without affection in my own life."

For pity's sake. Was she honestly expecting him to make a declaration of undying love? They scarcely knew each other.

It was if she thought they were acting a scene in a play.

What would he have to say to break through that smooth, porcelain composure? For Mary's sake, he couldn't very well blurt out that he'd just come from making love to another woman in the great outdoors. He was reaching about in his brain for something at least a bit less cruel than *I cannot imagine ever developing the slightest romantic feeling towards you,* when a great shout went up on the Green.

"Great heavens," he said. "What is going on over there?"

"Oh," said Miss Lawton, waving a hand vaguely in the direction of the crowd. "It's Mrs. Trumbull and Mr. Bassett. Apparently, they are engaged to be married. They came running in a few minutes ago to make the announcement." Her words held a faint edge of impatience, and she fluttered her lashes at him, as though he were an incompetent actor who'd forgotten his lines.

To John's great relief, the necessity of speaking again was deferred by the sudden appearance of Thomas Wilkins, who came hurrying towards them, calling, "Lord Parkhurst! If I may beg a moment of your time."

Mr. Wilkins' cheeks were flushed and his eyes were twinkling with his usual good humor. "My lord, Mr. Bassett and Mrs. Trumbull...well, the happy couple wish to head to Gretna Green tonight!" He came a bit closer, and his voice dropped to an amused whisper. "And as a clergyman, it is my professional opinion that the two of them really ought to be bound in holy matrimony as soon as humanly possible. Before Bassett has a chance to change his mind."

John chuckled. "You suspect he is not firm in his purpose?"

The vicar leaned closer still so Miss Lawton could not hear him. "And I suspect another happy event may be in the offing for the two of them, if you take my meaning. Which would leave the lady in some distress, were she not speedily married."

"Ah. I see."

Wilkins nodded. "Might they be permitted to borrow one of your carriages, my lord, to get them at least to the first coaching inn?"

John laughed now. No—all the world was not as polished and false as Annabel Lawton. Wilkins was as frank and open-hearted as his sister. "They may take my carriage as far as Scotland, if they like," said John. "What sort of village would this be if we had a heartbroken woman running our foremost public house?"

The vicar grinned. "Thank you, sir. I know it will be much appreciated. And I intend to accompany them at least partway myself to, ah—provide any necessary spiritual guidance."

"To remind the gentleman of his moral obligations," said John.

"Every mile of the way, if need be."

In his friendly manner, Wilkins clasped John's arm and led him over to the crowd, where Mrs. Trumbull and Mr. Bassett were standing hand in hand, encircled by their friends. Miss Lawton followed placidly behind.

"Mr. Bassett," called John as they drew near. "I hear you are to be congratulated, good sir."

"Yes, my lord," Mr. Bassett answered, looking rather stunned by his own news. "Yes, I am. Mrs. Trumbull has—she has—" He gulped rather loudly. "She has agreed to make me the happiest of men."

Beside him, Mrs. Trumbull beamed. Bassett's expression as he looked at her suggested he might be considering fainting, but then he grinned and gave her a smacking kiss on the mouth, and everyone cheered again.

The vicar clapped his hands together and raised them for attention. "Lord Parkhurst," he announced, "has granted the happy couple the use of a carriage, to speed them to their nuptial bliss."

Another cheer went up, and John could not help feeling carried along on the tide of happiness. Surely no one in Birchford would have thought the matronly innkeeper and the handsome young sexton would have made a match, yet here they were, embarking on a future together, and making all their neighbors quite merry. How then could anyone be shocked by his own choice of Mary—who was nearly of an age with him, and so very good of heart, and so worthy to be a beloved wife.

"And the carriage is not all," John declared spontaneously. "I shall give these two good friends of ours a purse of a hundred guineas as a wedding present!" He nodded at his steward, who raised his mug of ale in acknowledgment of the command. "And I shall host a wedding breakfast for them upon their return to Birchford, so that they may begin their life together in the happy spirit they deserve."

The cheering swelled again, and this time, the townspeople—quite well lubricated at this point, he suspected, by the hard cider and punch and whatever more potent beverages had been smuggled onto the Green—moved as if in one

LARA ARCHER

body to lift up the newly-engaged pair and dance them around on their shoulders, at least until the vicar and the Parkhurst steward pulled the two of them down to usher them off as quickly as possible to their waiting carriage.

The departure of the happy couple made no dent in the jollity of the gathering. The rest of the crowd continued dancing as the fiddlers launched into a tune popular in alehouses, which had several bawdy verses about a nymph and a shepherd and what they did with his crook and his pipe while the lambs all ran away. If the villagers remembered the words, no one seemed offended in the least.

Throughout the revelry, Miss Lawton had her confident mask firmly in place, and smiled beatifically around at the merry-making as though John's act of beneficence came from her as well. She was practicing to be the local viscountess, perhaps, as she no doubt assumed she soon would be.

His stomach went queasy again. He was going to disabuse her of that notion, and he was going to do it tonight. She would not return to Lawton Grange still anticipating a proposal.

But before he could draw her away from the crowd again to finish their conversation, Lord Lawton himself suddenly emerged from the crowd and clapped him on the shoulder.

A smile was on the man's face, but his voice as he leaned close and whispered in John's ear was full of sarcasm: "Well, there's a fine union for young Mr. Bassett—a lusty widow twice his age, who'll no doubt make him a cuckold three times over before the year is out. You see what comes of letting people chose on the basis of their desires."

Anger instantly began to heat in John's chest. "Sir! I hardly think—"

"But no hard feelings, boy," said Lawton, cutting him off. "No hard feelings between us. Let me prove it to you."

Lawton reached across to one of the tables and hoisted a

copper pitcher and big serving spoon, which he clanged together to get the crowd's attention. "My friends," he boomed in a commanding voice. "I have something I wish to share with all of you as well."

The dancing slowed quickly to a halt, and all faces turned to him.

"Good people of Birchford," Lord Lawton pronounced, "you know how greatly I esteemed the late Lord Parkhurst, this young lord's father."

A cheer went up for the memory of John's father—a genuine cheer, for the prior lord of the manor had been well beloved.

Lord Lawton craned his neck about like an eagle surveying the landscape from the top reaches of a pine tree. "And you know how much my friend's son resembles him. The very best aspects of him. And I know that this young viscount cares for all his tenants as much as his father did."

The crowd cheered louder.

"You all know that the good vicar's sister, Miss Wilkins, has been hard at work for years raising money to build a country hospital for the people of surrounding villages," said Lawton.

Was it John's imagination, or did the man's hand tighten on his shoulder when he made reference to Mary?

"I wish to mark this day," continued Lawton, "by offering to provide half the land needed for that hospital to be built." Cheers rose again from the crowd, and Lawton held up his hand to quiet them. "I will offer a piece of the unentailed land that currently attaches Lawton Grange, running along-side the Parkhurst estates. Provided, of course, that Lord Parkhurst is willing to offer a comparable piece of land from his side of the boundary."

John stiffened, listening for the catch, for something treacherous beneath Lawton's kindly words—was this somehow a trick to expose his relationship to Mary? Had Lawton seen them going into the woods together?

But the man's voice sounded sincere and cheerful. And he had truly loved John's father. Perhaps he was genuinely trying to make peace.

Mary's long-cherished project ought to be completed, after all. What better wedding present could he give her than to help her help the villagers she so deeply loved? So he raised his own voice to the crowd. "By all means, Lord Lawton. I will gladly match your gift, and provide a cottage and a salary for a new doctor as well. For the sake of the good people of Birchford and of Thurlow, and of all the villages around us."

Lawton leaned in privately again, and said low and kindly, "We shall name it in memory of your father."

The thought took John's breath away. A sudden longing to see his father rolled through him, tugging at his heart. "I would be most grateful for that, sir."

Lord Lawton raised his voice for the crowd again. "And the hospital will stand as a permanent reminder of the unshakeable bond between our two families, between the Lawtons and the Parkhursts, a bond the former viscount and I always hoped to solidify well into the future."

Lawton put an arm around John's shoulder, and John found himself awash in emotion. Losing his best friend must have been hard for Lord Lawton. Pompous as the man could be, he clearly had a heart.

For a moment, it was almost as if John could feel his father's presence close by them, placing a hand of benediction on each of their shoulders. Telling them all would be well between their families, after all.

So lost was he in that sensation, he did not fully attend to Lord Lawton's next words to the crowd. Not until it was too late.

"It gladdens my heart," boomed out Lawton, "to know we shall build this institution together, in the memory of my dearest friend. And it gladdens my heart further still to know that it happens as another dream is brought to fruition as well, with our families are joined in the union of his son and my eldest child."

The words were said so quickly, so smoothly, John at first did not fully register their meaning. Not until he felt Lawton's head bend towards his once more and heard a hoarse whisper: "You must have known I'd never let you shame your father, boy. You'll thank me for this later."

And by then, the crowd was whooping so loudly, no one would have heard him had he shouted at the top of his lungs that Lawton was lying, that he had no intention of marrying Annabel.

The world seemed to pitch, entirely unreal, a nightmare version of itself—and a dozen hands were hoisting him into the air, tossing him up onto the shoulders of two strong farmers, and he saw Annabel being lifted up as well.

She was laughing joyously, and the crowd began to spin the two of them round and round, with the fiddlers sawing away madly at some new raucous tune, and a drummer pounding as loudly as if the crowd were heading into battle.

And all he could think was *Mary*.

As best he could with the townspeople whirling him about, he scanned the edges of the crowd. Sweet heaven, let her be at the vicarage now, brushing the tangles out her hair, hearing none of this madness. Let her know nothing until he had time to stop the nightmare and bring out the truth.

Everything was reeling.

And then—dear God, he did catch a glimpse of her.

Mary.

She *was* there, at the far edge of the crowd. Her mouth gaping, her eyes wide in astonishment. And horror.

She must have heard everything Lord Lawton said.

He called out her name, trying to make her stop where she was and stay and listen to him, but she could not possibly hear him over the music and the communal shouting. He pushed against the shoulders of the burly farmers who carried him, trying to get down, but they seemed to think he was merely losing his balance, and gripped his thighs to keep him from dropping, laughing like fools. He reached a hand towards Mary as best he could while they spun him, reaching as far as his arm could go, willing her towards him, but the spinning was so fast, his outstretched hand swung towards Annabel Lawton instead, who clasped it eagerly in her own.

He turned his head back, trying to catch sight of Mary again, trying to meet her gaze with his so she would *know* this was all madness, this was all lies, just an enormous mistake that had no bearing whatever on what was truly going to happen between them.

But Mary had already turned her away.

And then she fled.

MARY'S HEART THUDDED DULLY, and the breath caught in her lungs. She ran without feeling her legs beneath her, racing for home, but knowing home would give her no real shelter from the storm breaking inside her.

Just moments before, she'd been riding a wave of utter happiness, believing her life was suddenly charmed, thinking everything was turning out a thousand times better than she ever could have imagined. She and John had lain together. She and John loved one another. She and John would live out their lives together in a kind of bliss she'd never imagined possible for herself.

And then, when she'd been drawn up to the Green by all the jubilant shouting and cheering, she'd heard Lord Lawton's words, and that sweet castle in the air had come crashing down.

She'd been a fool, and John was marrying Annabel Lawton after all.

Dear God, how had she been so stupid, so completely, utterly stupid? *Of course* her life wasn't charmed. *Of course* she wasn't heading for bliss.

She'd let herself believe a fairy story, and fairy stories had nothing to do with real life. In real life, handsome, wealthy, charming viscounts didn't marry poor clergymen's daughters, any more than they married governesses, or the dairy maids they bedded, or, for that matter, the opera dancers they wooed with jewels and flowers, then left at dawn to return to their proper wives.

By giving herself to him in the woods, she'd just joined the ranks of those sorts of women—the sort to be casually wooed and swived and abandoned, and not to be seriously thought of again.

She could scarcely believe it of John.

He had always been her friend. Had always treated her respectfully.

How could he have lied to her? How could he have *used* her in such a way, after all that they'd meant to one another through the years?

Perhaps he even *believed* he loved her. Sweet heaven, he'd certainly made her believe he did. All the words he said to her tonight—words so sweet to her at the time, she'd felt intoxicated by their beauty and passion.

But as she scanned back through them in her mind now, she realized her besotted ears must have interpreted everything according to the wishes of her heart, not necessarily according to John's intentions. Because hard as she scoured her memory, she could not recall a single word John had said about marrying her.

Oh, Lord. *Not a single one.*

And had he ever once said he wasn't actually going to marry Annabel?

No, he hadn't.

Mary had even asked him, point blank, if he intended to marry the Lawton girl, and he hadn't told her *no*, he'd told her to *put it out of her head.* That *he didn't want to talk about it.*

He'd merely said he couldn't *love* Annabel. And, Lord knows, men of his class all too often married without the slightest love for their affianced spouse. All he'd said was that he was going to follow his heart, and *not worry what the world thinks.*

He'd never meant that he was breaking off the presumed engagement. He'd merely been declaring that he wanted Mary *too.* Following his heart meant only that he meant to enjoy her body *without* benefit of marriage—regardless of the propriety of the situation, regardless of how wrong it was, regardless of how much their neighbors would all condemn them.

He was only offering to make her his mistress.

His *mistress.*

Oh, dear Lord.

And he'd done exactly that. Quite thoroughly. Outdoors on the forest floor.

The great canopied bed of his forefathers would be reserved for his proper viscountess, while Mary could be taken on a layer of pine needles, with only the moon for a covering.

And she'd spread her legs gladly, and moaned, and clutched at his hips—just as a mistress was meant to do.

Not a wife.

CHAPTER 14

*D*awn broke foggy and cold, the sun a vague paleness in a gray sky.

John only gradually become aware of the reason he was able to watch the sun rise—the same reason he was stiff as a board, and damp with dew, and getting poked all along one side of his face by the needles of a yew bush. He'd spent the night outside the vicarage, first pounding at the door and then the windows, long past the point when he realized the effort was futile, and finally settling in for a vigil on the stoop, thinking Mary had to come home eventually, or if she were hiding inside, come out and talk to him before the neighbors spotted him there.

Now, even as he forced his aching limbs to stretch and bring him upright again, he knew it was no use to knock. The vicarage was as dark and silent as it had been the night before, with a tomblike stillness within. The vicar, of course, had hurried off to Gretna Green with Mrs. Trumbull and Joe Bassett last evening. Mary must not have come home at all, or must have fled from home before he reached her door.

Dear Lord. The sight of Mary's back as she ran from the

cheering crowd on the Green, her shoulders so rigid, her hands clenched in fists, would never leave his brain.

What must she have thought when she heard Lord Lawton's announcement that he was betrothed to Annabel? What must she have believed of him? To make love with her as they had, so passionately, their souls joining as surely as their bodies had, and then to have his marriage to another woman announced before all the world...

The thought sent a wash of shame and agony through him.

Mary had clearly had difficulty enough believing him when he'd told her she was lovely, and desirable, and a far more worthy choice of mate than Annabel Lawton could ever hope to be. It had taken all his tenderness, all his kisses and caresses, all his promises to make her believe he loved her. And then Lord Lawton's lie had confirmed all her worst fears.

If only he could go back in time, he'd punch the man in the mouth to stop those lying words from coming out of it in the first place, honor and his father's memory be damned.

When Mary had run from the Green last night, he'd fought and kicked his way down from the farmers' shoulders, intending to race after her. But once he got on his feet again, another knot of villagers swarmed him, clapping him on the back and shouting their congratulations. By the time he'd wrenched himself free of them as well, Mary Wilkins seemed to have vanished from the face of the earth.

Heart sinking now, he searched the stable in the back of the house.

Thank goodness, the Wilkins's old nag was right there in her stall, tossing her mane at him when he approached. So she at least could not have been the means for Mary's escape —not that the poor beast could have carried anyone very far, even on her best day.

The horse stamped and whinnied, clearly hungry for breakfast, so he pumped some fresh water and filled her trough with a bucket of fresh oats. At least he could do that much for Mary's sake.

Had Mary left on foot, then? Gone to a friend's home to hide from him? Perhaps locked herself up in some recess of the church off limits to laymen?

He had to find her, wherever she was, and make her listen to him.

He was just giving the horse a final pat on the head when stable door behind him creaked. He turned on his heel.

Mary?

But, no, it was little Tommy Harrow from the village—one of the schoolboys Mary taught. The urchin stopped in sudden fear to see the viscount standing there. "Milord?" he said, eyes blinking.

"Tommy," said John. "What are you doing here?"

The boy looked as if he wanted to ask him the same thing. But he said, "I've come to see to the horse, sir. Miss Wilkins asked it."

"Miss Wilkins?" His heart thumped. "You've seen her? Where is she?"

The boy blinked harder now, and his Adam's apple bobbed up and down. "I'm—I'm not supposed t'say. Not to—to nobody, sir."

"Not to me, you mean? Specifically, you're not supposed to tell *me* where she is?"

The boy's cheeks blazed. "She—she made me promise, sir."

"Of course, Tommy, and you're a good boy. But there's something she doesn't understand. Something I need to explain to her. I need to find her, and you need to tell me. You must know I would never do wrong by Miss Wilkins."

The boy stood, mouth gaping, clearly torn between his

fealty to the Parkhursts and his loyalty to his schoolmistress. "You—you can't find her anyhow, sir. She's gone off."

His breath caught. "Gone off where?"

"I can't say, sir."

He grabbed the boy's shoulders. "You can say. You *will* say."

The boy's eyes squeezed shut in panic. "She—she went off north, sir. With Sam Brickley. In Sam's wagon."

"*North*?" Oh, no. The image of Sam Brickley coming from behind the schoolhouse, hitching up his trousers, spiked into John's mind. "North as in Scotland? North to Gretna Green?"

"I wouldn't know, sir."

John dropped his hands from Tommy's shoulders, and the boy fled.

Dear Lord, Mary was a practical woman, but would she really move so quickly to marry another man?

But why wouldn't she, if she believed he himself was marrying another woman?

Especially if she worried their lovemaking in the woods might have gotten her with child.

No doubt, Sam Brickley was a decent man. He was clearly attracted to Mary. And having lived in Birchford all his life, he must know full well what sort of extraordinary woman Mary truly was. If Mary asked him now to save her, to marry her, would Sam take her as his wife?

He might.

He very well might. And if they went through with it fast enough, it wouldn't matter whether his own engagement to Annabel Lawton was real or not—Mary would be lost, forever.

A wave of nausea swept through him. Sprinting out of the stable, he raced home, got his best horse, a fat purse of gold coins, and a parcel of bread and cheese from his housekeeper. He had no intention of stopping any sooner than he absolutely needed to.

On the way out of town, he passed the Brickley farm—and indeed there was no sign of the man plowing that morning, as he otherwise would be sure to do this time of year. And no sign of the strong cart horses that would usually be at pasture in the Brickley's orchard.

John's stomach squeezed tight as a fist.

He drove his horse to the limit, skirting the busier roads around York as he guessed Sam would, heading towards Wetherley to pick up the North Road. He stopped at the Hogshead Inn there, the most likely place for the pair to stop, and sent his exhausted mount off with the grooms.

Hurrying into the main room, he elbowed his way to the innkeeper, who was behind the bar polishing glasses. He described Sam and Mary, asking if the man had seen them.

"Oh, aye," said the innkeeper, brightening. "Came in past midnight last night. Big cove, black hair. Appetite like a wolf."

John really didn't want to hear about Sam Brickley's appetites. "And was a young woman with him?"

The innkeeper rolled his eyes now. "Aye. But she wouldn't touch a bite, meat nor drink. Sat crying in the corner, she did. Talking to that clergyman fellow."

"*Clergyman?*"

"Aye. What came in with another man and woman, in a fine coach, with a fat purse. They had the roast beef with mustard, they did, and plenty of—"

"I'm sure they were well fed," insisted John. "Please, just tell me if they're still here."

"No, sir. Didn't even take rooms. Ate by the fire and then left in the wee hours of the night. Took fresh horses. All five of them in the coach, bound for Scotland."

Damn. So Mary and Sam were definitely headed to Gretna Green.

And Mary must have confessed all to her brother, if she was weeping while she spoke to him. And Thomas would have no grounds to disbelieve her story—that she had allowed herself, sinfully, shamefully, to be seduced by a man who would never marry her.

No doubt, the vicar would have the same response to her situation as he did to that of Mrs. Trumbull and Mr. Bassett: ensuring a respectable marriage took place as quickly as possible.

Fear gripped him, more deep and visceral than anything he'd ever felt on the battlefield.

Why on earth had he made that offer to Mr. Bassett and Mrs. Trumbull, to give them his coach and a pouch of gold? The fleeing party would have had a hard time keeping ahead of him if he hadn't equipped them so well.

And the gold had probably allowed them to take the best horses the Hogshead Inn had to offer. If they travelled through the night, they could reach Gretna Green some time tomorrow.

He had to catch them, but his own mount couldn't go further today.

Looking about at the crowd of men in the inn—several of them apparently peers or wealthy merchants traveling between cities—John withdrew his heavy purse and held it up to view. "Who amongst you has the finest, fastest, strongest horse?" he called out. "I'll pay triple what the beast is worth if you'll give him to me right now!"

And so he went, inn by inn, switching horses every chance he got so he could ride hard, his purse growing lighter and lighter. But the party he pursued had many hours head start on him, and they weren't stopping any more than he was.

He could not afford to pause to rest. At Middleton Tyar, he turned to the west, then rode through the night to Carlisle, with the great hulking shadow of Barnard Castle looming on the horizon to guide him north.

By the time he crossed the Scottish border, he was bleary from lack of sleep.

For a tiny border town, Gretna Green managed to be as confusing as any metropolis, its residents loathe to cooperate with a desperate, glowering man who had the signs of "trying to stop a wedding" all over him. After all, such men were very bad for local business.

He spent what seemed like hours going from building to building, until at long last, in the back room of a public house, he suddenly came upon a familiar pair at a corner table with their arms slung around each other—the sexton of St. Michael's and the owner of the Fox & Crow, both looking quite merry and roaring drunk.

"Oh, thank goodness!" he cried out. "Mr. Bassett! Mrs. Trumbull! I've been searching everywhere for—"

"That's Mrs. *Bassett*, now," interrupted the sexton, his voice proud but noticeably slurred. "We're here enjoying our marital bliss!"

Mrs. Trumbull—Mrs. *Bassett*, rather—howled with laughter and collapsed sideways upon her new husband, kicking her feet. The pair did indeed seem blissful, though whether due to love or to drink seemed debatable.

"And many years of happiness to you both," said John. "But can you tell me where—"

"Oh, come now, lamb," cried the new bride affably, apparently forgetting his title in her nuptial joy. "Have a drink with us!"

"You're payin' for it, after all!" added the groom, and burst into a guffaw at his own witticism.

"Indeed. And glad I am to do so," said John soothingly.

"But, please, if you could tell me, where can I find the Wilkinses. And—and Mr. Brickley." His whole soul contracted as he braced himself for Mr. Bassett's correction that it was now Mr. *and Mrs.* Brickley.

But Mr. Bassett wasn't the one who answered.

"Oh, them," said his bride. "They parted ways with us just after we crossed the border. Just as well they didn't stay for the weddin'—that poor Miss Wilkins, she wept like a babe the whole way north, and I don't think she'd have stopped even for our vows."

Miss Wilkins. Oh, thank heaven. John breathed again for the first time in what seemed like hours, and his head spun like a top. *Mary isn't married. She isn't married.*

"Some gent done her wrong, if you ask me," said Mr. Bassett, leaning forward with a sage expression and planting his elbow squarely in a platter of fried oysters. "Sam Brickley kept whispering with her, urgent-like, and I heard him ask her to marry him, to set things right for her, if you get my meaning. But he weren't the bloke what did it in the first place, you could tell by the way she looked at him."

John's heart jammed its way up into his throat. "And—and what did she say to him? To—to his proposal of marriage?"

"Can't have been yes," said Mr. Bassett. "Sam hired a horse at Carlisle, and went home alone."

"Looking like rainclouds had opened over his head," added his spouse.

The relief that rolled through him made John clamp his hands to the edge of the table to keep from sinking to his knees.

The new Mrs. Bassett's eyes narrowed on him suddenly. "It weren't you who done her wrong, Lord Parkhurst, were it?" Of course, she remembered his title now, and he clearly wasn't a *lamb* anymore. "That girl is a right angel among us, and if you done her any harm, lord or no lord, you'll meet with the wrong side of my boot!"

Mr. Bassett sat up straighter, looking suddenly more sober. He reached into his pocket and drew out the purse of gold that was his wedding present and tossed it back toward John. "No disrespect, my lord. But I'll take no gift from you if you did harm Miss Wilkins. She's a good one, and she cried like her heart was broke. If you used her, then cast her off for that frippity little Lawton girl, it weren't well done, it weren't well done at all." He paused, seemed to realize how boldly he'd spoken, then gave his forelock a tug and added, "Beggin' your pardon, my lord." His gaze, though, remained hostile.

John gaped at the two of them, shame and outrage doing war inside him. "Blast it all! It *was* me who made her cry," he admitted, "but only because she misunderstood my intentions. Because Lord Lawton told a lie, that I was marrying his daughter. Which I'm not going to do. I mean to marry Miss Wilkins, believe me, if only I can catch her before she does something foolish."

Both the Bassetts became instantly more friendly again at those words.

"Well, that's all right, then," exclaimed said Mrs. Bassett, smiling upon him beatifically once more. "Marry her. Make our girl a proper lady!"

Mr. Bassett nodded vigorously. "If you're to catch her, you'll have to head back down to Penrith. That's where they were going, back south to see another clergyman friend of the vicar's. Mr. Chat-something was his name. Chattington, maybe. Chatterley. They've gone in your carriage, at any rate, since we weren't in need of it no longer."

"We thought we'd stay up here awhile, and have ourselves a proper wedding trip," said Mrs. Bassett, and with an innkeeper's nimble fingers, she whisked the pouch of gold back toward herself. "With your kind generosity, of course."

"Penrith?" John repeated. That was maybe two hours to the south. Back in England, where no one could marry as hastily as here. *Thank God*. He still had time.

He might even be able to eat half a meal before he left, perhaps sleep for a short spell so he wouldn't drop right off his horse on the way.

"You'd best hurry," said Mr. Bassett suddenly. "I think maybe the vicar had some notion Miss Wilkins might...well, find a match with his friend. Mr. Chatsworth, that was his name."

John fled back out the door.

An hour and a half later, he was in Penrith, pounding against the door of yet another vicarage, his head reeling from lack of food and sleep and rattled from so many hours on horseback.

By the time the door opened—revealing a rather stunted older gentleman with enormous ears and a nose like a small cabbage, and with a dinner napkin tucked into his collar—he had no mental energy left for manners.

"You can't marry her," he declared flatly.

The gentleman blinked at him, then, surprisingly enough, offered a kindly smile. "I beg your pardon, sir. Marry whom?"

"Mary."

"That's what I was asking. Marry *whom*?"

Impatience made John's head ache. "You are Mr. Chatsworth, aren't you?"

"Yes, I am."

"And Mary Wilkins came here to you, didn't she?"

"Ah, yes, *Mary*," said the old man. "Of course, of course. Wonderful girl!"

"Well, then. You must forget all about her. You're can't—you're not—you've got...you've got the wrong sort of *ears*."

Muzzily, John realized he was going about this all the wrong way. "And anyhow, I love her."

The man regarded him as though he had quite lost his wits. Which, quite possibly, he had.

And then a terrible thought occurred to him—the Wilkinses hadn't come down here, then driven Mr. Chatsworth and Mary back up across the border to be married, had they? His exhausted mind could scarcely do the math, but surely they would have had just enough time to make the round trip, then deliver the couple back to Penrith again.

He stared at the old man in horror. "Are you—are you already married?"

Mr. Chatsworth chuckled. "Well, yes. Since you ask, as a matter of fact I am. Most delightfully and happily so."

John staggered, putting his fist to the doorframe so he wouldn't topple over. "Happy. Of course, you are happy." All the blood seemed to have drained from his body. "You are the most fortunate of men."

"Exceptionally fortunate, indeed, sir."

John felt as if he would just sink straight through the dirt at his feet, and never come up again.

Mary was lost to him, after all.

And married to such a man!

And all because he had not waited until they were firmly married themselves before he'd made love to her in the woods. What an utter fool he'd been!

Before his legs truly gave out beneath him, though, an extremely rotund, extremely florid-faced woman of advanced years came trundling up from behind the old gentleman, untying a gravy-spattered apron from around her belly. She smiled, looking like nothing so much as an amiable turnip. "Mr. Chatsworth, what is it?"

"A visitor," said the old man, touching a hand to the

woman's back and drawing her forward. "And this, good sir, is my lady wife, Mrs. Chatsworth."

This was Mrs. Chatsworth? *Oh.* Strength bore John up again. "Your *wife*? This is your wife?" All of a sudden, he wanted to kick up his heels and dance a jig. "You were not a bachelor, then. Thank God!"

"I thank God myself for that fact every day," said Mr. Chatsworth. "And have for forty-three years. But I would ask why it's such a cause for celebration for you, sir."

"Oh, Lord! There's no time to explain!" said John. "Where have they gone? The Wilkinses? Thomas and Mary. I don't see my carriage here. I beg you, tell me where I can find them."

An expression of understanding dawned on the old man's face, and a new intelligence. "Ah, yes. I believe I understand all this now." The expression became a bit of a glower. "You are the young *viscount*, I suppose?"

Another pulse of shame. The sensation was becoming all too familiar. "They told you about me."

Now Mrs. Chatsworth's amiable face soured. "Oh, the viscount, are you?" Her voice went tight with disdain. "You have not done well, sir, I must say. Not well at all, by that sweet girl."

But Mr. Chatsworth looked him carefully and consideringly up and down. "You do look dreadful, if I may say so, my lord. Haven't slept, perhaps? Haven't eaten?"

"No, sir. I've—I've been trying to catch up to Mary. To beg her to marry me. To beg her *again*." He gave a sheepish smile. "I have actually been trying."

Just as with the Bassetts, the declaration that he wanted to marry the woman he'd ruined performed a marvelous transformation in the attitude of the Chatsworths.

"Come in, come in, lad," said the woman warmly, laying a motherly hand on his arm and urging him towards the dining room. "Have a bit of good supper with us, while one of our boys sees to your horse. You'll be with your Mary soon enough."

"But where is she?"

"Oh," said Mr. Chatsworth, looking suddenly alarmed. "She and her brother took the carriage home to Birchford. Tomorrow's Sunday, you know. Mr. Wilkins must be there in time for church. He's got to call the banns, sir—for your marriage to Miss Lawton."

CHAPTER 15

$\mathscr{I}$t was pouring rain as Mary sat in her usual spot in her family's pew in church. After the warmth of the past few days, today was almost wintery, the glory of spring vanished like a mist. And just as well. She could scarcely bear to face the day ahead as it was, and sunlight and balmy breezes would have mocked her past the point of tolerance.

Thomas had offered to delay the saying of the banns—he would find some excuse—but Mary told him he must go forward with them. And she must be there to hear them with the rest of her neighbors, her spine straight, showing Lord Parkhurst that she knew full well now of his perfidy, and that she would never again let him demean her.

She would get through this. She would hold her chin high, however pale and sickly her face might look.

Sam Brickley, in his kindness, sat beside her. He'd stayed by her since she first ran from Birchwood, like a loyal guard dog. "Just if you need me for anything, Mary," he'd said, by which she knew he meant he'd fight the viscount bare-knuckled if the man dared approach her again. He knew everything that had passed, and, bless his good heart, did not judge her for it. And he'd offered marriage, several times, quite earnestly, though she'd repeatedly told him no.

But where was John?

She'd been fortifying herself to see him—forcing herself again and again to imagine him sitting in the Parkhurst pew just ahead of where the Lawtons sat, or perhaps sharing a pew with his soon-to-be bride's family in acknowledgement of their coming union.

At the moment, the Lawtons were in their customary seats, Lord Lawton and his four lovely daughters together, showing every sign of calm complacency. But the viscount was conspicuously absent.

Too ashamed to show his face before the vicar, whose sister he'd debauched?

She hardly heard the service going on around her, and stayed uncharacteristically mute through the prayers and the hymns, staring blankly at her hymnal, which might as well have been written in ancient Greek for all she was able to attend to it.

Her ears pricked up, though, when Thomas began to speak the words she dreaded: "This morning, I publish the banns of marriage between John Robert Spenser Hereford Hollings, Viscount Parkhurst, of Parkhurst Hall, Birchford, in the parish of Selby, Yorkshire, and Annabel Elizabeth Lawton, of Lawton Grange, Thurlow, in the parish of Selby, Yorkshire. This is the first time of asking." He paused a few heart-rending seconds. "If any of you know cause or just impediment why these two persons should not be joined together in Holy Matrimony, you are to declare it."

Thomas paused again. Utter quiet in the church, and the silence seemed to rumble like thunder.

Thomas's voice rose louder than before. "You are to declare it," he repeated. "*Now.*"

Despite her better judgment, Mary's gaze went to the Lawton pew again. Rosamund Lawton had her head turned toward her sister Annabel, and seemed to be giving her a significant look of some sort, but Annabel held herself perfectly still.

Mary's lungs constricted. Of course no one was going to speak. Everyone around her was delighted their lord was taking a lovely, elegant wife. No one but Thomas and Sam had any idea what had happened between her and the viscount, or how much she was suffering.

Thomas sighed loudly from the pulpit, and she heard the rustle of his prayer book as he prepared to move on to the next part of the liturgy, the first of the banns having properly been said.

At that moment, the church's red doors banged open.

Everyone turned, and in limped a man made half of mud —hatless, his clothing askew and damp, one hand pressed to his ribs as he made his way up the aisle. One cheek was bleeding from a long scratch, and his hair was plastered to his skull, soaking wet. Only slowly did he become recognizable as John Hollings, Lord Parkhurst.

"Stop! Stop the service!" he said, in a voice that rang with command.

Mary's heart lurched. She'd spent the last few days trying to hate him, trying to drive any tender feelings from her mind, but now seeing him before her—battered and covered in ooze—everything instantly softened inside her, and she wanted to rush to him. Only Sam Brickley's big form blocked her from leaping out into the aisle.

"Steady, Mary," Sam whispered gruffly, gripping her elbow. "Let's hear what the man has to say."

The viscount stopped three-quarters of the way down the aisle, leaning heavily against the side of a pew. "Forgive me... everyone," he panted, seeming to struggle now to catch his breath. "I'm afraid I fell off my horse coming here. Two different times, in fact. I—I haven't slept in rather too long."

The entire congregation seemed frozen in place, twisted backwards in their seats to gape at their lord.

"The second fall," he added ruefully, "sent me down the banks of the River Ouse. And rather a significant way downstream."

Mary told herself to look away, to look at the floor, to hide behind Sam's broad back, but she couldn't tear her attention from the viscount. Good Lord—his eyes looked half-sunken in his head, great bruise-like dark circles underneath them. Where on earth had he been this morning? And what had he been doing?

And then, as though he felt her focus on him, he turned his face to her. His expression shifted instantly, but she could hardly describe the emotion behind it—he looked astonished to see her, which was quite ridiculous, since she belonged nowhere so much as at St. Michael's, but somehow he also looked relieved, as if he hadn't been quite sure he'd find her alive.

His eyes were wide, insistent, desperate.

If she didn't know better, she'd almost have sworn he was *pleading* with her.

Which...he had *no business doing*. He'd determined his own destiny very well on his own, and this morning's service was just another step in making it official.

And yet, the force of that look made her heart swell painfully, as though it might burst.

She squeezed her eyes tight shut, and felt tears humiliating press against her lashes.

No one moved for long, confused moments. But then Lord Lawton rose to his feet and clapped his hands together as though a bleeding, limping viscount were a cheerful sight, and said, "Oh, there is Annabel's betrothed. And not a moment too soon, my lad. Of course you were rushing to get back for the reading of the banns. I should have told all our friends Parkhurst had urgent family business in York—gone to retrieve a necklace that belonged to his grandmother, is that not correct, Lord Parkhurst? To give my Annabel as an engagement gift—and clearly overwrought himself in his hurry to return to her side."

The viscount glared at the man, holding up his own hand as if to block Lawton's speech. He took another step forward, but stopped, wincing. "I'll ask you not to speak for me, Lord Lawton," he said. "Not to speak for me ever again."

At the pulpit, Thomas cleared his throat loudly. "You may wish to know, Lord Parkhurst, that I've just finished saying the first of the banns. For you and for Miss Lawton. I was asking if anyone knew of any cause or impediment," he said, with a definite note of suggestion in his voice, "why the two of you should not be joined in Holy Matrimony."

John's gaze swung from Lord Lawton back to Mary herself, still full of baffling emotion. Mary felt dizzy, overwhelmed, and was grateful for the strength of Sam's hand beneath her elbow.

John drew breath to speak.

Before he could say a word, though, Annabel Lawton herself leapt to her feet. "Wait!" she cried. "I know a cause!"

Every head swiveled to her in disbelief.

Thomas blinked down at her from the pulpit. "Miss Lawton?" he asked. "What cause?"

Annabel nervously licked her lips. "Well—the cause that… I've changed my mind. I don't care to marry him."

Her father and her erstwhile fiancé both looked at her with almost identical expressions of disbelief.

She continued on blithely. "A lady can do that, can't she? Call it off? Throw a man over? It is her prerogative, is it not?"

"That's true," volunteered Sam, giving Mary's elbow an

encouraging squeeze. "A lady can do that. And no one would blame her."

"In that case," said Annabel, "I wish to change my mind. Lord Parkhurst and I, we simply do not suit. He is too—he is too…" She waved her hand at the viscount uncertainly, looking him up and down with her brow slightly furrowed, as though she were seeking a suitable flaw.

What on earth was she doing? Annabel Lawton had been working for months to bring the viscount to heel and make her his viscountess. And now she wanted to *reject* him?

When Annabel's pause went on too long, her sister Rosamund popped up beside her.

"He is too unconscious of fashion!" Rosamund declared, her chin lifting rebelliously. "Anyone can see that."

"Yes," echoed Annabel instantly, nodding her head as though her sister had just uttered the wisdom of Socrates. "Far too unconscious of fashion."

John stretched out his arms, making a show of his muddy, ruined garments.

"And he is unwashed!" added the youngest Lawton girl, Vanessa.

John helpfully lifted one foot to display his earth-clotted boots, as a distinctly confused murmur swept through the congregation.

Something more was going on here than the surface words implied, but Mary could not for the life of her decipher what it was. Annabel surely could not be rejecting John for his momentary lapse in attire. The viscount might not be in the very first stare of London fashion, but he was an exceedingly handsome man, and—with the exception of this morning—his clothes were always tasteful and excellently cared for. Not to mention that they fitted his body superbly.

Lord Lawton's face had heated to boiling. "Are you all mad? What sort of reason is that for rejecting a marriage?

Lord Parkhurst is a fine young man—the leading peer of this county! The best match any young woman could reasonably hope for." He turned his wrath directly on Annabel, stabbing a finger at her. "And you, young lady, will do exactly as you are told!"

Annabel's jaw jutted out. "No, sir. I will not."

"You will," commanded Lord Lawton. And then to John, with look of lightning in his eyes, he said, "Young man, go change your clothing, and appear before us as a gentleman! And then you will, by God, get down on one knee and beg Annabel's forgiveness for your...your crimes of *fashion*."

John lifted a challenging eyebrow. "But I have no wish to change, sir," he said. "No wish at all to change."

"You see!" said Annabel grandly. "I certainly can't bind my life and soul and fortunes to a man who thinks like *that.*" Her eyes looked earnest, but her mouth had begun twitching slightly, as though she were having some sudden difficulty keeping a straight face.

Rosamund, for that matter, seemed to need to keep scratching at her nose, and Vanessa was staring down at her feet, her shoulders shaking as if she were either crying or laughing.

John gave a shrug. "I'm afraid, Lord Lawton, that my flaws cut too deep in any case. And the greatest flaw of all: I know I do not have the power to make your daughter truly happy."

At that, Lawton puffed up like an outraged peacock, and turned his fury on his eldest daughter once more. "Listen well, young lady. If you persist in this absurdity and do not marry Lord Parkhurst, you may rest assured that you will never have a dowry from me! See if you like marrying a more...*fashionable* man if he hasn't sufficient blunt in the bank to support you in the lavish manner in which you have been raised!"

Rosamund's eyes flashed, and she said, "If you cut off Annie's dowry, you shall have to cut off mine as well! I won't accept a penny of it!"

"And mine!" shouted little Vanessa, stomping a foot. "I won't take a shilling!"

The remaining daughter, Lucinda, quiet until now, gawked at the rest of them like they'd all gone stark mad, but when Rosamund elbowed her, she squawked out, "Mine, too!"

"There!" said Rosamund in triumph. "Then we'll go off and marry colliers or—or *highwaymen*, and all your grandchildren will grow up in rags, or worse, and won't that be a fine credit to the Lawton name!"

"Indeed!" said Annabel. "And it will be your own fault! I know the law—well, Rosie knows it. She's been studying up. So I know I'm far too old for you to command me to marry anyone."

"*What?*" roared Lawton. "I am your *father*, and you most certainly are *not*—"

"She is!" insisted Rosamund, with remarkable firmness. "Annabel is twenty years of age, so her signature must be on the marriage documents, or they aren't valid in the slightest! I can show you the relevant legal statutes, if you'd like."

Lord Lawton was opening and closing his mouth like a fish. At last he blustered, "Enough of this balderdash! Before you throw your life away, Annabel, tell me one flaw—one *genuine* flaw—that could keep Lord Parkhurst from being an excellent husband to you!"

Annabel heaved out a great breath, a sort of tremor passed across her lovely face. "For heaven's sake, Papa. Lord Parkhurst would be a terrible husband for me." She seemed to be struggling with something inside herself, something she didn't want to say. "Can't you see the truth?"

"What *truth?*"

"The truth that he's—he's never truly wanted me."

Mary looked to John. The expression on his face was still hard to read. He watched Annabel with as much surprise as any of the other dumbfounded parishioners, but he was clearly making no protest against her claim.

"What are you talking about?" replied Lord Lawton. "The man is mad in love! Why, when he came to declare his intentions to me, the passion he expressed—"

"Did he?" snapped Annabel. "Did he express passion, truly? I find that rather hard to believe. I'm not a *fool*, Papa! From everything I've seen, the man has never enjoyed a single minute he's spent in my company. And, quite frankly, I found every one of those minutes utterly exhausting. Trying like a ridiculous prancing *spaniel* to please him any way I could, when it's clear every word from my mouth gave him the headache."

Lord Lawton looked at his daughter as though she'd sprouted a second head. "Absurd!" he bellowed.

Annabel's eyes shone with unshed tears. "It's true! He thinks me foolish and insipid and hopelessly spoiled!"

"And Annabel is not in the least foolish," declared Rosamund robustly to the whole church, wrapping a supportive arm around her sister. "Nor is she insipid."

"She is a bit spoiled, though," added little Vanessa, frankly.

"Hush, Nessa," said Rosamund, though her voice was somewhat lacking in its former conviction.

"Spoiled or not," continued Annabel, hoarse with anguish, "there's no hope Viscount Parkhurst will ever even *like* me, much less love me."

"Poppycock!" said her father. "You are the most attractive young lady in the county!"

All at once, Annabel's cheeks went dusky red and the tears began to roll down her lovely cheeks, as though she'd been holding in great pain for a very long time. Her arms were visibly shaking. "Apparently I am *not* the most attractive lady! If Lord Parkhurst found me so attractive, then why—" she paused dramatically and turned towards the pew where Mary herself sat.

And Mary was quite startled to see Annabel's finger stab straight at her.

"Why," continued Annabel, "does he stare at Miss Wilkins so intently all the time, and why did he choose to dance with *her* in his arms on May Day night? Why are they alone together at every possible opportunity?"

A gasp swept through the crowd, and every head now swung to look at Mary, the faces taut with astonishment. Cold and hot together swept up Mary's body, from her toes to the very top of her head. She wanted nothing more than to turn and run.

No, she begged silently. *No more, Annabel, you've said enough.*

But the girl took one more deep breath and blurted out the rest of what she had to say. "And *why* did he run off into the woods with her on May Day night—and stay with her there for more than an hour—and come back...*disheveled*. Just in time for Papa to announce his—his engagement to *me*?"

Another gasp went up in the congregation, roaring horribly in Mary's ears. Her knees turned to jelly, and she clutched Sam's forearm for support. At the pulpit, Thomas's face went as pale as the Geneva bands about his throat.

"*No*, Papa," concluded Annabel on a sob. "I shall never be Lord Parkhurst's lover. Because I suspect that *Mary Wilkins already is!*"

The room exploded with exclaiming voices, the sound buzzing and thundering through Mary's skull. The air went hot and thick and hard to breathe, and all the light was fading to black. The floor seemed to rush upwards towards her face, and only Sam Brickley's arms catching her pulled her back from it.

She was vaguely aware of Thomas's voice echoing from behind her. "And do you have anything to say to these claims, Lord Parkhurst?"

"Aye," said John, his voice seeming to come from very far away. "I most certainly do."

But whatever it was he was about to say, he didn't get to say it.

The church doors banged open once more, even more violently this time, and another figure staggered in.

It was Donald Evans, clearly deep in his cups again and listing heavily to one side.

The drunkard's jaw was vivid black and blue where Thomas had punched him the other night after he'd manhandled Rosamund Lawton so rudely. The man looked wretched and pathetic and likely to topple over at any moment.

But in his hands, he held a musket.

And, *oh, dear God*, the muzzle pointed straight at the pulpit, where Thomas stood.

CHAPTER 16

*J*ohn spun as quickly as his bruised leg and mud-encrusted trousers would allow to face the back of the church.

The town drunkard stood there with a bloody *musket* in his hands, red-faced and wild-eyed, his voice ringing out harshly. "No one strikes Donald Evans and gets away with it," the man cried. "Not even a man of the cloth!"

Even exhausted as he was, John's battlefield instincts kicked straight in. "Donald!" he said, using his sternest command voice, while positioning his body between the gun and Mr. Wilkins. "Put that thing down!"

Donald stopped, uncertain for a moment, and the barrel of the gun wobbled towards John in the man's unsteady hands. "No disrespect to you, milord. But my head's not stopped clanging since the preacher hit me, and I'll not stand for such treatment, or I can't call myself a man!" His eyes were even redder than his cheeks with drink and outrage.

Damn it—reason wasn't going to get them anywhere. Mary had been hurt enough; John damned well wasn't going to let her brother be killed by an addle-pated inebriate.

He sprang towards the gun.

But it was already too late. With a grimace, the drunkard pulled the trigger, sending up a flash of sparks and a thick cloud of smoke that stunk like bad eggs.

If Donald had been shooting straight, the bullet would have hit John square in the chest. But as fate—or drunkenness—would have it, the gun's upward kick took the man by surprise, and the shot whizzed over John's head.

A pained cry came from the pulpit, a scream came from Mary, and Donald puffed out his chest and said, "I know I may drink a spot or two now and again, but I deserve respect as much as—"

The rest of the man's declaration was cut off by Old Mr. Dockett whacking Donald on the back with his cane, and then silenced entirely as John tackled him bodily to the ground.

Holding down the still-struggling sot was no easy job—drink really did seem to give him supernatural strength—but John still managed to turn his head back over his shoulder to see if the bullet had harmed anyone.

Dear Lord—the vicar was slumped over the pulpit, apparently still conscious, but with his eyes squeezed shut in pain.

"You can't keep me down! " Donald was shouting, wriggling with all his might.

John gave him another fist to the face so he could have a matching bruise on the other side of his jaw, and the wriggling stopped entirely.

In the next moment, Sam Brickley came barreling down the aisle to keep Donald pinned. "I've got the blighter. You go to Mary." The man's dark eyes locked meaningfully with John's. "She'll be needing you."

John rushed to the pulpit, where already a small crowd, including Mary, the local baker, and, of all people, an hysterically sobbing Rosamund Lawton, were easing the wounded vicar to the floor. Wilkins was half in a swoon, but groaning, so he still clearly lived. His loose, dark vestments made it hard to gauge the seriousness of his wound, though his white neckcloth was spattered scarlet with blood.

John called out to the congregation, "Who can ride to Middlethorpe for Dr. Ausland? My horse is outside. Take him."

"I'll ride!" answered Ben Brickley, Sam's equally strapping younger brother, already running for the door. "I'll have the doctor back in a trice. God keep Mr. Wilkins!"

John knelt to help with the fallen vicar. He glanced at Mary, but she wouldn't look at him. Her whole focus was on her brother.

And blood was seeping out onto her hands from somewhere near Wilkins' right shoulder.

"Don't lay him flat!" said John. "Keep his head and shoulders up."

"But he's in *pain!*" cried Mary.

"He's losing blood," said John, calmly as he could. "We need to keep the injured place raised up. Trust me. I'm quite used to bullet wounds." He glanced at her again. "Army, remember?"

For a moment, Mary met his eyes, and he thought he detected a flicker of relief there. "Of course," she said.

John motioned to the baker. "Get behind him. Let him lean back against you."

"No!" insisted Rosamund Lawton, elbowing the baker out of the way. "I'll do it." And even as tears rolled down her cheeks, she slid quite efficiently behind the slumping Mr. Wilkins and knelt there, her arms holding him gently about the waist, pillowing his shoulders on her bosom, nestling his head in the crook of her neck. The vicar's blood stained her lovely sprigged muslin frock, but she seemed to pay it no mind.

Mary put one hand to the back of her brother's head and clutched his fingers with the other, weeping silently, while John worked to loosen his neckcloth and preaching bands.

Rosamund sobbed again. "Help him, Lord Parkhurst, please!" she begged, then leaned close to the vicar's ear and whispered, "Hold on, Mr. Wilkins. You must hold on."

At the girl's words, Wilkins' eyes flew open. "Rosamund," he murmured, in a sleepy, marveling tone, as though he'd been awakened by an angel's voice.

"Yes, Mr. Wilkins," she answered fervently, pressing her cheek to his temple. "I am here." Her cheeks flushed with color. "I mean, we *all* are here. And you—you must stay with us. We will not let you go."

"Mr. Wilkins will be fine," said John, tugging the bloodied neckcloth free, and hoped he was right.

The local barber, Mr. Croft, appeared by John's side now, pulling what looked like a rather rusty old knife from his boot.

"Careful what you do with that!" said John.

"Just cutting loose his robes, my lord," said the man, and busied himself doing just that.

As the barber cut through the fabric, John felt Mary's hand on his shoulder.

"Please," she said softly. "Don't let him die, John."

Their eyes met fully for the first time since they'd parted in the woods on the first of May. A torrent of emotion seemed to pass between them—pain, regret, passion, hurt. A powerful need swept through him to gather her in his arms, to make her finally, finally listen to the truth of everything. He wanted to beg her forgiveness, tell her he loved her, but he knew that wasn't what she most needed to hear right now. "I won't let him die, Mary," he said. "I swear it on my soul."

The moment the barber was done his work, John leaned in again, stripping away the bloodied fabric and examining the flesh beneath. Indeed, the outer curve of the shoulder was badly torn, the all-too-familiar gash of a musket ball. A small bore one, by the looks of it, thank heaven, though blood was welling up at a sufficiently alarming rate.

No fragments of bone, no sign that any scraps of cloth from Wilkins' shirt or robes had lodged in the wound. That was sheer good luck—heavens' angels had indeed been looking out for the clergyman today.

"A flesh wound," John declared. "Good and clean."

From behind the injured man, Rosamund Lawton looked at him with beseeching eyes. "But there is so much blood."

Indeed, Wilkins looked terribly pale. Roused again by Rosamund's voice, he looked about him, caught sight of his own wound, and instantly went limp again, eyes rolling back in his head.

"Thomas!" cried Mary.

"It's all right," John assured her, even as he looked around for something with which to staunch the bleeding. "That's the normal response—better than being awake for the pain. Pressure will cut off the flow of blood. I need a pad of clean cloth."

"Here," said Mary, pulling the linen fichu off from the neckline of her dress.

"Good. Make a pad of it, and press it to the wound," he instructed her. "You'd best be the one to do it—your hands are far cleaner than mine."

She did as she was bid, but at the first pressure, Wilkins' eyes fluttered opened again. "Damn me," he groaned softly. "Hurts…"

Horrified, Mary began to withdraw her hand. John pressed his fingers down on top of hers. "Keep pressing. With the heel of your hand, Mary. Hard as you can. Or he'll lose more blood. He's young and strong, and can take a little pain. You must have confidence."

Steeling her expression, Mary did as she was told. Good, sensible Mary. He could feel the power of her concentration, as though she were willing her brother to live. As if she were determined that the fierceness of her heart, her love, her loyalty, could bear her brother up and fight off death itself.

And surely she was right about that. Death, frankly, wouldn't stand a chance against Mary's heart.

A fierce wave of love for her welled up in his own.

John glanced around at the others. "Now we need a longer strip of cloth to bind that tight until the doctor comes."

"My shawl might do," said Rosamund, and she wriggled a bit so the length of fine woven silk slipped from her shoulders.

"Perfect," he said, catching it. "Now, Miss Rosamund and Mr. Croft, lean him forward a bit, gently as you can, so I can wind this around him. Keep that pressure on, Mary, until the shawl holds the pad, then press again from the outside."

John wrapped the length of silk around Wilkins' torso twice, trapping the pad against the wound, and drew it tight. His arm brushed Mary's side as he worked, and he couldn't deny the simple pleasure he took in the contact. It felt so good to touch her, even that little bit, as if he'd been deprived of oxygen the last few days, and was finally able to take some in.

"There," he said at last, making a knot. "That will hold him."

Mary looked at him with searching eyes. "He will truly be all right?"

"No doubt it hurts like the devil," he answered, "but you must trust me. I've dressed many wounds, and this should end in nothing worse than a dashing scar." Unless serious infection sets in, he thought, but he wasn't about to mention that part aloud.

"Thank God," whispered Rosamund, and pressed her cheek once more to the vicar's—who, John suspected, would have gladly accepted full awareness of his pain could he have been awake enough to feel the girl's touch. Clearly, one Lawton girl at least was capable of deep affection—though she'd face a long, hard fight against her father if she truly had her heart set on a poor, untitled clergyman.

John heaved a tired sigh. "All right then," he said, "we should get Mr. Wilkins off this cold floor, and under blankets, in a room with a fire. Shock is still a risk. The less we jostle him, though, the better. If we had a blanket here to carry him on, something sturdy—"

"The altar cloth," said Mary. "It's large enough, and a strong brocade." And, not bothering to ask anyone else's opinion, she lifted away the candlesticks and Bible, and stripped off the cloth with her usual efficiency. "I've no doubt the Lord would give His blessing for its service."

With the help of Sam and Geordie, the third towering Brickley brother, they carried Wilkins the short distance to the vicarage. Mary helped, but stayed on the opposite side of her brother, away from John. The two of them stayed in step the whole way, moving smoothly, her skirts even brushing the toes of his boots once or twice, but she would not meet his eyes again.

CHAPTER 17

*H*ours later, Mary watched as Dr. Ausland leaned over Thomas's bed, securing a clean new linen bandage. He'd given them good news: the ball glanced off bone without causing fracture, and the major arteries were untouched. Thomas would have to miss all the sheep-shearing this year, but he might be healed enough to help his parishioners with the last of the haymaking in July. "And no passionate sermons for a while," the doctor joked, though Thomas seemed too dazed by laudanum to hear him. "We can't have you waving your arms about, exhorting your flock to mend their ways. Stick to quiet bits like the Beatitudes."

Despite the doctor's good nature, no one in the room laughed. Rosamund Lawton stood like a carved Madonna at one bed post, her expression distressed as if her own life hung in the balance. Sam Brickley hovered at the foot of the bed, hat in hand, in quiet guard dog stance.

John was with them, too—washed now and dressed in fresh clothes one of his footmen brought him—but he hung back in the shadows near the door.

Mary herself sat by the bed, tightly clasping her brother's

hand, but her mind could not settle with the viscount in the room. Against all good sense, his presence tugged at her. The weight of him there seemed to make the floor slant in his direction.

She wanted to talk to him. She wanted to weep.

She had no idea what to think.

John wasn't marrying Annabel Lawton now, that was true. He hadn't objected in the slightest when Annabel threw him over. And when Annabel said it was Mary he truly wanted, he hadn't denied the claim.

But...but...he *had* entered into the engagement to Miss Lawton in the first place.

And he *had* made love to Mary under false pretenses while knowing full well that engagement was in effect. And if he hadn't done so, Mary wouldn't have had to stand in front of all her friends and neighbors and publicly be branded a harlot, within the walls of her own church.

Without question, she had every cause to hate the viscount.

Heaven knew, if Donald Evans hadn't burst in with his musket and shot poor Thomas, all of Birchford might be pillorying her right now, and her brother might be looking at the end of his career.

Of course, Donald Evans *had* burst in, and Thomas *had* been shot.

And...John had quite probably saved Thomas's life, staunching the flow of blood from his wound.

He'd stepped in front of Donald Evans' *gun*, for pity's sake, to try to keep Thomas from getting shot in the first place.

Oh, Lord. She wasn't sure if she wanted to push John down the stairs, or pull him into her arms.

So lost was she in these thoughts, when Dr. Ausland laid a hand on her shoulder, she jumped nearly a foot.

"Your brother should rest, now," the doctor said. "Lord Parkhurst prevented the worst of the blood loss, so I shouldn't worry for him through the night. We must expect fever of course, but I'll be back first thing in the morning to check on him, and I expect I'll remove his bandage then and let the wound drain—that should lessen the chance of serious infection. Meanwhile, keep the fire built up in here, and have someone with him to be sure he keeps still, but otherwise leave him be."

He held out his arm to Rosamund Lawton in offer to escort her from the room.

But Rosamund shook her head. "I can sit up with him," she insisted. "He has only his sister here, and she can't be expected to stay up all night alone."

When the doctor blinked at her in surprise, Rosamund blushed. "Laudanum," she said, "is as good as a chaperone."

"I suppose that's true," said the doctor, chuckling. "The vicar's not likely to wake at all before morning. And Miss Wilkins could certainly use the help."

"I would be thankful for it," Mary said, smiling at Rosamund. "I'll just see all the gentlemen out, and make some tea for the two of us, then come back and sit with you, Miss Lawton."

"No need to bring me tea, Miss Wilkins," insisted Rosamund kindly. "Please get some rest, at least for an hour or two. I shan't be able to sleep tonight in any case. I promise to wake you if there's the slightest trouble."

The poor girl. Tear streaks were still visible on Rosamund's cheeks, which looked dreadfully pale with worry. Blood covered the bodice of her dress and spattered her skirts. They'd all washed up a bit already using water Mary heated over the fireplace grate, but Rosamund's once-pretty dress was a lost cause. "First let me find a clean frock for you," said Mary. "You shouldn't sit in those clothes any longer."

Rosamund glanced down as though she just now realized what a mess she was. Her cheeks went even more pale at the sight. "Thank you, Miss Wilkins. I'd be grateful for that."

"Though I'm afraid I can't offer you anything near as fine as your own clothes."

Rosamund blushed again. "I promise I shall not mind."

"All's well, then," said Dr. Ausland cheerily. "Two ministering angels for our minister, and all the gentlemen get to sleep." He offered Mary a courtly bow. "Your brother really should come through this nicely, Miss Wilkins. You're lucky the viscount was a veteran of battle. He did well in staunching the wound."

She glanced at John, who gave her a dark, unreadable look.

What was going through his mind right now?

She couldn't very well speak to him with other people in the room, and he couldn't remain in the house with her and Rosamund after the other men left. Mary's reputation was in tatters as it was.

Though she could hardly let him leave without acknowledging what he'd done for Thomas.

Stiffly, she walked over to him, stopping a more than respectable distance away. "Thank you, Lord Parkhurst. I'm so grateful for all your help today."

The look in his eye only became darker and more unreadable. "I do have my skills," he answered in a soft, sardonic tone. "Believe it or not, I'm not always the useless prat you think me."

Now that was puzzling. "I've never thought that. I've never thought any such thing."

"No?"

"No, of course not." What in heaven's name was he talking about?

Some further gesture seemed required, but she had no idea what would be appropriate, or what would suffice. Embracing him would be wrong, surely. A dreadful mistake in every way. So she reached out her hand instead and clasped his. Something more than a polite handshake, but not a gesture of romantic love. A gesture of…respect. Of gratitude. It would have to be enough.

The muscles of his face relaxed, not quite into a smile, but into something less distant than before. But all he said was, "Good evening, Miss Wilkins. I can show the other gentlemen out for you." And then he released her hand, and headed down the hall towards the staircase.

A pang went through Mary as he went, and she clenched her fists to ward it off.

Dr. Ausland followed the viscount, but Sam paused before leaving and leaned in close. "Don't you worry, Mary Wilkins," he whispered low. "All will be right as rain before morning, I feel it in my bones." And he winked.

Now *him* she did embrace. "Thank you, Sam. For everything, these past few days. You've been so much more generous than anyone could ask."

He squeezed her hard against him, then set her back on her feet. "You can count on me. Whatever you need. Whatever you choose. And if anyone in this town is fool enough to breathe a word against you, they'll take it back, or meet with my fists, I swear it. Man or woman."

She hadn't expected to laugh anytime soon, but she laughed now, with a rush of tenderness for Sam's kindness. "I don't deserve you. You're the very best of friends."

"I'd gladly be more, and you know it," he said, and for a moment he brushed the edge of his thumb along her collarbone, where her seed pearl necklace had hung. "But I see which way the wind blows."

"What wind?"

"You're a lovely girl, Mary Wilkins, and you deserve every happiness," he said, and gave her a wistful smile. "Whatever happens, I thank you for the memory of May Day night." With one last wink, he too turned and disappeared down the stairs.

Mary felt herself flush.

If only she returned Sam's feelings, her life would be so much simpler. But her heart didn't bend that way. She sighed, listening to the men's footsteps as they went downstairs, to their deep voices in the foyer, to the front door as it slammed shut.

John was gone.

She had no idea when she would see him again, or what on earth they would ever manage to say to one another. It was more than her mind could take in just now.

She was rather grateful for the interruption when Rosamund came up behind her and said, "About that dress you offered, Miss Wilkins? This one's become rather...*stiff*. I should be glad to be out of it."

So she busied herself helping the Lawton girl, fetching more water to warm in the pot on the hob and taking it to her in Mary's own bedroom, so she could take off her dress and scrub her skin where the sticky blood had soaked through. Mary found fresh clothing for them both, though it shamed her a bit to see how awkwardly her drab and too-small frock fit Rosamund's far more fashionable form, squashing her fine bosom and erasing the elegant curve of her waist.

"Let me get that tea," Mary said. "I'm sure we both could use it."

"Don't worry about me," said the girl. "I don't think I

could manage to drink or eat just now. I'll just sit with him. You should take some supper, if you can, Miss Wilkins, and then try to sleep awhile. I'll wake you in the night if I find myself nodding off." At the moment, Rosamund hardly looked or sounded like the heiress she was. In truth, she looked quite sweet and innocent in the simple, borrowed gown.

Impulsively as she'd hugged Sam Brickley, Mary threw her arms around Rosamund and kissed her cheek. "Thank you, Rosamund. Dr. Ausland was right—you are a ministering angel."

Rosamund pulled back shyly, and pink color stole over her cheeks once more. "Don't say so, Miss Wilkins. I—I owe you an apology, really. For—for everything with Annabel. What she implied about you and Lord Parkhurst. I know she didn't say it to hurt you."

"You shouldn't apologize. All this must have caused her a great deal of—"

"No, Miss Wilkins," the girl insisted. Her mouth twisted, and she seemed to be rallying herself to say something difficult. "I must confess something to you now. Just so you know the exact truth. So you can throw me out of your house if you wish. *I'm* the one who told Annabel to keep an eye on you and the viscount. That's why she saw you go into the woods together. That's why she was watching out so carefully for his return."

"Oh," said Mary. She wasn't really sure what to think about that.

"I didn't tell her out of malice, I swear that to you. I never meant to hurt you. Or—or anyone in your family." Her blush deepened. "I just wanted Annie to know the viscount wasn't in love with her. Before she waltzed herself blithely into a marriage that would have ended up being a daily heartbreak. Her heart's tenderer than you might think, and she *does* deserve to be loved." Rosamund's bright blue eyes pleaded for understanding. "I just—I wanted to protect my sister."

Mary nodded quietly. "I do understand," she said, but her own heart felt strange and aching and hollow. Had Rosamund not intervened, would Annabel and John be planning their wedding now? Whatever John's feelings for Annabel, or lack thereof, would he ever have stopped that wedding on his own?

Rosamund seemed to sense Mary's distress, and said, "I'll just go sit with Thomas now—with Mr. Wilkins, I mean. If you don't mind."

Rosamund turned and left the room, leaving Mary standing dully in place, staring out the window at the sun setting in the darkening sky. She knew she ought to move, ought to find something to eat, ought to at least try to sleep, but all those options seemed impossibly hard at the moment.

But she couldn't let her whole life stop.

She couldn't let this defeat her.

She squared her shoulders. Perhaps she could at least manage making a pot of tea.

Finding her way downstairs in the last faint streaks of daylight, she went to the kitchen. The shadows of the house seemed far less comforting than they usually did. Would it even *be* her house much longer, if the town folk chose to believe the innuendo Annabel had voiced in the church?

Innuendo that was, of course, accurate in absolutely every detail.

Even if her neighbors simply *wondered* if the story might be true, even if Thomas managed to hold on to his position as vicar, how could she carry on her life here in Birchford, facing sidelong looks each day?

How could she be the upright, trustworthy Mary Wilkins everyone had always known?

Lost in that thought, she reached absently for the box of

rush candles on the kitchen table, and was just touching one to the low embers of the kitchen fire when she nearly screamed.

A figure lurked in the shadows beside the door to the outside yard.

John.

CHAPTER 18

"Dear Lord!" she exclaimed, waving the sputtering candle at him as though it were a fiery brand. A strange mix of fear and joy flowed through her, making her heart thump madly. "I thought you left with the doctor and Sam."

"I did," John said, shrugging. "Just far enough for Dr. Ausland to think I'd really left. I've had my valet put him up at the Fox & Crow for the night, by the way, so he'll be nearby if you need him."

She couldn't seem to get her breathing under control. *John was here. He hadn't left her.*

But he *couldn't* be here.

He *shouldn't* be.

"Why did you come back?" She held the rush candle before her as if the little halo of light would somehow reveal his thoughts to her. All it did was throw flickers of orange and shadow across the handsome angles of his face, making him seem more a mystery than ever.

He ignored her question. "I meant to give Sam the slip too once we'd crossed the lane to the Brickley farm, and then double back here," he said, "but Sam caught me by the arm the moment the doctor was inside the inn and told me I'd better haul my arse back to talk with you." John's mouth pursed ruefully. "His precise words, not mine. He also told me he'd break both my legs, and quite possibly my neck, if I didn't treat you honorably." He gestured towards her candle. "Now blow that flame out, will you? If anyone walks past the vicarage, they'll see us, and then they'll feel sure Annabel spoke the truth about how we've been carrying on."

With a defiant gesture, she dipped the candle into the little lamp on the kitchen table, touching the flame to the wick so the lamp began to glow. "I want the light," she said. "People will believe what they wish to believe, evidence or no."

"Please, Mary. We can fix all this. You won't be ruined at all, if only you'll marry me."

She shook her head at him furiously. "I think we've had this conversation a few too many times already. I won't discuss it again."

"For pity's sake, sweetheart," he said, sighing. "Everything's changed. The whole village has heard we've been together. In the carnal sense. And you can't claim I have any obligation toward the Lawtons anymore—Annabel clearly wouldn't have me even if I begged her. So you need not feel guilty marrying me. Not to mention that your life in Birchford will be nearly impossible now if I don't make an honest woman of you. I can't see what objection you could have to my proposal at this point."

"Can't see what objection?" she hissed at him. Buried anger surged out of her, and she wanted to kick him or bite him or throw a pot at him. "Can't see what *objection*? You— you misled me! You—you *used* me! You may not have lied to me outright, but it was no better than lying! You thought you could marry Annabel for show and still have me as—as a sort of *side* dish. Like a—like a bowl of sugared carrots."

"Sugared *carrots*?" he asked. "What on earth are you talking about? I haven't changed my intentions towards you, sweetheart, not since that first morning when we got caught in those blackberry vines."

"Haven't changed your intentions?" She stamped her foot at him. "Well, I don't understand your intentions, John Hollings! It seems you've done nothing *but* change them. You showed not the slightest interest in me for months and months after you came home. And—and then you dallied with me in the woods. Twice. No, *three* times. And not ten minutes after the third dalliance, you were announcing your marriage to the lovely Miss Lawton!"

He looked at her squarely, as if willing her to read his mind—which she was still entirely incapable of doing. "Is that what happened, Mary? Is that really how it happened? On May Day night?"

"Yes, of course that's how it happened! I was there! I saw it all, I heard it all!" Hot tears burst forth despite her best efforts to keep them in, and streamed thickly down her face. "I left the woods by the far path, meaning to go back home, but all the cheering drew me back to the Green, and I heard everything Lord Lawton said."

"Indeed. You heard what *Lawton* said."

"I saw the crowd lift you on their shoulders! I saw you clasp Miss Lawton's hand!" She ran at him then, pounding her fists on his chest. "How could you do that, John? You let me think you—you let me think you *cared* for me."

He did nothing to defend himself against the blows, just looked down at her quietly, his gaze so intense. "How could you doubt that I care about you, Mary? Don't you know me better than that by now? "

Her hands fell uselessly to her sides, trembling with hurt

and blunted fury. "I thought I did. I don't know what to think." Under his gaze, all her defenses were collapsing, like a child's sandcastle as a huge wave hit, crumbling and washing out to sea.

Frustration came over John's features now. "You assumed the worst of me. You ran off that night before I could say a word to you. You didn't trust me, Mary. Why didn't you just *trust* me?"

Her mouth fell open in surprise. How was he was putting her on the defensive, when he was the one who'd wronged her? Wronged her quite spectacularly. When she'd always been so loyal to him.

He blew out a heavy breath. "I chased after you straight up to Scotland, do you know that? Barely ate or slept for days. And damn near broke my neck—twice—rushing back here to stop the banns this morning."

A sort of shock ran through her. "What? You went to...*Scotland*?"

"God, Mary, I was so afraid," he said, running a hand fitfully through his hair. "I thought you were going there to marry Sam Brickley. Or—or Mr. Chatsworth."

"Mr. *Chatsworth*?" The world seemed to float around her suddenly, less substantial than before, and she wished to heaven she had more light than her one guttering lamp. "Are you quite mad?"

"Sam's willing to marry you now, Lord knows, if you say the word. And I don't doubt Mr. Chatsworth would be willing, too, if he weren't already happily wed."

She blinked hard and shook her head in disbelief. "Why are we even discussing this? What difference should it make to you whom I was going to marry, if you were going to get married yourself? I certainly wasn't going to accept being your mistress, whatever you might have assumed of me! And, anyway, for your information, I wasn't going to marry Sam, no matter what. I told him no, quite clearly, several times. *I* at least would never marry where I don't love."

John's eyes went wide. "And neither would I!"

"Oh, so you're saying you *did* love Annabel?"

"Of course not."

"Well," she said, putting her fists on her hips, "one of those statements has to be a lie, because you *were* going to marry her. Can you deny I saw what I saw on the Green? Can you deny that Thomas was reading the banns for your wedding this very morning?"

John stepped back from her, spine stiff, shoulders squared, looking every bit the soldier he'd once been. His gaze turned suddenly fierce. "Do you know what the real problem is? Between us? Annabel's supposed claim on me wasn't really your main objection. You told me several times that we shouldn't marry because our *stations* in life are so different, because a viscount must marry a grand lady, not someone of lower status than he."

"And I was quite right to say it. Like it or not, that *is* the way of the world."

"Ah, but my supposed *superiority* wasn't quite the issue, either, was it?" He pointed a scolding finger at her. "Because deep inside, you also believe the reverse."

"What?"

"You think *I'm* the one who's unworthy."

"*What?*"

"You think I'm spoiled and thoughtless. More selfish than you, less honorable than you."

A dizzy, disbelieving feeling swept through her. "That's not true, John! That's never, ever been true."

"Then why did you underestimate me so completely? Why didn't you *trust* that I meant what I said to you? Why didn't you believe I'd never, *never* turn my back on you?"

"Because—because…" Oh, Lord, her head spun. And she

wasn't going to repeat it all again, about his engagement, about his hand grasping Annabel's as they were twirled about on their neighbors' shoulders on the Green. If John didn't understand how wrong his behavior was, she couldn't even bear to look at him.

"I—I want you to go, John," she said. "Go and not come back."

His eyes squeezed shut, and the breath rattled out of him. "Don't say that."

"I have to." Her throat seemed to be closing up. "I don't know what else to say."

He stepped closer to her, then. He touched his hand to her bodice, against her ribcage. Her skin tingled, and an electric shock went through her belly. It was the very spot where he had marked her with his mouth just a few days before. The red spot he'd left on her flesh was still there. "That was the sign, Mary," pressing his fingers against the mark. "That was the only one you should have paid attention to. Of us being bound together. That was more marriage contract than anything Lord Lawton's solicitors could dream up."

Tears filled her eyes again. It was pleasure and pain to have him touch her, a delirious mix of anger and longing, and she had to turn away lest she throw herself against him and beg him to take her in his arms.

"That night on the Green," he said, "you heard Lord Lawton announce my marriage to Annabel. But let me ask you again: did you hear *me* say anything?"

"I…" She racked her memory for the details. She knew she'd heard his voice, but couldn't for the life of her remember what he'd said. "I don't know. But—but I didn't hear you *object*. And—and I saw your hand in—"

"In Annabel's, yes. When the dancers spun us, and she took hold of it. But did you see me looking at her? Did you see where I was looking? Did you see whom I'd been reaching towards?"

"I don't know. I didn't stay to study you."

He nodded. "You ran. You ran and didn't wait to hear from me."

Why did he keep saying that? She pressed the heels of her hands against her eye sockets, trying to still the terrible wavering within her. She knew she shouldn't let him keep talking, but the thought of letting him go was too awful to bear. "All right," she said, half choking on the fresh tears she fought to hold back. "Tell me. What would you have said if I'd stayed?"

He set his hands to the sides of her arms, then, and turned her fully towards him. The frustration in his expression was mixed with such tenderness, he nearly broke her heart. "You are the most stubborn, willful creature, Mary," he said.

"*That's* what you would have said?"

"No. No, that's not what I would have said." He stroked his hands up her arms, sending waves of need through her. His fingers skimmed her shoulders gently, then her throat. At last, he cupped her jaw with his spread fingers, lifting her face to his. "I would have said, *Look at me, Mary. Look in my eyes, and know the truth.*"

Her insides were shifting about, as though her internal organs were all trying spontaneously to rearrange themselves. She tried to shut her eyes against him, but the sheer force of his gaze compelled her to keep them open. His expression warmed her, sent a faint trickle of hope through her blood.

"Are you looking?" he asked, his eyes so intense upon her. "*Really* looking?"

She was trembling all over. "Yes."

"Do you see me, then? Do you remember who I am?"

"Of course. You are Viscount Parkhurst."

"*Not* Viscount Parkhurst," he said firmly. "Not to you."

Something turned over inside of her, something vulnerable and frightened. His face was so dear to her, so familiar, so beautiful. His bright blue eyes had always looked at her with such kindness, laughing with her so many times, gleaming with mischievous excitement so often in their youth at all her teasing and her dares.

"*John*," she whispered. "You are *John*."

And so she looked at him long and hard, at this man she had loved and trusted for so many years. She looked into the very heart of him.

And it was as if the world had been out of focus for days. As if she'd been viewing everything though a rain-streaked windowpane, and now the sun was warming the blurring drops away.

Yes, this was John.

Her John.

Her oldest, dearest, truest friend. Not some *viscount*. Not some status-conscious aristocrat whose motives and heart she could never understand.

Just *John*.

And the John she knew would not have betrayed her. John would never betray her.

She'd been so stupid to think he would.

And...sweet heaven, *that* was why he kept reminding her he hadn't spoken a word about marriage when Lord Lawton had made his announcement. The thought sent a shiver sweeping from the top of her head down to her toes, followed by a flush of warmth.

"That night," she gasped, as suddenly all the pieces fell into place in her mind. "That night on the Green. When Lord Lawton said that you were going to marry Annabel. Oh, dear God—Lord Lawton *lied*."

A smile broke out on John's face that matched the warmth spreading through her. "There's my clever pirate queen. I knew you'd puzzle it out, if you just gave me a chance. Lawton thought to shame me into making the marriage, after I'd told him in no uncertain terms that morning I would not agree to it."

"Oh, John!" she cried, pressing both hands against her mouth. "Oh, dear Lord! Forgive me. You have to forgive me...I was just so...shocked. And frightened. And hurt. And —and—"

"Hush, Mary," he said. And gently, he pulled her hands away from her mouth and guided her arms around his neck. "There's nothing to forgive. Because your worst sin—your very, very worst one—was never that of underestimating me. Not truly." His arms came around her waist, pulling her closer. "Your worst sin, my love, was that of underestimating yourself."

"*Myself?*"

"That's really what kept you saying no to my proposals, wasn't it, for so long? You didn't believe I *ought* to choose you. Despite abundant evidence from me to the contrary, you couldn't see yourself as desirable enough."

She felt herself flushing. "Well—for pity's sake, John, I'm plain as mud."

"You are the farthest thing I know from plain." His body pressed hard against hers, giving her direct evidence even now that he desired her very much indeed. "You are a dazzling creature, Mary, who roams the woods like a wild thing, who dares me to climb into the treetops to look for giants, whose hair flames like a Beltane bonfire in morning sunlight. And the most beautiful woman my eyes have ever seen. I've never desired any woman as I desire you. And never could. And never will."

Oh, sweet John. She clung to him as surely as if a magnet

pulled her, to his body which was warm and solid and smelled of everything good and fresh on earth.

It felt safe and thrilling all at once. Like home, and also like an adventure. As it had always been between them.

He murmured low against her ear. "And if you're still worried about how you'll manage as a viscountess, I think you will make the best one imaginable. Precisely *because* your mind has no interest in elegant parties or—or in finding the perfect bauble to decorate your hat."

She gave him a poke in his ribs. "Are you sure you've been paying attention to actual viscountesses? I assure you, your own mother always wears impeccable hats."

"True enough. Her headgear is superb. But you, my love, have a superb *heart*." He kissed the top of her head tenderly, then drew her back away from him just enough that he could look directly into her eyes. "You make me a better man, Mary Wilkins, every minute I spend with you," he declared. "And that means I'll be a better lord to the people of Birchford. Isn't that the whole purpose of the peerage—to have the power to help the people? It's clearly what you've always believed. And, as I recall, it was the theme of a goodly number of sermons by your father when we were young."

"Ah. So you did pay attention to him sometimes?"

"Always. Even when you and I snuck under the back pews to play cards."

She laughed.

"Oh, sweetheart," he said. "I have no more interest than you do in a frivolous London life. What more entertainment do I need than festivals out on Birchford Green with all our neighbors? And nobody plans those better than you."

"I see," she said, raising her eyebrows at him. "So I'm the practical choice of wife?"

He nodded, his eyes twinkling. "Very practical. Very, very practical, indeed." And then he slid his hand between their bodies and beneath the neckline of her bodice. His fingers closed over her breast, just above the shift, his palm brushing the thin linen over her nipple. "A viscount has so very many needs to be taken care of." His voice went husky. "Urgent needs. So a viscount must always think of practicality."

A delicious shiver went through her. "Keep talking," she whispered.

"Everywhere I walk now, I see all the practical things I missed when I was a boy." As he spoke, he spun their bodies around and pushed his muscled bulk against her, forcing her backwards several steps, until she felt the solidity of the kitchen cupboard at her back. "I see improvements I need to make to the lands and farms. Which fields need better drainage, which need to be left fallow."

Even as her eyes shut in pleasure, she chuckled. "Oh, John Hollings, you do know how to sweet-talk a woman."

"I know how to sweet-talk *you*," he said, and now his words were spoken between kisses along the curve of her neck. His free hand wandered over her belly, down her hip. His strong fingers gripped her thigh for a moment, then slid up between her legs towards the joining spot at the apex, so sensitive even with the layers of her clothing between them. "I know you'll want to hear I've noticed which cottages need new roofs."

"New roofs," she agreed with a gasp. "Always a fine idea."

"Hmm," he said. "We must be practical, above all things." The hand that had been playing with her nipple dragged her bodice down to bare her breast. His hot mouth found its way there in a moment, and dragged that exquisitely sensitized nipple between his lips, drawing out a spark of sensation that made her gasp.

"Oh, John."

"I've noticed a school that could use more books," he murmured against her flesh, his tongue pausing for a moment to lick a tantalizing whirl around her aureole. "A muddy main street that could be paved."

"So romantic," she teased, but her words came out on a shuddering breath. A deep ache was growing in her belly, along with a tightening between her thighs.

"It is romantic," he insisted, "when I imagine doing it all with you."

It was a marvel to her that he could keep speaking, for she could no longer keep track of his hands and mouth as he played them over her body and made short work of undoing the fastenings of her clothing.

"What seemed a dull burden to me," he said, tugging loose the laces of her stays, "suddenly blooms with life. Forget new roofs—we can build new, modern cottages for all our tenants. We'll make that country hospital of yours the rival of anything in London. I'll offer the good Dr. Ausland double whatever he's earning now if he'll move here as soon as possible and be our first physician."

She was panting now, and rational words were getting harder and harder to form. "You could do all those things without me."

"Not nearly so well. And not nearly so enjoyably." With quick jerks of his hands, he pulled her sleeves and bodice down, and loosened her stays and lifted them free, so she was bared nearly to the waist. In the cool air, her nipples peaked to hard points, and ached for the continued attentions of his mouth.

She wanted him now, right now, right here as they stood, without a moment's delay.

But, as always, his patience was far greater than hers.

He drew back from her and took her in with his hot gaze. "There," he said with satisfaction. "Now you look like a proper pirate queen. Except for one more thing."

He slid his fingers into her hair and slowly, one by one,

pulled loose the hairpins that bound her tresses tight against the back of her skull. When all the pins were gone, he brushed out the mass of her loosened hair with his fingers, lovingly, spreading it across her shoulders, stopping to kiss the curls.

"This stuff drives me mad," he murmured, dragging a lock sensuously over his fingers. His eyes burned into hers, then, and she knew, despite his patience, that he was as lost to desire as she.

"And these lovely things drive me mad as well," he said, and dipped his mouth again to lick and suckle his way across her breasts, fitting his mouth to each nipple until she cried out and writhed against him.

The sound of her own cries made her suddenly aware of something. "John, Rosamund Lawton is right upstairs."

He chuckled against her breast. "And refusing to leave Thomas's side. She'll stay where she is, I'm sure of it." He gave her another lick that made her jerk in his arms. "I do believe she loves him."

And before Mary could object again, he suddenly slid to his knees and knelt before her, his hands raising the hems of her skirts.

"I should mention, Mary," he said, his voice low and rasping, "that making you a viscountess is not a one-sided deal, purely for my advantage. I'll see to it you get something out of the bargain, too." His big, warm hands slid their way up her bare legs.

"Oh, dear," she breathed. "I believe I'm seeing some advantage already."

"Even London can offer pleasure, you know." And his mouth followed where his hands hand gone, kissing at her knees, nipping at the tender flesh of her thighs. And then finally, finally going where it had gone that morning when she lay sprawled half-naked on the ground by the blackberry vines, to that sensitive nub at the joining of her legs. He kissed her tenderly there, and then—making her cry out in frustration—pulled back again to speak. "You'd love the entertainments at Vauxhall," he told her. "It's like a fairy garden at night, full of people in masks, music, and the most marvelous fireworks."

And then he licked her on that nub, and it was as good as fireworks, the pleasure bursting like colored sparks through her limbs, through her head, making her exclaim with wonder.

His hands went where his mouth had been, working the same magic, while his deep, thrumming voice kept caressing her just as effectively. "The theaters can be splendid, too," he said. "Not to mention the Royal Menagerie, where you'll come face to face with lions. Which might be the closest you'll ever come to meeting truly worthy adversaries."

His fingers were stroking and stroking so marvelously, sending delirious waves of arousal through her, punctuated here and there by licks and kisses, until all her muscles save those that clenched in her belly and thighs went slack and pliable, until her arms and legs and breasts seemed to be glowing from within with pure, golden light.

Oh, Lord. Her legs were trembling, and her knees were going to buckle soon.

She would either explode in a moment, or topple to the floor.

But he still was not done with her. "And I'll get you a proper horse," he promised, sliding his hand deeper between her legs, between her slick folds, stroking her there as well. "A truly fine one, not like that old nag of your brother's, and you can learn to ride, really ride."

At that, three of his long fingers slipped up inside her wet, heated sheath, stretching her deliciously. Their pressure against her swollen flesh had a sharp, hot sweetness that made her bite her lips and squeeze shut her eyes.

Thankfully he put one hand around her hip and pressed his chest to her knees to support her, because the heat that spiked through her threatened to melt the very last of her strength.

"Imagine that, Mary. I've been imagining it—you at full gallop, your cheeks flushed and the wind pulling your hair loose. I should love to see you ride like that."

And at last he stopped speaking, and worked her with both hands and mouth, his tongue laving her, his fingers thrusting inside her with a rhythm that did indeed rock her like a racing horse, making her clench against him with her thighs and pump her hips up and down as the pressure and pleasure built and built within her. She was flying, hurtling, and her fingers grasped at his golden curls as though they were a horse's mane.

Even behind her closed eyes, colors flared.

A few more strokes of his hand, and with a cry, she arched her back and shuddered against him, the walls of her sheath pulsing and clutching at his fingers, that sensitive nub seeming to melt into outward-pulsing circles of pure flame. Her soul rushed with it, bursting beyond the boundaries of her flesh, merging with the light that sparkled everywhere.

John held his mouth and hands against her for long moments, while the thundering of her heart and the rasping of her breath quieted, while that ethereal part of her that had leapt beyond her body slowly returned to solid form within her.

She was barely conscious of John rising quietly to his feet, and putting his arms around her waist once more.

"Look at you," he whispered once he stood before her again, his voice hushed, reverent. "My Mary. My beautiful, beautiful girl."

Her hands, somehow, were still tangled in his hair, and she drew his mouth against hers.

His kiss was desperate now, and tinged with the salt musk of her body.

She didn't know how long the kiss went on, but some time later, he pulled back from her again. "You haven't said it yet," he murmured. "That you will marry me."

Her heart seemed to clench at that; her breathing hitched. There was joy in the thought, warm and pure and glorious, but also something else, something that made her feel the solid ground was slipping from beneath her feet.

"I'm afraid," she admitted.

His arms tightened around her, anchoring her. "Afraid of what?"

"Afraid I'll—I'll seem ridiculous as a viscountess." Her breathing quickened now, as she confessed the truth. "Like a wren dressing herself up in another bird's bright feathers."

He chuckled low in his chest, and leaned back so he could look at her in full. "Mary, my love, if you could but see yourself right now, and how gloriously flushed and glowing you look, you could never, ever doubt the power of your beauty."

Heat spread through her at his words, and she clutched at his shoulder, holding fast. "I don't think a viscountess could appear like this in public."

"That's a damned shame," he answered, his eyes raking lasciviously over her bared breasts. "But if I make love to you enough, the whole world will see your glow even when you're fully clothed. Every peer in England will be mad with jealousy that I won you. *You*. Exactly as you are."

She squeezed shut her eyes, trying to let the heat in his voice burn away the chill of her fear. John did love her, she did not doubt it any longer. He really did see her as beautiful.

Could she truly see herself as he saw her?

"Just trust in me, Mary," he insisted. "I swear I'll remind

you every minute of every day how desirable you are. Until you cannot doubt you are the very embodiment of Aphrodite herself—a goddess of love and beauty."

"Aphrodite? *Me*?"

"My Aphrodite," he said, and set about proving it with his mouth on her breast and his hands lifting her skirts once more. His powerful form backed her against the cupboard again, and she could feel the pressure of his shaft, hard and ready, pushing against the restraint of his trousers. One of his hands slipped behind her knee, raising it up, pulling her leg around his thigh.

"One more thing I must say," he said between the kisses he was pressing to her breasts and throat. "I love you, Mary Wilkins. With all my heart, I love you."

"Oh, John," she answered. "I love you, too. With all my heart. And always have."

"Thank God for that," he said, and set his mouth hard against hers.

And then she reached between them to the closure of his trousers, and began to work the buttons free. The pressure of his straining manhood against the fabric made the job harder than it had to be, but he didn't complain about her fumbling fingers as they brushed against the outline of his shaft, and when at last it sprung free, he certainly didn't object to her fingers grasping him and stroking him up and down, causing him to swell ever harder against her palms.

All the while, their mouths worked against one another, their tongues tangling, their breath meshing, drawing them deeper together.

He had her skirts up around her waist again, baring her legs completely, and wanting to see him bared as well, she pulled at his jacket, yanked up the hem of his shirt. He paused in his ministrations to help her, shrugging out of the jacket and whisking the garment over his own head.

Her little lamp had already sputtered out, but the embers of the kitchen fire still cast enough orange light to highlight the hard ridges of his chest and shoulders, and limn the hollows between his muscles in tantalizing shadow. He looked utterly male, utterly commanding, dangerous and powerful and glorious.

And entirely hers.

She skimmed her hands along his chest and over the hard plane of his belly, enjoying every inch of his masculine beauty. "You know, viscount," she said, panting with arousal, "you look rather rakish at the moment, like a pirate king, yourself." She gave one of his nipples an experimental lick, and rejoiced at the way he jolted and sighed. "When I wanted to be a pirate as a child, I had no idea this sort of wickedness could be a part of the deal."

"This will be yours every day and every night, my love, if only you'll marry me. A pirate marriage, if you will, full of every wickedness you and I can imagine." Sliding his hands lower, he gripped her buttocks and lifted her up so her legs were nearly around his waist. "Let me show you a little of what I mean, and perhaps you will be convinced."

The firm head of his member pressed against her swollen, slick folds, and it was all she could do not to impale herself upon him instantly. But she held back for a moment as she remembered John limping into the church that morning. "You shouldn't try to lift me, John. I'll hurt you. You're injured."

A low growl came from his throat. "Pirates laugh at injury," he said. "And, believe me, love—at the moment, I'm feeling no pain at all." His eyes met hers, burning with need. "All I need right now is to be inside you again. To claim my most precious treasure."

And steadying her back against the cupboard, he thrust up inside her, stretching her, filling her gloriously.

It felt so good, so incredibly good, to have him inside her, the sensation of pressure so deep and so hot. His desperate need for her fired her own desire, and she pushed her hips downward to meet his thrusts, gripping him with her thighs, locking her legs over his clenching, surging buttocks.

Heat pooled in her belly, and a high sweet pleasure began to sing through her blood. Sparkles and streaks of golden light began to flash behind her closed eyelids. How could he raise her to this peak again and again, so quickly and so completely every time?

The slide of him in and out of her, the feel of his hard shoulders beneath her arms, the musky smell of him, the sound of him groaning as his own arousal grew—they were indoors now, but the heady magic of it spiked through every nerve ending, as surely as when they'd been outside beneath the murmuring pines and the stars and the moon.

Only...there was another sound accompanying them now, and not that of rustling leaves or the songs of night-birds. It was the cupboard, banging and rattling as the teacups within clattered together in rhythm with John's thrusts.

"John!" she cried breathlessly. "The noise! Miss Lawton will hear...might come down..."

"Damn it all," he grunted, and swung around towards the kitchen table. A push of his hand to clear a space and he lay her down on her back. "Spread your legs wider for me," he commanded, and leaned down over her, his biceps pressing the backs of her knees up toward her shoulders, splaying her, opening her more deeply to him than ever before.

His feet still on the ground, he pumped into her harder, harder, leaning his weight forward on his elbows now, spearing his fingers through her wildly disordered curls.

This deep possession thrilled her, pushing her higher towards a climax that she knew would soon shake her to her core. She gripped his back with her legs, her ankles pressing just below his shoulders blades, and his muscles rippled beneath her calves as he rocked and rocked into her.

The rough roar of his breathing matched the wild thundering of her blood, and the boundaries of her flesh and his seemed to blur as they had before—their muscles clenched and strained together, and heat bloomed through them, and soon she was soaring, and he was soaring, and the bright, clear light that filled her filled him, too, and as one they pulsed outward into what seemed to be a warm, velvet, star-filled sky.

The pleasure of it was blinding, obliterating, beyond flesh, beyond names, beyond time or space. There was only that pure, sweet brightness that meant her soul merging with his.

And they hung within it for what seemed like an eternity.

The world rocked and pulsed and glowed, larger and wider than before, and her heartbeat shimmered in time with it.

Gradually, though, she became conscious of John's weight upon her, a separate form from her own. Her breathing steadied, her heart slowly resumed its normal human dimensions, once more allowing itself to be contained within her chest.

The smooth, familiar wood of her kitchen table was at her back, the pots and pans she'd scrubbed a thousand times hung on their hooks around the walls above them, the flaxen curtains she'd stitched as a girl hung over the window.

But John was still with her—warm and solid, his chest rising and falling against hers, his hair brushing her cheek, the scent of him surrounding her, the fullness of him still inside her.

How extraordinary.

It seemed impossible and inevitable all at once. And she

could have this. Always. This miracle of making love to him could become part the life she lived.

A dream in reality.

John gave a sleepy, contented sigh and rolled his weight off of her, stretching himself out beside her and drawing her snugly against his chest, as though this were a perfectly normal thing for a wealthy viscount to be doing, to be lying half-naked on a table in a humble country kitchen, with his head against the salt cellar and the sugar bowl at his back.

And contrary to anything she would have expected just moments before, she laughed. "Dear Lord, John—remember I told you how many people have confessed their sins at this table?"

He chuckled, his ribcage rumbling against hers. "Then it's very appropriate that we're here. And how can anyone blame sinners if their sins make them feel like this?"

"It's rather hard to believe anyone gets anything virtuous done at all."

He propped himself up on one elbow and look down at her tenderly. "And I must say, you look utterly delicious laid out like this—the most alluring meal imaginable. In future, I fully intend to take you on as many tabletops as possible."

"I hope you will."

"See, there's another advantage to marrying me. I have a great many tables at Parkhurst Hall, of varying heights and dimensions. And also divans, and ottomans, and a quite sturdy desk in my study…and a well-stuffed leather armchair I'd definitely like to try. A good many stairwells, too. And linen closets. Not to mention the stables. Even the ice house offers some tantalizing possibilities. I look forward to mapping out the whole estate with you."

She laughed and buried her face in the warm crook of his neck, her hands exploring the wonderful contours of his chest and ribs.

He pressed a kiss against her ear. "We really must be married now, Mary," he said. "Miss Lawton would have to be deaf not to have heard some of that."

A hot blush swept over her. "Do you think so?"

"I don't know which of the two of us was shouting louder at the end. But don't worry—laudanum is powerful stuff. At least your brother won't have heard a thing."

He pulled her up then, so she was sitting on the edge of the table, and gestured for her to put her dress to rights. He yanked his trousers back up over his hips and buttoned them hastily. No one could have said they were properly dressed— he was still shirtless, and his shoulders bore small red marks she supposed she must have made with her fingernails at some point in the proceedings, and his hair looked to have been through a mild hurricane—but still, he knelt down formally by her feet.

"I'm asking you now, officially, Mary Wilkins," he said, taking both her hands in his. "Will you have me? Will you marry me? Will you be my match in this world and the next? Will you help me make a life I can be proud of?"

She looked deep into his eyes, those loving blue eyes that had always seen the best in her, that truly saw her as beautiful and worthy of cherishing. And her heart melted.

"Yes, John," she said. "Yes, of course. I am yours. I have always been yours. And I cannot imagine any life I would want if I could not live it with you."

"Hallelujah!" he cried, and jumped up to grab her in his arms and kiss her soundly. "And as a clergyman's daughter, you know you can't go back on your word. That would be shameful, you know."

She found herself laughing again. "I won't go back on it. But, oh, heavens, John, what on earth are we going to tell people? Annabel told everyone we went into the woods together on May Day night. How will we ever explain?"

"We'll tell them the truth."

"The truth?" And visions of all they'd done together flashed through her mind—the tangle of blackberry vines, his lips against her breast, her back against the hawthorn tree on May Day morning, their naked bodies intertwined outdoors under the open night sky and here on the kitchen table in the vicarage, his shoulders above her, his sweat on her skin, his hips surging into hers. "I'm not sure any of that is going to help my reputation."

"No, Mary. The *truth*." He took her hands in his again and smiled at her with his eyes sparkling. "The only truth that matters, which is that I fell in love with you and your good, true heart. And we were alone together so long in the woods on May Day night because I was proposing to you. Which is exactly what I was doing, as a matter of fact. Perhaps not with words, but with my body."

She drew in a deep breath, drawing the scent of him inside of her. "I did understand you correctly at the time, didn't I? Even if I got myself confused about it later."

"Yes, you did. You understood everything perfectly, that I was promising myself to you forever, and you to me. Though we'd best not give the neighbors all the details of exactly how. Let's let them believe I got down on just *one* of my knees."

Mary laughed, pure happiness bubbling through her. "Then perhaps you might ask me once more, John, if you don't mind. In just the way you did before."

And so he put his mouth to her breast and began to show her what he meant, all over again, as he intended to do every day, for the rest of their lives.

www.ingramcontent.com/pod-product-compliance
Lightning Source LLC
Chambersburg PA
CBHW022202170626
46807CB00005B/2312